THE
MARRYING KIND

THE
MARRYING
KIND

by Elizabeth Cadell

WILLIAM MORROW AND COMPANY, INC.
New York   1980

Library of Congress Cataloging in Publication Data

Cadell, Elizabeth.
  The marrying kind.

  I. Title.
PZ3.C11427Mar   1980   [PR6005.A225]   823'.9'12   79-20088
ISBN 0-688-03581-7

Book Design by Michael Mauceri

Printed in the United States of America.

    2   3   4   5   6   7   8   9   10

Chapter 1

Rain had been coming down steadily since morning, and the sky held a threat of more to come. The local weather expert had foretold that spring would come in weeping, and for once he had been right: the end of March and the first three weeks of April had been a time of almost continuous downpour. The river that at other seasons flowed sedately round the base of the low hill was running swiftly and had overlapped the top of its banks. The fields among the widely spaced farmhouses were in several places under water.

A visitor might have thought it a cheerless scene. But to those who lived here, this peaceful valley appeared as picturesque in these conditions as it did under a summer sky.

In a cottage that stood about half a mile from the largest farmhouse, Laura Seton glanced at her watch and realized that if she was to be in time to meet her sister at the bus terminus, she should set off now. She put on a mackintosh, tied a scarf over her hair and, opening the front door, engaged in a battle to eject three puppies and prevent their parents from entering. The two cats, she decided, could stay inside.

Before closing the door behind her, she paused to give the room a brief survey—and at once realized that this was a mistake. She should have gone out without looking. She gave an impatient sigh, re-entered the living room and embarked on a token tidying. Hammer and nails—those could go under the big chair. Dogs' tinned food, cats' tinned food—on the shelf under the counter at the kitchen end of the room. The panel of the screen she was embroidering—prop that against the wall. Books . . . if you hadn't finished putting up shelves, you couldn't clear away books; they could be stacked on one side of the stairs leading up to the attic. Put coffeepot and cup into the sink. No time to make the bed, so close the sliding door to the bedroom. The two rugs . . . it was a pity that puppies couldn't be taught to wipe their paws—and it was a wonder that no carpet-maker had as yet thought of marketing a rug with an all-over paw pattern.

And that, she decided, took care of the tidying. She thought it wasted labour. It was a living room and she lived in it and there had been nothing in sight that she did not need, or would shortly need, or had recently needed. But if Jess had stepped in and seen it as it was . . .

She went out and got into her car. As she drove past the farmhouses to the village of Crossford, she found herself wondering how her sister could have exchanged this peace and spaciousness for the pressures of life in London. But Jess, she recalled, had wanted change—and Crossford was a changeless place, quiet, serene, concerned only with the rural problems that arose with each successive season. She and Jess had been born here, in the only house built on the hill; in twenty-three years they had seen nothing that could mar or disturb the placid, pastoral scene.

She came out of her reverie and concentrated on her driving. As she reached the outskirts of the village, she saw the bus coming across the bridge that spanned the river and connected Crossford with the busy town of Waterside.

To those awaiting its arrival at the village, the first view of the bus from London—sixty miles to the south—was glimpsed as it turned into the main street of Waterside. As it approached the bridge, watchers invariably received the impression that it was slowing down. The drivers called this an optical illusion; none of them had ever admitted to slackening speed on leaving the town. The men who in bygone days had driven stagecoaches had maintained that it was not they but the horses who slowed down, understandably reluctant to cover the last three unnecessary miles. Despite these denials, the illusion of a decrease in speed had ceased to be a debating point, and had passed into legend.

The terminus for vehicles coming to Waterside had from time immemorial been the coaching inn called The Bell and Bottle. Here drivers, horsemen, travellers of all types and conditions had found warmth and good fare and good cheer. This was their journey's end. On the other side of the river there was only Crossford, a village which had no outlet and which, seen from the town, was a single straggling street with muddy tributaries leading to farms and ending in impenetrable woods.

The Crossford farmers who had business to transact in Waterside had for centuries cantered uncomplainingly over the ford. But with the coming of a regular coach service, their wives had begun to complain; why, they demanded, couldn't the coaches travel the extra three miles to the village? The drivers, emptying tankards in the snug parlour of The Bell and Bottle, told them why: Neither they nor the horses contentedly champing oats in warm stables were going to splash across a muddy ford to oblige a few farmers or their wives. Then why, persisted the wives, couldn't a bridge be built? A bridge, stated the town authorities firmly, would be built only if the farmers paid for it.

The farmers regarded this as the end of the matter. But nagged and harassed by their women, they were at last compelled to dip into their gold reserves. The bridge was built. Thereafter, public transport drove across it to the village. But as Crossford offered no comforts comparable to those to be found at The Bell and Bottle, Waterside remained the official terminus. The extra miles were made grudgingly, or—on the days when the road was under water—not at all. Flooding in spring was a frequent occurrence. At these times, the floodwater on the Crossford side formed a shallow lake on which the children of the neighbourhood launched homemade craft.

An enterprising boatbuilder, coming to the district after more than usually severe flooding, had visualized a future marina and had brought half a dozen dinghies and canoes to the lakeside and erected a large board stating that these were for hire. At the close of the disastrously unsuccessful season, he had come to the conclusion that the farmers either were landlubbers to a man, or were unable to read. He departed, leaving two of the dinghies to rot among the reeds and furnish further fun for the children.

The bus terminus at Crossford was the village inn, a neglected-looking building with an adjacent petrol pump and service garage. Behind were fields. Some distance along the riverside road were a smithy, a cobbler's shop and a small general store.

When Laura reached the bus stop, the rain had dwindled to a drizzle. Outside the garage was its owner, Conrad Lester, now nearing thirty but once an active member of the Crossford teen-age group to which Jess and Laura Seton had belonged. He was washing a car, an operation Laura thought superfluous. She stopped her car close by, got out and addressed him.

" 'Morning, Con. Why don't you let the rain do that job for you?"

"Hello, Laura love." He stopped work, hitched up his oil-stained dungarees and went to lean against the petrol pump. "Why don't I let the rain do the job? Rain wets a car; it doesn't wash it. And this car needs special treatment. It belongs to—"

"I know. I've seen it around."

"It's the first job he's brought me. I thought he was going to bypass my humble establishment and use the posh garages over in Waterside—but no." He paused to look in admiration at the car on which he had been working. "Beautiful, isn't she? First time I've seen this new model. D'you know what they cost?"

"No."

"A long row of figures." He sketched them in the air. "But this chap can afford it. You ever come across him?"

"I've only spoken to him once. In a car park."

"He's a good looker. Fine, upstanding chap. But he doesn't talk much, did you notice? Opens his mouth, says a couple of words and then shuts it. Look at that rain again. You can't blame the bus drivers for not wanting to come to this dump, can you?"

She tried without success to keep her eyes from the inn's uninviting facade. She remembered that when Conrad's father had been alive, it had had a trim, spruce look. The interior had been clean and tidy, the rooms occasionally let to travellers had been comfortable, the food plain but good. The public bar and the small lounge overlooking the street had been a popular meeting place for the local farmers. Conrad and his brother, Clive, had worked in the garage; their widowed father had managed the inn, and the cooking and housekeeping were done by his somewhat sour-tempered sister, Minnie. But on his death, Minnie announced that she was retiring; having worked hard all her life, she was now going to enjoy herself. Let Conrad and Clive marry and bring their wives to run the place.

Conrad and Clive went wooing, but no woman would agree to move in until Aunt Minnie had moved out. The inn became shabby, and then frowzy. Dirty curtains hung in the windows, refuse appeared in buckets at the doors. The inn sign, once a colourful representation of the three pigeons that gave it its name, now swung with two of its birds in a moulting state and the third obliterated. Conrad and Clive cooked their own meals and looked after themselves.

Soon Clive accepted an offer to go over to the bar of The Bell and Bottle. He sold his share of his inheritance to his brother, and Conrad was left alone.

He had no difficulty now in following Laura's thoughts.

"It's an eyesore," he said, "and it's getting worse. If she'd go and live with her sister up at Whitby, I could get a woman to move in. But she's going to stick. Costs her nothing but her food, so she can spend all her dough on living it up. When you think of the business we could've done, with all those workmen rebuilding your old house . . ." He shrugged in resignation. "Oh, well, that's life." His eyes went to the approaching bus. "There's been nobody coming in here all this week. Just a few parcels, and the two Transcombe kids going to stay with their grandma, and Mrs. Flickson going to meet her brother from China."

"Japan."

"All right, Japan. And today, only you. The only passenger I know who's coming is old Mrs. Weatherstone. I've promised to drive her up to her place. You travelling, or meeting someone?"

"I'm waiting for Jess."

He straightened and faced her, interest quickening in his eyes. "Jess coming?"

"Yes."

"She staying long?"

"No. Just the weekend."

"I see. Another of her here-today, gone-tomorrow visits. She's forgetting all her old friends. She hasn't been home for a long time."

"Four months. But this isn't her home," Laura reminded him after a pause. "Not anymore. Her home's in London."

"Well, there's nothing for her here, is there? Nothing for you either."

Conversation languished. The bus drew near and Laura tried to guess the reason for her sister's visit. Her telephone call had not been informative.

"Laura?"

"Nice to hear you, Jess. Any news?"

"I'm coming down to see you."

"Good. When?"

"Friday. Only for the weekend. I've got to talk to you."

"Anything special?"

"In a way. I can't go into it over the phone."

"Something serious?"

"Not for us. It might worry Claud."

Claud was their father, who from their infancy had expressed a preference for being known by his name.

"Have you seen him?"

"No. I've seen Aunt Magda."

"She's in London?"

"Yes. She's going back to Waterside on Friday evening. I'm coming down in the afternoon. My car's giving trouble; I'll have to come by bus."

"I'll meet you."

"Don't cook anything. I've got to take off weight. See you. 'Bye."

Laura, replacing the receiver, had reflected that it would be nice to have news of Claud. He seemed to have gone to ground. Not that there was anything new in that; he had always had a way of disappearing and reappearing.

The bus drew up at the garage. There were only two passengers: old Mrs. Weatherstone, who was swung out on the arms of Conrad and the bus driver; and Jess, who stepped out without assistance. Her only luggage was a small plastic case suspended from her shoulder. She offered a cheek to Laura and then addressed Conrad.

"Nice to see you again, Con. I've just been talking to Clive."

"He's back on the job, is he? He was off with flu, last I heard."

"He's back in the bar. He told me he was thinking of getting married."

"That's as far as it ever gets—thinking," said Conrad.

"I reminded him that when he was fifteen, he promised to marry me. So did you. Hello, Mrs. Weatherstone. I didn't recognize your back view on the bus. How's your wicked husband?"

The old lady gave a cackle, displaying new teeth that had been the reason for her journey into Waterside. "He's fine, Jess dearie, he's fine. He'll want to see you, if you've got time to look in. We miss you here, you know."

The bus driver was climbing into the cab of his vehicle for the return journey. He drove away, but Conrad did not notice his departure. He was musing over the change that a few years had wrought in the two Seton girls. Who would have guessed, he asked himself, that a pair of free-ranging, unfettered young hell-raisers would have turned out like these two? Poise, easy manners, no affectations, and friendly feelings towards all their old companions. Their good looks were no surprise; they'd been good to look at, one so dark, one so fair, when they were chasing round the countryside in scuffed shoes and reach-me-down clothes. You could say they'd brought themselves up. A mother who let the food burn to a cinder while she stood at the kitchen door with a paintbrush, catching the colours of a sunset before it faded. A father who painted portraits some of the time, but shuttled between Crossford and London and Paris most of the time, doing nobody knew quite what. A house that had been half-ruined when they bought it and which went on falling apart through the years of their occupancy. And Jess and Laura running round with the neighbourhood kids, tough, tireless and able to swear in three languages: the English they spoke with their mother, the French they spoke with their half-French father, and the Midland dialect they used at the Waterside school. Well, that was all over. Their mother was dead and their father was still shuttling and Jess had gone to live in London and looked thinner and smarter every time she paid a visit to her sister. You couldn't, he admitted, say that Laura was either thin or smart—but if he had to choose, he'd choose Laura every time.

He came back to the present and picked up Mrs. Weatherstone's bag. "I'm driving you, Missis," he said. "Let's get going."

"I could take her," Laura offered. "We go past the farm."

He turned to look at her small, dilapidated car. "No offense," he said, "but I think she'll be more comfy in my van. I dunno how that thing of yours keeps running."

"You said you'd try and find me another."

"I could find you a dozen—secondhand, third, fourth—but you won't raise your price. They're not giving 'em away anymore."

"She spent all her money on her house," Jess reminded him.

"So she did. She should've bought herself a nice little place in London, same as you did." He paused on his way to the van. "Talking of houses," he added, "what d'you think of the carry-on up at your old house? New wing, new front, new everything else."

"And greenhouses," piped Mrs. Weatherstone, "and stabling. They say it's like what it was when those monks had it."

"That's how it was meant to be," Jess said. "And that," she went on to Laura as they got into the car, "is what it might have been if we'd had any money. Though I doubt whether we'd have used the money to change it. We liked all those empty rooms and odd corridors and leaky attics. I couldn't face it again, but it was a wonderful place to grow up in."

"Yes," Laura agreed. "It was."

Their parents had bought the house shortly after their marriage. It had been built about a century earlier by monks, who during their brief occupancy had had little contact with Crossford and none at all with Waterside. The house was in a bad state of repair and had been known simply as Up-the-hill. This label held no attraction for Claud Seton or his wife, but while they were turning over new possibilities, people in the district began to refer to the house as Seton's. Seton's it remained. And in spite of the extensive rebuilding now being carried out by the new owner, it was understood that there was to be no change in the name.

"Must have cost a lot to do up the place," Jess remarked.

"Yes. What are you groping for?"

"Boots. Didn't you bring a pair of yours for me? I can't wade through mud in the shoes I've got on."

"No mud. The yard's been paved."

"You mean we can actually walk dryshod from the car to the cottage?"

"Yes."

"Thank God for that."

There was silence for a time. They had left behind the village street, the weed-choked lake, the uninviting front that Crossford presented to strangers; now they were driving along the lovely, unspoiled valley. Some distance ahead was a farmhouse that had been owned and occupied for centuries by a family named Sheldon. Beyond the spread of its outbuildings was a small, newly built cottage. This, with four surrounding acres, was now Laura's home.

"When was the road up the hill to Seton's repaired?" Jess asked as they passed it.

"It's only just been finished. They didn't only repair it, they widened it."

Jess's eyes were on Laura's cottage. "I see you've put a wall round your property. About time," she commented.

Laura smiled. Jess's remarks were frank, brusque and at times scathing, but they were delivered in a careless, take-it-or-leave-it way that disarmed her hearers. When they stopped at the door, she spoke with grudging appreciation.

"It's pretty," she acknowledged. "All the same, you ought to get out of it."

"I might, one day. Don't get out of the car yet—the dogs will be all over you."

Parents and puppies were pawing at the windows in an attempt to get in. There was a deafening medley of bass barks and treble yapping. Laura got out, restored order and then opened the door on Jess's side.

"All right now," she said. "How do you like my newly paved entrance?"

"Great improvement. Why don't you put shrubs in tubs on either side of the front door?"

"Too towny. I don't want a Mews look. As soon as I've earned a bit more money, I'm going to extend the wall down to the garage."

"You're actually making money?"

"Raking it in. I delivered eighteen orders yesterday. Come inside and get dry."

They went in. The living room was very long. At one end was a counter behind which were a small stove and a sink. In the center of the room were grouped some comfortable chairs, a sofa that could be extended to make a bed, and a small round table. Behind sliding doors were a bedroom and a bathroom. Against one wall was an open-tread stairway which led up to the attic bedroom and bathroom that had been planned for Claud Seton but which he had never occupied. A door behind the counter opened into the large kitchen in which Laura did the cooking and deep-freezing which, begun tentatively, almost as a hobby, had to her surprise expanded until she now supplied meals not only for festive occasions in the district, but also for a growing list of regular customers.

Jess, looking round the living room, made no comment on its lack of order; she had learned to accept the fact that Laura's idea of gracious living was to have everything within arm's reach. The disarray was a reminder of their old way of life, to which she herself had no desire to return. She had changed; Laura was still as she had been, as their mother had been until she died: happy doing tasks that interested them, contented, oblivious to their surroundings. Laura remained a countrywoman; she, Jess, had made her home in London. Each had got what she wanted.

Not at once. When their mother died, eighteen months ago, there had been a family meeting attended by Jess and Laura and, when they had succeeded in locating him, their father. The future was mapped out. Seton's was to be sold, if a buyer could be found for so dilapidated a property. Claud, who had no income apart from what he earned, would take the proceeds of the sale, leaving to Jess and Laura the money they had inherited from their mother. He stated firmly that he did not want a fixed base; he would continue to use hotels when he was in Paris; when he came to England, all he would need was a studio, if possible where there were no visitors to disturb him, a green retreat surrounded by fields. Having made this clear, he bought part of a disused warehouse in the Deptford district of London, converted it and used it as a studio.

Jess wanted no fields. She planned to buy a flat in London, not far from the place in which she worked. Laura could share the flat with her and look for a job; in their spare time, they would try and find a modest country cottage in which they could spend weekends.

Laura did not look long for a job, and did not look far for the cottage. Mr. Sheldon, the district's leading farmer, who had known her all her life and who—like the members of his family—did not want to see her go away, as Jess had done, offered to sell her four acres of his land. When she had bought them and set about building, she had no clear idea what she wanted from life, but she had learned what she did not want: she did not want to live in a town or in a city. She needed open spaces, rural surroundings, woodland walks; she wanted to tramp round the paths she had known since childhood. She wanted to live what she thought of as a jeans-and-sweater existence, free from social obligations. Above all, she wanted to live at a leisurely pace.

She had not planned to keep animals, but from somewhere had come dogs, two cats of assorted antecedents, two stray ducks and an aged Shetland pony. Mr. Sheldon gave her a cow and the cow gave her a calf. She was offered more live-stock—rabbits appeared in the arms of small Sheldons but were sent back when she learned that she was expected to eat them. Chickens were offered and rejected for the same reason.

Jess, having shed her mackintosh, was lying on the sofa. She was wearing a skirt and a woollen sweater. Her hair, short, springy, looked almost black against the sofa's pale cover. It was hair that required no more attention than a comb drawn through it—to the envy of Laura, whose hair hung fair and straight and stubbornly resistant to styling.

Their characters were as contrasted as their colouring. Jess was impulsive, impatient, a good judge of people but not al-ways charitable in her assessments. Laura was energetic when doing anything that interested her, and at other times lazy. She had none of Jess's need for companionship, none of her easy way at social gatherings. Each in her own way resented interference, but Jess's reactions to it were direct, Laura's less so.

Laura was at the counter, making preparations for tea. "Tell me about Magda," she said.

"Not until I've had some tea," Jess said. She did not offer to help. Arms clasped behind her head, she looked slowly round the room. "I suppose" she said, "this might have turned out even more like Seton's."

"It would, if I'd been left to manage by myself. But I've been lucky. Jim Sheldon came over, unasked, and offered to plow three of my four acres. Don Weatherstone came and asked if he could rent one of my fields to plant vegetables—he takes them into Waterside and sells them from his van. It ended by my not charging him anything, but I can take all the vegetables I want. Old Granny Sheldon said she'd start beekeeping and share the honey, if I'd share the cost. Mrs. Transcombe puts my washing into her machine and her daughter does my ironing and milks my cow, and I give her most of the milk. Old Mrs. Flickson says she hasn't enough to do now that her son's married and his wife has taken over the house, so she comes twice a week and cleans for me. There was only one difficulty: I had no idea that this business of selling deep-freeze food was going to be such a success, and for a time I found I couldn't get away from the phone—orders were coming in all the time. So I went to see Winnie Transcombe—she works at the Waterside Hotel switchboard—and we agreed on a fee, and now all orders are phoned to her, and I call her once a day and write them down."

"If you hadn't had all that help . . ."

"I know. Squalor, as Magda used to describe conditions at Seton's. But I've discovered something that you probably knew all along: that I'm like Mother. Remember what she used to say about housework?"

"Yes. 'Do only what you comfortably can, and forget the rest.'"

"Such *wisdom*, Jess. In that great ruin of a house, with two children and a husband who kept going away and didn't do much even when he was around, not a single laboursaving gadget, no electricity until right at the end, no car, just that pony we had to catch, and that cart with the wobbly wheels, and a great stone-floored kitchen . . . if she'd let all that get on top of her, where would we have been? So she concentrated on producing one square meal a day, and then she—"

"—let us run wild. It was a good life. Free."

Too free, Claud's mother had decided on one of their frequent visits to her. She was French, rich and selfish, but she interrupted her habit of spending money lavishly on herself long enough to pay the fees of a boarding school in England.

It was during school holidays that Jess and Laura, bringing

girls home for visits, had first begun to understand that life in a large, cold, half-furnished and ill-equipped house was not everybody's idea of bliss. The realization had come as a great surprise to them both. It had not greatly altered Laura's outlook, but for Jess it had been the beginning of the road that led in time to London and a series of jobs in a photographer's, a Chelsea boutique and an interior decorator's. She was now designing jewellery.

"Speaking of freedom," she said, "look; I'm free." She held up a ringless hand, and Laura looked at it with a worried frown.

"You don't mean that Wilfred—" she began.

"All over."

"I'm sorry," Laura said.

She spoke with genuine regret. Among the confusing variety of Jess's men friends, Wilfred Downes was the only one who had links with home, the only voice that spoke a language she recognized. She had been surprised to find him in favour, for he did not conform to the pattern set by the other men Jess knew. He was a solicitor with an office in London, stolid, serious and, in matters unconnected with Jess, a man of sense. His father, a successful surgeon, had retired and bought a large house in Waterside, and Wilfred came down frequently to visit his widowed mother and his two sisters.

"What went wrong?" she asked.

"Oh, all those early-morning exercises he did, with the window wide open and snow blowing in on my pillow. He was always a health maniac, if you remember, raw carrots and nuts and sunflower seeds, but it's got worse. Now he goes in for muscle building, so every morning, up, down, in, out. So I said Out."

"But—"

"And it was his fault that I got landed with Hollis. He

21

tried to get rid of him, and couldn't. Hollis has got suckers; he adheres. He needs his glasses changed; he can't see when he's not wanted. Wilfred saw."

"But, Jess, that makes four. Iain, Ivan, I forget who next, and now Wilfred."

"That's right. Four."

"Why get engaged to them, when you know very well it isn't going to last?"

"Don't blame me; blame them. I make it absolutely clear, right at the beginning, that I've no intention of getting married until I'm at least thirty. Getting engaged isn't my idea; it's theirs."

"But why let them move into your flat?"

"They move in because I won't move out. Bernard's given me a lovely ring. I can't show it to you because it's being made smaller."

"Bernard?"

"You'll like him; he's nice, and he's not as jealous as Wilfred was. He's Bernard Shotton, brother of the sports commentator. You know?"

"No."

"Don't you *ever* look at television?"

"Now and then I—"

"How do you expect to keep in touch? Even if you live in outer space, you can at least try to follow what's going on in places where things do go on. To say you've never seen or heard of Miles Shotton is like saying you don't know who the Prime Minister is, not that that would surprise me. Miles Shotton is the top sports commentator, as you'd know if you were switched on—you and the television, too. Bernard's his brother."

"I see. You really like him?"

"Yes."

"But this Mr. Hollis—is he still around?"

"Not Mister. Hollis is his first name. He's called Hollis Hinchcliffe Howard."

"She sells sea shells. Do you want Indian or China?"

"China, with lemon."

"What does this Hollis do?"

"He hangs around. He sticks. However hard you try, you can't get rid of him."

"Who is he?"

"Some kind of soil analyst. Most of his jobs are in the region of the Persian Gulf and in those Arab states—he goes and comes, but he doesn't go often enough and he doesn't stay away long enough. Then he comes back and reattaches himself to me and my friends."

"Where did you meet him?"

"Through Wilfred's two sisters. He couldn't glue himself to them, because they were always on the move from one concert platform to the other, so he transferred himself to Wilfred, and that's how I got landed with him."

"Hasn't he got a home?"

"He's got two. His mother's got a house in Salisbury, and he's got rooms in some dreary house near my apartment block. But he has to talk, and talking to himself is no fun, so he looks for an audience. When he finds one, he stays with it. The only thing you can do with anybody like him is to transplant him. I'm trying to find someone to pass him on to."

Laura carried the tray to the table and handed Jess her cup with a saucer on which were slices of lemon. "Anything to eat?" she asked.

"No. Between buying this skirt, and wearing it two weeks later, I put on eight ounces. I was getting gross."

Laura thought that she was getting gaunt, but did not say so. They had long ago clarified their widely differing ideas on weight.

"Why did Magda want to see you?" she asked.

"She didn't. She rang to tell me she was in London for a few days. I went to see her because I was afraid that if I didn't, she'd come and see me, and I couldn't have stood that. So I went. What upset me was something she said." She paused to drink her tea. "You know, you're like Mother in another way: you have this calming effect. When I came down today, I was tense. Worked up. Now I'm not."

"That's not me; it's the country air."

"No, it's you." She held out her cup to be refilled. "Before I forget, I want to ask you about this man who's bought Seton's—Falconer."

"His first name's Finch. Wouldn't you say that was an odd name for a man?"

"If you ever run into him—"

"I suppose it's no odder than Robin."

"I suppose not. If you ever run into him, could you—"

"Or Merlin."

"Look, we've played that. Can we proceed?"

"Sorry. You were saying?"

"If you ever run into this man, could you say a word to him about having a sister in the interior-decorating business?"

"But you gave that up."

"I know I did, but if I got Ivan a job as big as this one's likely to be, he'd give me a nice rake-off."

"You still see Ivan?"

"How can I help seeing him? He's taken a flat just up the road, and he keeps coming in to borrow things."

"Well, no rake-off. You're too late."

"Why? Has the job been given to another firm?"

"I don't know. But he wouldn't give it to anyone I recommended. We've, so to speak, crossed swords."

"You've had a row?"

"Not exactly a row. He discovered that someone had removed the plaque with the inscription that was above the door of the chapel at Seton's. He thought it had been removed after the house was sold."

"He's right. Claud went up there the next evening and took it down. You knew that."

"Not until I saw it among the things he was packing when he went to Paris."

"This Finch wanted it back?"

"Yes."

"Did you say he could have it?"

"No."

"Quite right."

"Not quite right, quite wrong. If Claud took it, it should be given back. But I like people to ask politely."

"And Finch didn't?"

"No. We met for the first time when I was getting into my car one day last week. In Waterside. It was just after the market had closed, and I was on my way home and I wasn't looking my best. I—"

"Let me guess. You were wearing that same old mackintosh, and your hair was hanging in streaks like this morning, and you were carrying an armful of cabbages."

"I was carrying a wastepaper basket I'd bought."

"Have you any idea how lovely you'd look, if only you'd take some trouble?"

"Yes, I have. Have you any idea how you'd look if you tried being a cook and a delivery van? Do you want to hear about this Finch, or not?"

"Yes."

"His car was parked next to mine. He was just getting out. Nice clothes—best-tailor look. I recognized the girl who was with him—she played Fanny Burney in the Fanny Burney film."

"They're engaged."

"I know."

"You surprise me. You actually switched on your television?"

"I didn't have to. The whole of Crossford and Waterside knew about them. How could I help knowing?"

"Was there much local gossip?"

"Not when she ditched Lord Torringdon. It was only when people realized that the Falconer she'd ditched him for, was the Falconer who'd bought Seton's, that the gossip started. Then everybody got used to seeing him coming and going to Seton's to see how the rebuilding was getting on, and the interest died down."

"Does he often come?"

"Yes. She only comes now and then, and only for an hour or so. He stays. He's got a room or rooms fixed up at Seton's. I think people have forgotten all about that affair."

"It was rather more than an affair. She and Lord Torringdon were going to be married in two weeks, and she changed her mind overnight and got engaged to his closest friend, Finch Falconer. Well, go on. You met him in the car park and she was with him. And then?"

"I don't think he would have asked me about the plaque then, but she said—meaning me to overhear—'There's that girl who used to live at Seton's, ask her about the chapel inscription.' He mutttered something about some other time, but she said 'If you don't, I will,' so he came over and said that the plaque had been removed after the house had been sold. I told him he should go and see the lawyers who arranged the sale of the house. Then I drove away, but I was angry and I grazed one of his fenders as I backed out, and I didn't stop to apologize. So I don't think I could go and ask him about interior decorating."

"Pity. What does he look like?"

"Didn't you just say you'd seen him on television?"

"Not him. Her. He didn't appear."

"He's tall and broad."

"Good-looking?"

"Yes, except that he's got a sort of built-in frown. Not an angry frown; a suspicious look. Conrad services his car and says he doesn't waste words. He didn't waste any when he talked to me. Go on about Magda. Was she at her usual hotel?"

"Yes. I can't understand why they don't throw her out—she acts as if she owns the place. But she always gets a room when she wants one, and she always gets the room she wants. I know she's an Honourable, but I wouldn't have said that cut any ice nowadays."

"It doesn't. It's all those receptions and lunches and dinners she gives in her official capacities. She held three big receptions at the Waterside hotel recently: Aid to Refugees, Retired Horses and Women Militant. Go on."

"The first thing I had to listen to, of course, was her account of how overworked she'd been. Then came the usual grouses about expense. Can there be, anywhere, a woman more cheeseparing than she is?"

"No. What did she say that worried you?"

"She was talking about a picture that she'd had stored when she gave up her house. She'd written to that firm that deals with her pictures—I've forgotten the name."

"Mellish and Son. It used to be Mellish and Sons, but one of the sons had a row and walked out—about three or four years ago. Go on."

"She wrote to them to say that she was going to sell a picture—a Zollard. She had an answer from the son. He said he had reason to believe that the picture wasn't genuine; it was a copy."

Laura was frowning. "Zollard? That was the picture Mother liked, wasn't it?"

"Yes. When Magda gave up her house, it went into storage like all her other pictures and silver and valuables. Everything, she told us at the time, was to be Mother's when she died. But

27

it was Mother who died, and since then, Magda's been selling off items. She offered this Zollard to—guess."

"Can't. Who?"

"Finch Falconer. But before she could show it to him, she got this letter saying it was a copy. So she stormed up to London to have it out with Mellish and Son, but old Mr. Mellish was in hospital, and all the son could tell her was that the brother—the son who walked out—had told him it was a copy. Magda must have accused him of switching the picture, because he assured her that it hadn't been out of their hands except for the time when, following her instructions, they sent it to be cleaned before putting it into storage. And that's when I began to worry."

"You mean this is where Claud comes in?"

"I don't know. I don't know whether he comes in or not. There's no connection in Magda's mind—as yet—between the firm's letter and Claud. But if they tell her who did the cleaning, she'll get her nose to the ground."

"I don't see . . . Oh, you mean this firm was the one that occasionally gave work to Claud?"

"Yes."

"But why should you think that he—"

"I'll tell you why. The picture was stored five years ago. Where were we—you and I—five years ago?"

"At a boarding school in Sussex."

"The fees of which were paid by Claud's mother. Five years ago she died, leaving Claud nothing but debts. So no more fees. So we got ready to pack up and leave school and come home—but what happened? We didn't come home. Claud sent us to Paris. We spent two blissful years at the École Eugénie. Not cheap, the École Eugénie. There hadn't been any money to keep us at school, so where did the money come from to pay large fees to Madame Luard and Mademoiselle Justine? Two years' fees plus those little extras like theatres and expeditions and . . . well, you remember. In those days, Madame Luard and Mademoiselle Justine had never set eyes on Claud, so he couldn't have used his charm to persuade them to take us for nothing."

"He would have needed more than charm. Strictly business, those two."

"Quite. So for two years we were there, and the fees were paid by Claud. So where does that leave us?"

"It leaves us hinting that Claud switched the picture, sold the original and stored the copy. I don't believe it. I don't believe it for one moment."

"Why not?" Jess leaned over to put her empty cup on the tray, and then leaned back. "Why not?" she asked again. "What do we really know about Claud?"

"We know that he's good-looking and amusing and—"

"What hard facts can we assemble?"

"He's a portrait painter."

"You have to qualify that. He's a portrait painter who doesn't often paint portraits because he doesn't like getting involved with people, and sitters are people. Go on."

"He married Mother, who was an orphan with quite a lot of money which—"

"—was in trust, and doled out in snippets. He himself was the son of a rich man who died just after Claud was married, and who left all his money to Claud's mother, but forgot to put in any instructions about doling it out to her in snippets. Result: she got through the lot. That was a terrible thing to do—to leave her only son without a sou. But just think back, Laura, at how *beautifully* she lived. Remember all the times we went to stay with her? First that heavenly house in Paris, and then expensive rented villas in Cannes, rented chalets in Gstaad and Zermatt and Cortina, cruises in the Mediterranean, that fabulous hotel in Istanbul . . ." She stopped on a deep, nostalgic breath. "When I remember to say my prayers, I put in Grandmère, with thanks."

"So do I."

29

"Well, you see? She left Claud nothing, not even enough to pay our last term's fees at school. And just then, Mellish and Son or Sons hand him this picture, this Zollard, and tell him to clean it before it's put into storage. Look into Claud's mind. He'd feel certain that it wouldn't be taken out of storage until Magda was dead—and then it would have belonged to Mother. It would have seemed to him, it would have looked to him like money for jam—a wise, sensible thing to do."

"Claud would never—"

"—stoop so low? How do we *know*? This is the first time in your life or in mine that we've considered exactly what Claud is, or what Claud does. We know what Magda thinks of him. She never believed he had a rich father when he married Mother. She thinks he married her for her money, and she thinks the proof is in the fact that he has never done any regular work—what she'd call work—in his life. She thinks he's Cadgers, Incorporated."

"Claud restores pictures."

"So we've always understood. But as far as we know, only two firms have ever given him any restoring to do: Mellish and Son, in London, and Lavalette, in Paris. The rest of the time, he goes round out-of-the-way picture dealers in London and Paris, picking out neglected work and restoring it and reselling it. What else do we know about him? We know that when he was at Seton's, he was good company. He was fun. He was—"

"He was a crook, if he switched that Zollard."

Jess got up, walked to the window and looked out. Then she turned to face Laura.

"Yes," she said. "You've got the idea. I thought you'd be upset if I talked about it."

"Of course I'm upset. But I'm puzzled, too."

"What about?"

"The picture. Why all this fuss? I've never heard that a Zollard fetched a big price. It's—"

"Will you use your head? Money matters more than anything else to Magda. She paid for that picture. Having paid for it, she now suspects that firm of having cheated her. Money, money, money. If she'd lived in the old coaching days and a highwayman had said: 'Your money or your life,' she'd have been dead on the spot. She'll keep at that firm because they bought the picture for her and told her that it was genuine. She'll find out that it was given to Claud to be cleaned—and once she knows that, she'll see her chance to go after him. Whether he is or isn't mixed up in this won't matter to her; she'll go for him tooth and nail."

"Tooth and claw. We shouldn't just be talking about this. Isn't there something we can do?"

"Yes, there is. Somebody's got to go across to Paris and talk to Claude. I can't go. I've got orders that'll keep me busy for some time. You'll have to go."

"*Me?*"

"You. What's to stop you?"

"What's to . . . You don't imagine, do you, that people who own animals can just go off and leave them? And I've got orders coming in, just as you have. I can't—"

"People who own animals usually make some arrangement with neighbours to do the feeding in times of emergency. This is an emergency. Haven't you ever left this place and asked someone to take over for a few days?"

"Yes. Sue Sheldon takes over."

"Then all you've got to do is walk over, tell her you've been called away, and—"

"You think it's as easy as that?"

"Easy or not, Laura, this is what I just called it—an emergency. That means it's urgent. Magda's waited for over twenty years to get at Claud. She won't ask for proof. If there's even a vestige of suspicion, she'll talk, and it'll be all round the district, with embellishments. I know you don't want to leave your dogs and your deep-freezing, but you can shake loose if you want to—and you've got to want to now. You've got to go and warn Claud. You know where to find him."

"No, I don't."

"Where else would he be except at the Eugénie? He's never stayed anywhere else since it was made into a hotel."

"He wasn't there when I rang up on his birthday, ten days ago. They said he'd been there, but he'd gone away."

"All the more reason for going over. You can find out where he went."

"And what do I say when I find him, if I find him?"

"You simply say you decided to take a brief holiday in Paris and didn't want to leave without seeing him. Tell him a few items of news, and then say casually that you ran into Magda and found her in a rage because she'd been told that the Zollard that had been stored wasn't a genuine Zollard, but only a copy, and had he by any chance seen the picture, and if so, what was his opinion?"

"Where does that get us?"

"Nowhere. It alerts Claud, that's all. Whether he switched that picture or not, he's got to be told that Magda's out for blood. He'll take it from there. He knows how much she loathes him and he knows she's longed for a chance to get at him. The least we can do is warn him. Will you go?"

There was a prolonged silence.

"Yes," Laura said unwillingly at last. "I'll go."

"When?"

"Well, this week will be—"

"You can't think in weeks. You've got to go as soon as you've fixed things with Sue Sheldon. You can do that today or tomorrow. You can leave on Monday."

"Monday! I—"

"And go by air."

"Why air? I like going on the night ferry."

"I know you do. But this isn't a pleasure trip. You'll go by air, and I'll book you a flight first thing on Monday. You can get away on Monday afternoon; there's no travel rush at this time of the year. Go straight to the Eugénie Hotel; if Claud isn't there, find out where he went, and follow him. You won't have to go far; he doesn't stray out of Paris. You'll get your tickets at the airport. Is that all straight?"

"I suppose so."

"Good." Jess ran her fingers through her hair. "Thank God that's off our minds. Now we can relax. I hope you didn't tell anyone I was coming down."

"Conrad knows, and Clive knows."

"Yes, I forgot. That'll mean that all the old crowd will be told, and I'll be expected to make the rounds. Has Mr. Sheldon got any more horses?"

"Yes. Two. Want a ride?"

"Don't you?"

"Yes."

The rest of the day followed the pattern of all Jess's visits—a succession of meetings with former companions who still lived in the neighbourhood, a drink session at The Bell and Bottle and dinner at Waterside's newest restaurant. Not until midnight did Jess and Laura get back to the cottage, attended by a guard of honour who were invited in for a last drink—which, traditionally, was cocoa.

When the last car had driven into the night, Laura gave Jess a choice: Claud's room upstairs, or the sofa bed downstairs?

"Oh, down here," Jess said unhesitatingly. "Then we can talk."

"Shouldn't we switch on the television and look at Bernard's brother?"

"Laura, don't try to be funny. It doesn't *suit* you."

They left the sliding door open and lay in the darkness. This was how it had been, not so long ago. They had shared a room at school; there had been a communicating door between their rooms at the École Eugénie, and they had talked in the darkness. This was as it had been before Jess decided to go to London and Laura decided to stay in Crossford. This was perhaps how it would seldom be again.

"Sleep well," Laura said at last.

"In a minute. I've been thinking about Claud and Mother. Claud and Helen. Funny how we always called him Claud but never called her anything but Mother. I suppose a psychiatrist could make something out of that. Would you have called theirs an ideal marriage?"

"No. Ideal relationship, yes. But marriage—no."

"Why not?"

"Because I think marriage is a relationship in which couples get together more than Claud and Mother ever did."

"They loved each other."

"They didn't really know each other—not in the way most married couples get to know each other. He used to drift away, and drift back, and Mother would say: 'Do help yourself to anything you want, dear,' and go on with her painting or sculpting or sketching, and he'd take a look and tell her what she was doing wrong, and then he'd take over the cooking because he didn't like the way she cooked. They never got into what you could call a domestic routine."

"I suppose that's true. The only family get-together was when we sat down to dinner. I suppose they loved their children, but you can't say they spent much time watching our development, can you?"

"No. If Claud had ever given us any advice, it would have been a warning to keep out of complicated situations. His way of coping with people was to dodge them. He took no interest in women when he was at Seton's. Do you think he kept away from women in Paris?"

"Yes. If he hadn't, I think Mother would have known. But she didn't have to worry; what Claud loved was herself, his painting, peace, French cooking and French wine—in that order."

"If I marry a wanderer like Claud, I won't think I'm enjoying an ideal marriage," Laura said.

"You want someone who's always around, getting in the way?"

"I want someone who'll talk over the household bills, and read the school reports and blow up because the kids aren't at the top of their class. I want a face behind a newspaper at breakfast, and arguments about where to go for holidays. That's marriage."

"That was. But we're streaking for the space age. You frighten me sometimes, Laura, you really do. You're still holding views that went out with bustles. As we've got on to marriage, there's nobody round here I'd like to see you settle down with."

"There's no hurry."

"Don't you ever *want* a man?"

"Only to do the weight lifting. Isn't it time you settled down? Four men in under two years might sound a modest total in some circles, but I think you're overdoing it."

"I'll make a note. Speaking of Claud—"

"Tomorrow. Go to sleep."

"Magda tomorrow. With luck, she won't come until the evening."

"The luck would be if she didn't come at all. But that's too much to hope for."

She came before Jess and Laura had finished their breakfast coffee. Having brushed aside the dogs and entered without the formality of knocking, she stood for some moments in the doorway, surveying with compressed lips the unmade sofa bed, the untidy bedroom beyond, the cups left unwashed from the night before, the cats asleep on the chairs.

"Almost ten thirty," she said, "and still in your night attire. And as usual, everything in disorder."

Her voice was rather high, and not unmusical, but had a

note in it that suggested she was addressing serfs. She was tall, thin, handsome, well groomed and expensively though not fashionably dressed. Her chief characteristic, overriding even her parsimoniousness, was arrogance. Daughter of a baron, she had been told from infancy that she was Somebody, and she was to go to the end of her life believing it. She was without tact or humour, encased in smugness, armoured against snubs or slights, impervious to the effect she had on others.

Her marriage had been childless; her maternal instincts had centered on Helen, her husband's motherless niece. When her offer to adopt the child was rejected, she appointed herself unofficial guardian—an unrewarding role, for Helen, dreamy, detached, listened politely to the unending stream of advice and then acted as though she had heard nothing. Her decision to go to London to study painting, her subsequent marriage to an unknown portrait painter, took place without the knowledge of Magda, who, immersed in business matters after the death of her husband, surfaced to find her niece married and installed in a half-ruined house in an out-of-the-way village named Crossford.

She could not bring herself to reproach Helen, but she never forgave Claud. Her low opinion of him, freely and frequently expressed, appeared justified by later events, for having claimed to be sole heir of a rich father, he had inherited nothing and had contributed little or nothing to the support of his wife and children. He had done no regular work. He had absented himself from home at frequent intervals, and he had allowed his children to run wild with the children of the neighbouring farmers.

For some years after her marriage, Helen had seen little of her aunt. Two or three times a year, Magda descended on Waterside, inspected Seton's and expressed horror and disgust at what she called its primitive living conditions, suggested extensive and expensive improvements and then returned to her mansion in Bath. About five years ago she had sold this, stored its contents and installed herself in a Waterside hotel. After this, her visits to Seton's became more frequent and more trying.

On Helen's death, Magda's unwelcome criticism and advice were transferred to Jess and Laura. Nothing they could say or do to shake her off had the smallest effect; they could only be grateful for the saving fact that a large proportion of her time had to be devoted to her other commitments, which she called her civic duties.

Laura was folding the sofa bed, dislodging a cat and drawing up a chair for the visitor. Magda sat down and spoke irritably to Jess.

"Why didn't you tell me you were coming down to Crossford? I would have asked you to bring down some things for me."

"I didn't come by car."

"In that case, it'll be you, Laura, who will have to take me back to the hotel. I came in the hotel taxi, as usual, but I refused to keep him for the return journey. He now charges a waiting fee, which I told him was quite unnecessary." She leaned back and loosened her coat. "Laura, when are you going to do something about keeping this cottage in order?"

"One day," Laura said tranquilly.

"I've told you more than once that I can arrange for a cleaning woman to come over from Waterside two or three times a week. That one you've got is quite useless. You'll have to pay the Waterside woman the exorbitant wage they all ask now, but you can afford it. Do you two girls ever stop to think where you would be now if I hadn't had the foresight to advise your mother's lawyers to tie up her capital? Your father would have got through it all, just as he got through his father's money, if there ever was any of his father's money, which I've never for one moment believed. I can't say I approve of the way in which you used the money you inherited, but at least Jess had the sense to leave Crossford and shake off all those unsuitable childhood connections. Laura, what did you have to pay for having your entrance paved?"

"I haven't had the bill yet."

"You mustn't pay it before showing it to me. You insisted on giving the work to a builder I've no confidence in; everybody knows he overcharges. No, no coffee, thank you. I've got to get back soon; I've two committee meetings this afternoon. I really do too much. People are always telling me that I should take a rest."

"Why don't you go on a world cruise?" Jess suggested.

"Have you any idea how much a world cruise would cost?"

"It wouldn't cost more than you could pay."

"It would cost far more than I would agree to pay. And what pleasure can one get in travelling nowadays? There was a time when one could winter in pleasant, inexpensive places and be welcomed and well looked after by the natives. But no longer. As for cruising, I shouldn't enjoy it in the least. Imagine being with people one doesn't know and probably doesn't like, without any means of getting away from them."

"You could jump overboard," Jess suggested.

"I wish you wouldn't always be so flippant. Have either of you by any chance met the new owner of Seton's."

"I've seen him here and there," Laura answered.

"He hasn't shown any interest in the neighbourhood so far, but he may be waiting until he takes up residence. You know, of course, that he was mixed up in that affair between that actress and Lord Torringdon? Now she's engaged to this man Falconer, but I really can't imagine what she's going to find to do in a place like Crossford. I daresay she'll be like your father—more out of it than in it. This Falconer is what used, in my day, to be called a rough diamond. No shortage of money. It comes from his mother's side. His grandfather was the head of a steel firm in Sheffield; he married a woman named Finch and the firm became Finch-Falconer and made millions. Some of the millions have been spent on rebuilding Seton's.

Grandfather made them, grandson is spending them. His grandfather brought him up, I'm told; day school, scholarship to Oxford, no polish of any kind. Grandfather didn't believe in polish. It's a pity we've got to have that actress here. She had three fiancés before settling on Falconer: first that Air Marshal, then that film director who, they say, got her the Burney part. Then Lord Torringdon. I think there was a great deal more in that affair than the public ever got to know. All that's certain is that this man Falconer stole his best friend's fiancée. The reason I mentioned him was because I offered to sell him one of the pictures I had in storage. Did you tell Laura, Jess?"

"I told her you'd had a letter saying it wasn't genuine."

"I was going to write a very strong reply, but then I decided to go to London and see them. It was a wasted journey. Mr. Mellish was in hospital, waiting to undergo an operation. I was shown into the son's office. Not Edward; Edward was the son who left the firm, and a great pity that was, because he was the only one with anything you could call brains. He left four years ago, but it was he who told his brother that he thought the picture—a Zollard, you probably remember it—was merely a copy. Why, I asked, was I not notified at the time? Nobody could answer me. Where, I then asked, was Edward, who had given his opinion in the face of the experts who had said that the picture was genuine? Nobody knew where Edward was. Short of paying another team of experts, which I'm certainly not going to do, the only thing left is for me to wait until Mr. Mellish comes back to the office—if he ever does. That's the last piece of business they'll ever do for me, I can promise you that. I suppose your father is away as usual?"

"Yes," Laura answered.

"He has never once stayed in this house, has he?"

"No."

"I could have told you so, when you planned that room for

him. I knew that once he got his hands on the money from the sale of Seton's, he'd set about spending it. Jess, before I go, I must say a word of protest about the way you've treated poor Wilfred Downes. His mother is terribly upset."

"What's it got to do with his mother?" Jess inquired.

"She happens, strange as it may sound, to be interested in her son's well-being. I think it's a pity he couldn't have found a woman who would marry him and settle down."

"That's what I think, too. Tell his mother to help him to look."

"Don't be childish, Jessica; you know very well you're in the wrong. For years, he has never looked at another girl, and this is how you treat him. His poor mother—"

"—should be rather relieved."

"You were certainly spoiling his chances of finding anyone else. His mother isn't strong, and—"

"She's as tough as ski boots. I can't stop you from discussing my affairs with her, but— Oh, must you go?"

"Yes. Laura, will you kindly put on some clothes and drive me back to the hotel? I have only one more thing to say to you, Jessica, and that is that the Downes family are well liked and respected in Waterford; it won't do you any good to be talked of as callous and unfeeling."

"It won't do me any harm, either."

"I was going to invite you to come and have tea with me tomorrow, but I can see you're not in a social mood. Some other time, perhaps."

"Perhaps."

Laura returned from the bedroom, ready to leave. Jess watched them drive away, told the cats exactly what she thought of Magda, and then undressed, got under the shower and washed away her irritation.

Chapter 2

Monday morning was fine, but not warm. Laura, working hurriedly down the list of things that had to be done before her departure, wished that she could have found time to pause and think about her journey's end. Spring in Paris. They had had many, she and Jess, but never with Claud. He was as elusive on that side of the Channel as he was on this; never to be pinned down in Paris or in London.

Sue Sheldon—once Sue Transcombe, and a lifelong friend and companion—came over to ask if she could do anything to help.

"I don't think so, Sue, thanks."

"Suitcase packed?"

"Yes. I'm sorry to leave you with all the—"

"Forget it." Sue, small, quick-moving, efficient, picked up a list from the counter. "This the program?"

"Yes. I shouldn't have bothered you with all the details, but—"

"I'd rather have them. All animals have their likes and dislikes, and I'd rather know about them. Does the pony still get through that gate?"

"No. I fixed the latch."

"You're not going to hurry back, are you? You haven't seen your father for a long time."

"I'm not sure I'm going to see him now. The keys are on the table; don't lock yourself out."

"What have you done about the orders for deep-freeze meals?"

"They'll have to pile up until I get back. Sue, I can't thank you enough for taking over."

"You've done more for me. Remember when I brought the twins over and left them with you?"

"Yes. Frightening, but fun." She looked round the room. "Time to go."

She hurried past the eagerly following dogs and hoped they would not sense that she was deserting them. Not for long— but desertion it was. They would line up outside the door tomorrow, and she would not be there to open it and give them their breakfast.

She said good-bye to Sue and drove away. She had decided to leave her car at Conrad's garage, to be serviced during her absence.

"I hope to be back before the end of the week," she told Conrad. "Could you do whatever's needed, and—"

"You don't mean that, Laura love. If I did everything that car needed, you'd have a bill a mile long."

"Well, just the oiling and things, then."

"Bit sudden, this trip, isn't it?"

"In a way."

"Going to see your father?"

"Yes."

"Tell him from me he missed a grand opportunity of making a lot of dough. He should've been the one to open that new restaurant in Waterside. Clive says it's pulling in a fortune—and they don't know half as much about food as your dad does. How're you travelling this time—land, sea or air?"

"Air."

"Don't lose your boarding card, like you did once. And don't get stuck in the duty-free shop and miss the plane. You saw your aunt on Saturday, didn't you?"

"Yes."

"I bet she'll be busy this morning, catching up on the news. Have you heard about the row up at Seton's?"

"No."

"As a rule, I only get the tail end of any gossip that's going around here. But this time, I got it straight, as you might say, from the horse's mouth. He stopped here for gas, and—"

"Who did?"

"That architect chap. He was in such a toss-up that I thought I ought to ask him to stand clear while I filled up. Friday evening, this was. I'd seen her go by about an hour before that, driving *ventre à terre*, as you linguists say. That car of hers is so low-slung it's got its *ventre* practically on the *terre*."

"Whose car?"

"Pay attention, love, pay attention. The bus won't be here yet. I'm talking about the lady. The fiancée, if you want more French. She looked steamed up, too, but that's more or less her usual expression. She went by and then he came along, this architect, and I thought he was going by, too, but no; he stopped and told me to fill up. And while he was paying for the gas, along comes car number three—the big one. The boss's. Mr. F. Falconer's. And he stops, but he doesn't want petrol, he only wants the architect. I didn't even have to edge nearer to listen—I was right there, at their elbows, and I got it all, direct. The architect did all the talking, and what he said was that it was the end, the finish, the ultimate limit. I wish I could think of things like that: ultimate limit. That's what I'm going to say in future when I fill up a car: 'Sorry, can't fit any more, sir or madam, I've reached the ultimate limit.' He'd warned Mr. F. before, he said, and more than once. He'd warned him that if ever he came down here again and found that his plans, his orders had been countermanded, messed about by her, this lady we've been talking about, then he wouldn't stand for it. And that day, Friday, had been a proof that she thought she was in charge, and not him. Mr. F. was late driving from London—he comes most Fridays and stays over the weekend, but this Friday he was late, and the architect and the lady had got there first. She had time before the architect arrived to go round giving orders to the workmen—and she told them that this was being done with the architect's knowledge and say-so. He told Mr. F. that he got there to find everything to blazes. So he said that Mr F. could get himself another architect, or if he liked it better, he could take his fiancée and the two of them could go into the architect's business together. He'd send in his account, and Mr. F. could send his check, and good-bye. And with that, he got into his car and went, and Mr. F. went after him. So it looks to me like no more architect."

"He was a good architect, people said."

"The best. Famous. Internationally famous, which means that you don't expect to be messed about by young women who stray onto the site, even if they've just played the lead in a successful film. Here's your bus, love. Have a nice time, and don't stay away too long."

"I won't. Good-bye, Con."

"Good-bye, love. Looks like you've got a nice flying day."

It looked even better at the airport, but her mind was still on her house and the animals she had left behind. She had no anxiety about their welfare—Sue would look after them well—but she missed them and knew they would miss her.

The airport formalities, the safety precautions, seemed to her tedious and irritating. If she had gone by train, she thought impatiently, she would merely have had to walk onto the platform and find her seat and the train would have started. Now she was sitting in a departure lounge watching the time of the flight go by and listening to reasons why it was going to be further delayed.

Departure was at last announced. At the departure gate she saw a figure she recognized: Finch Falconer. He was one of the first in line; he did not turn and she did not think he had seen her. There was time, on the way to the aircraft, to study his impressive height and width and well-made clothes.

She thought Crossford an unlikely place for a man like him to choose to live in. He looked like a successful executive, our man in Wherever. He would look odd among the farmers and the dairymen.

Entering the plane, she remembered a further objection she had to air travel: lack of leg room. She was glad to find a window seat vacant, and made her way to it. Seated beside her she found, presently, a man of about fifty, and next to him, on the aisle seat, a witchlike old woman with a fierce expression and a varied collection of shawls and scarves which she unfurled before settling herself in her seat. From her conversation with the man, which was in French, Laura learned that they were mother and son. After listening for a time to his mother's complaints about the discomfort of her seat, the son suggested that she might be more comfortable seated between himself and Laura. To this the old lady answered in a carrying voice that she had been assured that she would be given a window seat, but if selfish young women pushed their way onto the aircraft and occupied all the best places, there was nothing for the old to do but endure.

There was some delay before takeoff. The old lady's complaints continued in a growl. After a time, the man turned to Laura, gave a stiff little bow and asked her if she spoke French. She said that she did.

"Then you have understood what my mother has been saying," he told her apologetically. "You must forgive her. She is old, she is fatigued. Travelling is not easy for people of her age."

"If she'd like this window seat, I'll change places with her," Laura offered.

Before the sentence was completed, the old lady was fumbling with her seat belt. Helped out of it, and out of her seat, by her son and a steward, she waited for Laura to vacate the window seat and then shuffled into it. There was no word of thanks and no change of expression; having made herself comfortable, she took a large rosary from her bag, leaned back and closed her eyes.

When they were airborne, the man expressed his gratitude. His name, he said, was Coulin, Henri Coulin. He explained that he had not been in favour of his mother's visit to England; she was not used to today's conditions. She had travelled only in her youth, when everything had been easy, no crowds, numerous porters, everybody anxious to assist. A young lady of today could not imagine how it had been in those old times. Today it was very different.

"I suppose it is," Laura agreed.

"You speak excellent French, mademoiselle. You have lived in France?"

"From time to time. My grandmother was French."

" 'Was.' She is not still alive?"

"No."

"I regret. But it comes to us all. You are going to stay in Paris?"

"Near Paris. Vauzel."

He gave an exclamation of surprise. Vauzel? He and his mother lived not more than eight kilometers from Vauzel.

"Then you must have known École Eugénie," Laura said.

The École Eugénie? Had not Mme. Luard been one of his best customers? His shop had supplied the École with most of its staples: sugar, cereals, rice, flour. His son had driven to Vauzel for orders. Such a splendid institution, such charming young ladies, and Mme. Luard and her sister Mlle. Justine so good, so respected. It was a pity that with the death of Mme. Luard, changes had come. From the École Eugénie, it had become the Hôtel Eugénie—but he was still one of its suppliers. Now it was Mlle. Justine who was in charge of everything. She had promised that she would continue to buy from him, and she had kept her promise. It had prospered, the hotel. Mlle. Justine had been wise to close the École; she could not have undertaken the care of the young ladies without her sister to help her. But she was a splendid manager, a house-keeper without equal.

Laura, listening, was sorry when Paris was reached. M. Coulin had been re-creating for her one of the happiest times of her life. On learning that she was on her way to the hotel, he put himself at her disposal. Ignoring angry mutterings from his mother, he told Laura that he would be happy to drive her to Vauzel. His daughter Nicole was meeting him, bringing his car. It was a large car; there would be room for all. He would be happy to drive to Vauzel, so close to his own destination, and leave Laura at the hotel.

The muttering became louder. M. Coulin warned the old lady in an undertone that this young lady spoke perfect French and could understand everything that was said. The warning had no effect; the old lady ceased to mutter and informed everyone within earshot what she thought of young women who conversed with strangers on journeys and begged lifts in their cars.

"Take no notice," M. Coulin advised Laura. "It is her nature."

They had left London in sunshine. They landed in a light drizzle. From a pocket, M. Coulin produced a beret. Putting it on, he at once lost his international look and became one of the illustrations in Laura's early French readers. Disregarding his mother's protests, he added Laura's suitcase to the considerable pile on his luggage trolley, and wheeled it to the exit.

They were leaving the airport building when Laura heard herself addressed.

"Miss Seton?"

She turned. Finch Falconer was looking down at her with the slight frown she realized was habitual. His air was formal, his manner stiff.

"I'm driving to Paris," he told her. "If I can give you a lift—"

She was surprised and grateful, but she was not sorry to be able to refuse.

"Thank you very much. It's very kind of you, but I'm going with this gentleman." M. Coulin, beside her, swept off the beret and bowed. "Thanks all the same."

"Not at all."

He walked away, leaving Laura to confirm Conrad's opinion of him as a man of few words. M. Coulin gathered up his mother and the luggage. His car, as he had claimed, was a large one. Behind it was a small one which, Laura learned, belonged to his daughter and son-in-law, Jean-Paul. There was a noisy and affectionate greeting among the younger members of the family, and then followed a discussion as to who would go in which car. M. Coulin explained that he was taking Laura to Vauzel, so she would go with him and his mother in the big car. To this, his mother voiced strenuous objections: he would surely want to have his daughter with him, when she had taken the trouble to bring his car? With Nicole seated beside him, with herself and her luggage at the back, there would be no room for anybody else, especially a stranger like this young girl who fastened herself onto people and insisted on being driven here and there. She could go in the small car with Jean-Paul.

"I have told you, Maman," M. Coulin whispered angrily, "that she speaks French and understands what you say."

"Then she knows that she cannot go in the big car."

"She will sit beside me. Nicole will go with Jean-Paul. In that way, they will be able to go straight home to the children, without delay."

To an accompaniment of friendly farewells from the daughter and son-in-law, and increasingly venomous comments from the old lady, the passengers took their seats. Nicole and Jean-Paul drove away. M. Coulin took the wheel of his car.

They had barely left the airport when rain descended—not a soft, welcoming shower but a sudden, heavy fall that poured down the windshield faster than the wipers could sweep it away. In the increasingly bad visibility, M. Coulin slowed down until they were travelling at little more than walking pace. After a time, there was a slight lessening of the downpour and they came upon the small car parked at the side of the road. Jean-Paul, getting out and putting up his coat collar, ran back to address his father-in-law.

"Nicole said we should wait for you," he told him. "It is hard to see, and ahead there are fog patches; you will have to be careful. I will drive slowly; you will follow."

They crawled on. Darkness fell. M. Coulin leaned forward and peered through the rain-washed windshield. Behind, his mother kept up a ceaseless fidgeting, arranging and rearranging her luggage and from time to time passing items over to the front, until Laura was sitting with her feet on a collection of miscellaneous packages.

Their progress was brought to a halt by Mme. Coulin's announcement that she wished to relieve herself. Her son sounded his horn, the two cars stopped, the son-in-law came through the rain and it was decided to go to the nearest café. It was some distance away, but they reached it at last and the old lady was hurried inside. Nicole went with her; Laura and M. Coulin waited in the car.

"Soon we shall be at Vauzel," he assured her. "It is a pity that the rain has made a delay. And travelling with my mother, it is of course necessary to stop often. You would not like to go inside and take some coffee?"

She said that she wanted nothing. The old lady reappeared and was once more settled at the back.

Before setting off again, Nicole had pointed out the necessity for haste; she had to get back to her children. She took the wheel of the small car, but her driving seemed to be erratic. The old lady guessed what was wrong.

"When I was engaged in there, you know what she did? She took something to drink. On an empty stomach, with her weak head. She will drive into something; you will see."

But it was M. Coulin who drove into something. The small car stopped without warning; he braked, but was unable to stop. The large car cannoned into the small car, and then came a succession of shrieks, reproaches, accusations, suggestions and countersuggestions. Everybody except the old lady got out and stood in the road to inspect the damage. There was not much damage to the large car; it could go on. One wheel of the small car, however, was buckled.

"You see?" screamed the old lady. "You see what comes from picking up strangers and going where they wish to go? Now how shall we proceed?"

M. Coulin recovered a measure of calm. "We shall push the damaged car to the side of the road," he said, "and we shall arrange for a garage to come and take it away. Nicole and Jean-Paul will come into the big car and—"

"And I," Laura said, "will be very grateful if you would find a phone and get me a taxi. I'm very grateful to you for having brought me so far."

The suggestion was a sensible one; it was decided to adopt it. But as Nicole and Jean-Paul prepared to squeeze themselves into the small space ceded to them by the old lady, Laura saw a car pass, slow down, stop and reverse. A window was lowered and Finch Falconer addressed her.

"Trouble?"

"Ah!" M. Coulin gave a cry of joy. "Monsieur, you are a friend of this young lady?"

"A neighbour," Finch answered.

"A neighbour! This is Providence. I heard you say that you were going to Paris. Could you go a little, very little out of the way and take Mademoiselle to her hotel?"

"Yes." Finch got out of his car. "Luggage?"

Jean-Paul displaced a mountain of Coulin luggage and retrieved Laura's suitcase. M. Coulin opened an enormous umbrella to form a shelter between the cars. Laura renewed her thanks and made her farewells. Mme. Coulin said that it was indeed Providence, for she could now sit in front and be comfortable.

The change from M. Coulin's crowded conveyance to the luxurious hired car uncluttered with luggage seemed to Laura a great relief. Beside her, Finch Falconer sat silent. She wondered whether his silence was due to shyness, or simply to a disinclination to converse. After consideration, she decided that it was not shyness; his manner was easy, almost relaxed.

"Friends of yours?" he inquired after a time.

"No. Monsieur Coulin knew the hotel I'm going to. It used to be a kind of school, and he supplied it with stores. He lives so near that it seemed sensible to accept his offer of a lift. I'm going to a place called Vauzel. It isn't far out of your way."

"Can you direct me?"

"Yes. It's a few kilometers from Malmaison. Does that help?"

"No."

There was another interval of silence. He drove steadily through the still-pouring rain, alert but at ease, to all appearances forgetful of her presence. She found herself wondering why he had come to Paris; was he in pursuit of his architect, or had he come to meet his fiancée? If he asked her why she was here, she would find it difficult to answer. It had seemed clear enough when she and Jess had talked about the picture and decided that Claud ought to be told what was going on—but now that she was in Paris, she thought it was going to be more difficult than she had anticipated to explain the matter to her father without revealing that she and Jess had suspected him of substituting a copy for an original. He couldn't deny the charge until the charge was made, and she could not imagine herself making it. Jess, she thought, could have done it; she herself could not.

She heard Finch speaking.

"This isn't the Paris they sing about. Do you know it well?"

"Yes. My sister and I were at this hotel for about two years, only it wasn't a hotel then, it was called the École Eugénie. It was run by two sisters. One of them died, and the other one closed the school and reopened it as the Hôtel Eugénie. That's where I'm going."

"Your sister—she's called Jess?"

"Yes. She lives in London."

"And you live in Crossford. What keeps you there?"

"I like it," she said lamely.

"That was Sheldon's land you built on, wasn't it?"

"Yes. It's the first time for centuries that the family has parted with any land, but Mr. Sheldon bought part of Seton's property from my father, and he's breeding horses. I suppose you know."

"No. I go to Seton's frequently, to see how it's getting on, but I can't say I've learned much about the district or about the people."

Once again there was a long silence. He broke it with a question. "Are you by any chance hungry?"

"I think I'll enjoy my dinner when it's put in front of me."

"Are you scheduled to arrive at any particular time? I mean, is someone waiting to give you dinner?"

"No."

"Then if you don't mind, I'd like to stop on the way. I missed lunch. It's now past a Frenchman's dinnertime. Would you dine with me?"

"Thank you. It sounds a nice idea."

"I don't know Paris well, and my French is elementary. You'll have to take charge. Can you find me a restaurant?"

They slowed down in front of more than one, but he did not like the look of them.

"Find me one," he directed, "that'll make us forget the weather."

"I don't know many restaurants in *les environs*," she said. "My father never came to see us at the school while we were

52

there, but he did meet us at Versailles and take us to a wonderful—"

"Versailles. Is that much out of our way?"

"Well, it's—"

"And if it is, does it matter? Versailles it is."

Once there, she had to feel her way to the restaurant. It
was not so very long, she recalled, that she and Jess had come
to the Palace with other girls from the school, walking round
it until they were ready to drop, taking notes for the essay
they were to write for the history professor, M. Philippe. It
was not long ago, but there seemed to her an unbridgeable
gap between what they had been then and what they were
now. Nothing could ever bring back, for her or for Jess, those
two happy years of interest and variety and companionship.
There had been so much to see, so much to do. Exhilarating
winters, enchanted springs, reunions in autumn after summer
vacations.

Finch spoke. "I came here last when I was twelve."

She was becoming used to his slow, deliberate speech. She
liked his voice, and the friendly composure that had replaced
the formality with which he had addressed her at the airport.
It felt strange to be with him in this warm, cushioned interior,
shut in by streaming windows. The streets, their lamps dimmed
by the mist, looked ghostly. The headlights of the car shone
on driving rain. When she lowered her window to read street
names, heavy drops beat on her face.

They passed the entrance to the Palace, and she leaned back
with relief.

"Now I'll be able to find the way," she said.

"What's the restaurant called?"

"Le Dernier Louis."

"Rather grim?"

"People say it doesn't refer to the king. It's so expensive
that it's believed to be the place where the courtiers spent
their last louis. The food used to be very good."

It was still very good. When the menus were brought, she found herself wishing that her father was with them. This was where Claud appeared at his most French, his most knowledgable. He knew all about good food; more, he always seemed to know what food his guests would like. Every waiter at every table that she and Jess had sat at with Claud had known they were serving an expert. Food—and wine. She had learned much from him. But she had also learned that men, taking women out to dine, did not care to have the ordering taken out of their hands.

Finch, she found, had no intention of ordering. He folded his menu and handed it back to the waiter.

"Up to you," he told her. "I like steak, in whatever form, and I like red wine. I don't like soup and I don't like having things cooked at the table. Now you can go ahead."

She ordered what she thought Claud would have ordered, and she heard no complaints from her host. It was a leisurely meal, and towards the end of it, the faint frown that Finch had worn had given way to a smile of appreciation, and his brief remarks to an easy conversational exchange.

"You must take me out again," he said. "There are holes in my education that need filling." He paused as coffee was placed on the table. "How long did you live at Seton's?"

"All my life. Jess and I were born there. My parents bought the house just after they married. I know you saw it more or less as a ruin, but we were very happy there. It wasn't until we were older that we began to see the place as other people saw it. You've done a lot to it, I'm told."

"Haven't you been up there to look?"

"No."

"Not interested?"

"Yes. But it seemed like . . ."

"Like?"

"Trespassing. I'll go and look at it when I get home."

"I'll take you round."

"Why did you buy it?"

He hesitated. "In a way," he said at last, "it was a mistake. I thought I'd found an ancestor. But I found that I hadn't."

"A monk?"

"Yes. The monk who built the house."

She waited. There seemed to be no more. He did not appear to be a man given to elaborating his statements. "Go on," she prompted.

"It might bore you."

"I'd like to hear."

"I was staying at an old inn near the Scottish border. There was a glass case in the hall with one or two old manuscripts. I glanced at them and saw the name Falconer. There are several million Falconers, but I don't suppose many of them were monks. I made inquiries and found that a Bruce Falconer, born in a village about ten miles from my grandfather's house outside Sheffield, became a monk. He quarrelled with the Order, walked out and went round begging until he got enough money to build a place for monks like himself, who wanted a contemplative life outside the recognized Orders."

"Seton's?"

"Yes. I went to look at it, and found it was up for sale. I'd discovered by that time that there was no connection between his origins and mine, but I'd got interested. I walked round the grounds, and then I went up with the house agent and then I decided to buy it."

"A semi-ruin?"

"I saw what it could be made into. The chapel was almost unspoiled. The whole place—house and its surroundings—had a kind of atmosphere. Not cloistral, exactly, but . . . different. The inscription over the chapel door was a quotation from the manuscript I'd seen in the glass case at the inn."

She would have liked him to go on to relate the sequel: the feud between architect and fiancée. But there was no more. His eyes were on the uncurtained window. Looking out, she saw a night very different from the one they had left when they came in. There was no sign of rain; there were no clouds. There was an emerging moon.

The bill was brought. Finch paid it, thanked her for giving him a perfect meal and led her out to the car.

"So far," he said, as they drove away, "I seem to have done all the talking. Now it's your turn. Tell me about that school that turned into the hotel we're on our way to."

She was leaning back, her head against the cushioned extension; she would rather have listened to him than talk herself.

"Well? Finishing school?" he asked.

"No. Claud—Claud's my father—wouldn't have been interested in a finishing school, even if there were any finishing schools nowadays. This one was for French girls who lived a long way from Paris and had never had a chance to get to know their capital. The two sisters who ran the school agreed with the courtiers of Louis the Fourteenth's day: If you weren't in Paris, you were in exile. The girls could take a two-year course—museums, churches, historical buildings, picture galleries from the Louvre onwards. Foreign girls weren't accepted unless they spoke fluent French; Jess and I qualified because we had a French grandmother—Claud's mother. Sometimes we went out with a professor, sometimes on our own, in groups of three or four. We weren't allowed to take taxis. We used the Métro, we used buses, we used our feet. We got to know Paris so well we could have worked as taxi drivers. We were taught French art, French literature, French history, even French food, though it was Claud who knew most about that. We were taught what the wines were, and where they came from. We were taken to look over vineyards. Jess and I felt, in the end, almost French. We would have liked to stay in France, but my grandmother had died and my father had no money. We went back to England, and Jess got a job in

London and I stayed in Crossford, the end."

"Not quite the end. Have you been back to the school since it was turned into this hotel?"

"Only once—for one night, on my way back from a package tour to Italy. I detached myself from the group and went out to Vauzel, but it wasn't really worth it—I arrived, there had been a big wedding and the guests had stayed on for dinner and nobody on the staff had time to stop and talk to me, and I had to leave before six the next morning. So I'm looking forward to seeing it now." She paused. "My father always stays there when he's in Paris. He spends half his time in France and half in England."

He did not, to her relief, ask what Claud did for a living. She did not want to embark on the subject of pictures. But the next moment, Finch broached it.

"Mrs. Pennerley is your aunt, isn't she?" he asked.

"She married my uncle."

"A nice distinction."

Anxious to change the trend of the conversation, she asked him if he worked in London.

"Most of the time, yes. I have to do a bit of shuttling between London and Sheffield. I was trained to work from an office desk, but after giving it a trial, I got myself a base in London, and now I go round lecturing on Sheffield steel, or inspecting steelworks, or interviewing trainees. My grandfather is dead, but he left me his house and I wouldn't have minded living in it—it's near some of the loveliest scenery in England. But I bought Seton's, and that wasn't a bad move, as it turned out, because it's about halfway between London and Sheffield."

Listening, she had forgotten that she was the navigator. "I'm sorry. You should have taken the other road. We're nearly there."

"You booked a room, I suppose?"

"No. If there isn't one at the hotel, I can go to one of the houses that take the overflow. Now we're on the Vauzel road."

The hotel was the only building of any size in the neighbourhood. It stood in spacious grounds, some distance from the road. Jess, on first seeing it, had said that it looked like one of the Loire châteaux reduced to pocket size. As they stopped before it now, Laura thought it had the same warm, welcoming look it had presented when she and Jess had come to it. There were lights in most of the windows. The entrance door stood open, revealing an interior more private residence than hotel. A uniformed figure appeared and came down the steps. Finch was opening the car door for Laura; she stepped out and was greeted by a cry of joy.

"Mademoiselle Laura!"

It was Louis, promoted from messenger boy to page. She remembered that he had lined his pockets by carrying clandestine notes between some of the girls at the École and their admirers.

"You are going to stay?" he asked.

"I haven't booked a room, but I'd like one."

"Please come inside. We will ask Monsieur Philippe."

"Monsieur Philippe's here?" she asked in surprise.

"Yes. Since a year. He is the manager."

She had no time to dwell on this surprising piece of information. M. Philippe was coming towards her, bringing with him one of the brightest memories of the past.

He had been one of the school's visiting professors. He had taught history—a tall, handsome figure in well-fitting trousers, silk shirts and flowing cravats. Outdoors, he wrapped himself in a voluminous black cloak which on windy days ballooned behind him in Batman fashion. He had a long face with large, sad brown eyes, and hair which fell in a lock on his forehead and was tossed back from time to time in a gesture which most of the girls thought the last word in grace, but which Jess had likened to a horse with fly trouble. It was generally agreed that he looked like Chateaubriand, but the majority of the girls were too sophisticated to fall victim to his charms. To those who did, he was careful to vouchsafe a no more than fatherly response.

Laura saw that a black formal suit had replaced the silk shirts and the cravats, but she did not think that it robbed him of any of his former magnificence. The wayward lock still lay on his forehead; the theatrical gestures were the same.

There was another surprise: Having come up to her and taken both her hands in his, he addressed her in English. The last time they had met, all languages but French had been prohibited, and his pupils only had his word that he spoke English flawlessly. It was far from flawless now.

"Mees Laura, you are a comedown from heaven. You are genuine, not false?"

She assured him that she was real. M. Philippe looked relieved and reverted to his native tongue. "We are happy to welcome you," he said.

"Thank you. Is my father here?"

"At the moment, no. He was here until last week. You expected to meet him?"

"I hoped he'd be here. Is there by any chance a room for me, Monsieur Philippe?"

"You should have telephoned," he said reproachfully. "You should have reserved a room. We are full, quite full. We are always full. Louis, bring in Mademoiselle Laura's luggage. We are full, Laura, but as your father is not here, I will put you into his room."

"Which one?"

"The one he always occupies. The room that was yours. He asked for it, the first time he came here. He has kept it ever since."

"Do you know where he is?"

M. Philippe seemed to hesitate. "No. When he goes away,

he goes without saying where he is going. This is all your luggage?"

"Yes. Is it too late to see Mademoiselle Justine?"

"Unfortunately, she is away. We expect her back tomorrow." He turned to Finch, who was standing beside Laura. "And you, monsieur—?"

Finch addressed Laura. "About going on to Paris," he said. "Like you, I didn't book. You said there were houses that took the overflow. Could they find a room for me in one of them?"

He had spoken at his usual unhurried pace, but it was too fast for M. Philippe. Laura translated.

"We have outside rooms, yes," M. Philippe said. "But I shall have to telephone. Will you please to seat yourselves for a little moment?"

They seated themselves. He telephoned once, twice without result. The third call revealed that a certain Mme. Simon had a vacant room. M. Philippe informed her that an English gentleman would shortly be sent to her.

"Louis will show the way," he told Laura. "But she will give only a bed. Monsieur must come here for his breakfast. Louis, go with Monsieur. And tell Gaston to take Mademoiselle Laura up to room number thirty-eight."

"What time do you have breakfast?" Finch asked Laura.

"Early, as a rule."

"Eight?"

"Make it half past. I'll meet you in the Round Room if it's wet, and in the garden if it's dry."

It was dry. It was not only dry, but warm. The tables were placed under trees. There was scarcely enough wind to stir the snow-white tablecloths. Laura came out of the building to find Finch standing by a little fountain, gazing into it.

"Counting the fish?" she asked.

He turned. The frown was back. One had to look at his

eyes, she found, to discover what mood he was in.

"Good morning," he said. "I'd got up to eighty-four—ten fish eight times and four on the ninth round. You're late."

"Sorry. I couldn't get to sleep last night, thinking about the time Jess and I were here. Good morning, Michel."

"Good morning, mademoiselle. It is like old times, I think."

"Before you start discussing old times," Finch broke in, "would you please explain to Michel that I'd like an English breakfast. Do they serve English breakfasts here?"

"Of course. But isn't it too hot for an English breakfast? What's wrong with croissants?"

"Nothing. But croissants and coffee only last me until about ten thirty. After that, my stomach begins to complain. I'd like bacon and eggs, please, and a couple of sausages and tomatoes and kidney, and toast and marmalade and coffee and—all right—croissants."

Michel led them to a table, and Laura gave the order. Before the food was brought, M. Philippe approached in the course of fulfilling his duties, one of which was to assure himself that everybody was happy.

"Your friend," he asked Laura, "does not speak French?"

"Not very well."

M. Philippe gave an understanding nod; not everybody could be a linguist. He addressed Finch in English. "You slept good, monsieur?"

"Thanks, yes."

"Your room—all right?"

"Yes."

"You come to France for business?"

"Yes."

"Sometimes it is for business, sometimes it is for the sport. My days for the sport are finished. Only, I still go to angle."

Finch glanced at Laura, and she came to his aid. "Monsieur Philippe likes fishing."

"Ah."

"You know Laura from long before, monsieur?"

"He's a neighbour," Laura said. "He bought our house."

"This is interesting. Laura," he confided, "is very clever. I know this from when she was my pupil. Is there anything you wish from me? What you need, tell me; I am here for that. And now here is your breakfast. I will leave you to eat it; you must be very angry."

He gave the graceful bow Laura remembered so well, and departed to address the occupants of another table.

"Why did he say I was angry?" Finch inquired.

"He meant hungry." She watched Michel setting out the dishes. "You shouldn't be hungry after getting through all that."

He was looking at the food with undisguised pleasure. "Looks good. But nobody can eat an English breakfast and talk at the same time. So perhaps you'd fill in a few facts for me, if you will. In between croissants."

She was studying him frankly. He was what Claud called a good morning type; in Jess's cruder terms, someone who didn't look dished up from the night before. He was without doubt good-looking, and would be better-looking if he lost his frown.

"What facts do you want filled in?" she asked.

"Claud. Why don't you call him by his right name: Father?"

"We never have."

"Why did you have to ask Monsieur Philippe where he is? Shouldn't you know? That's to say, shouldn't you check before coming over to Paris to see him?"

"This is where he always is, when he's not in London."

"What I'm trying to find out is whether you came over here to meet him, or whether you came to look for him. If you came looking for him, we have something in common: I'm here looking for someone, too."

"I hope you find him, her."

"Him. My architect walked out. I went after him, to his house in London, but he wasn't there; they told me he'd gone over to Paris to see a friend. I thought I might induce him to come back with me. He's too good to lose."

She wondered where his fiancée was. He appeared to be taking sides, and this wasn't her side. She watched him finishing his breakfast, and felt a strange sensation of emptiness. Perhaps she, too, should have ordered an English breakfast. She seemed to herself to lack her usual feeling of well-being. Her pleasure at being once more in this house had evaporated. She had to decide on her next move. Claud was not here, and nobody she had asked knew where he had gone. It had sounded easy, listening to Jess: Look for Claud, she had said, but where should one begin the search?

Diagnosing her empty feeling, she came to the reluctant conclusion that it was loneliness. On the previous evening, she had had a pleasant companion who had kept her from realizing the difficulties of her position. He had suggested breakfasting together, and here they were. But he had just stated why he had come to Paris; as soon as he had finished his coffee, he would get up and go away—to pick up his architect and go back to Crossford with him. Or without him. She would be left alone, a state which as a rule she enjoyed. She did not think she would enjoy it now.

He went inside to pay his bill. When he returned, the keys of the car were in his hand.

"I suppose you're staying on here?" he asked.

"Yes. For a few days, anyway. Thank you for rescuing me."

"Rescuing? Thank you for bringing me here."

She was standing beside him. He looked very large and very solid; reliable was the word that came to her mind. She was sorry that he was going to marry a girl who had had three fiancés.

"Good-bye," she said.

"Good-bye."

That was all. Not a word about seeing her again in Cross-ford. A pleasant interlude—over.

When he was gone, she walked slowly along one of the paths that led to the now deserted tennis courts. She knew that Michel was disappointed at her failure to stop and talk over old times—but she did not feel like talking. She wanted to think.

She was not given much time. She heard her name called, and turned to find M. Philippe striding after her.

"Laura, wait. Wait for me." He arrived at her side, panting. "I should take more exercise; I am getting lazy. Michel told me you had come this way. Will you come to the house? Mademoiselle Justine is back; she would like to speak to you."

Laura's spirits rose. She had always liked Mlle. Justine, who was shrewd, sensible, down-to-earth, and who had always been more approachable than her more reserved sister.

"In Madame's room?" she asked as they entered the hall.

"The same, yes. It is now Mademoiselle Justine's *salon*."

He opened the door, ushered her in, declaimed: "See, I have brought you a beautiful young lady," went out and closed the door behind him. Laura advanced to greet the familiar figure standing beside the window.

The same, she told herself—only more so. Unlike her tall, handsome sister, Mademoiselle had been small and plump and plain; now she was plumper and plainer. Her sister had directed the school and engaged the teaching staff; Mlle. Justine had been responsible for the domestic side, giving orders to servants, appointing caterers and chefs, seldom seen except when she supervised the layout of the food in the self-service dining room.

"My dear child." She kissed Laura on both cheeks. "How well you are looking."

"You, too, Mademoiselle Justine. It's lovely to be here again."

"Sit down, Laura."

Laura sat down. The room was familiar. In it Mme. Luard had received parents, interviewed the teachers and entertained pupils. The large desk had been removed; in its place was a small oak table. The full-length portrait of the Empress Eugénie, given, it was said, by the Empress herself to a member of the Luard family, hung on the wall opposite the door.

Mlle. Justine seated herself behind the table. Yes, plumper and plainer, Laura confirmed, but also smarter. Neat, as always, but not, as in the past, unadorned. A gold chain hung round her neck, and she wore a brooch which Jess might have designed. Her manner was as pleasant and as friendly as in the past, but Laura noted a considerable accession of dignity.

"Jessica is well?"

"Yes, thank you."

"She is working?"

"Yes. In London."

"Your father told me that you have not yet married. And you are living near your old home. You are happy?"

"Yes."

"There is time enough to look for a husband; you are very young. How my dear sister and I used to smile when we heard you girls chattering. Never about your studies; no, no. Always, always about love and so on. Do you remember a girl named Ginette Strauss?"

"Yes, very well."

"She is here, staying in the hotel. She has been here for three months. She talks of going away soon."

"I thought she went to live with her aunts in California."

"She went for a time, but she did not like it, and returned to France. She is, you will remember, very restless. She has already been married—and divorced. And now, Laura, about your father. The situation is the same as always: He was here, he went away, he is expected to return soon."

"Do you know where he is?"

"Yes. It is a rather long story, but I will tell it to you as briefly as possible." She leaned back and folded her hands on her lap. "We had here, for some weeks, an Australian lady. She is called Mrs. McClure. She is very rich, about forty, and in her way good-looking. There is a husband, but he is not seen very much; he did not come here with her. She heard that your father was a portrait painter, and she asked him to paint her portrait. He did not want to—as you know, he works only when he feels inclined—but she offered a very large fee, and at last he agreed to do the picture. This, of course, meant that they spent a good deal of time together." She paused, glanced out of the window and sighed. "It was a pity. She was susceptible; your father is not. But he is an attractive man, and she had not yet found out that he was not a philanderer. He remained absorbed in the work without, I think, seeing how enamoured his sitter was becoming. We all saw. One sees this in a certain type of woman—foreigners who think it is chic to fall in love with a Frenchman. I attempted a hint, but your father did not take it seriously. When the portrait was finished, it was very good, but Mrs. McClure pretended that she was not satisfied with it, and she took it with her to her apartment in Paris and asked your father to go there to do some alterations. He went to see her, to explain that he did not do alterations to his finished work. But after he returned, she did not send his fee, so he decided to go and do as she wished. I have the address of her apartment; I will write it down for you. I do not think your father is there, but she and her husband will undoubtedly know where he is. It is for you to find out."

Laura sat for a time, digesting this information.

"He wouldn't have liked altering the portrait," she said at last.

"This I know. But money is money, is it not? He is not rich. Perhaps I should not speak of this to you, but for the past year, I have been deducting a certain percentage from his bills."

"That's very kind of you."

"It was not entirely kindness. He is a welcome guest. He occupies your old room, which is too small and too near the staff rooms to be acceptable to many guests. The staff are fond of him. He gives no trouble. Sometimes he comes into this room in the evenings, to listen to music, to take coffee with me. Until Mrs. McClure came, everything was going very smoothly; I said to your father that we were like a little family party. I am sorry he is not here—but see, I have written down the address of the apartment and you must decide whether you wish to go there or not. If I were you, I would not telephone. Go there and see for yourself."

Laura took the paper with the address written on it, and rose to take her leave. Mlle. Justine walked to the door with her.

"There is no need for you to do anything in a hurry," she said. "If you cannot find out where your father is, stay here for a little while. Do some shopping; amuse yourself. And come and speak to me whenever you wish to."

Laura thanked her, and went up to her room. Seated on the bed, she reviewed the situation. Her first thought was that if Mrs. McClure thought she was going to get more than a portrait out of Claud, she was going to be disappointed. He would get his money and she would get her portrait and he would disentangle himself with his customary combination of charm and elusiveness. She felt that she and Jess had assessed correctly Claud's needs: he wanted ease, leisure and peace. What those added up to was freedom.

She was longer in coming to a decision as to whether she would call at the McClures' apartment in order to ask them where her father was. She looked at her watch: half past eleven. She could have lunch here and then go into Paris and call at the apartment and say that she happened to be in Paris by chance and wanted to get in touch with her father. A grown-up daughter might cool the situation a little, if there was a situation. But perhaps it would be better to go out to lunch and avoid having to join Mlle. Justine or M. Philippe. Ginette Strauss had made no sign; she was probably not interested in meeting former school friends.

She decided, finally, that whether she succeeded in finding Claud or not, she would not stay more than a day in Paris. She would ask Gaston to book her a seat on tomorrow's flight.

As she reached the hall, a girl came in from the garden. She was small, dark, slim, with hair that clustered in short curls round a somewhat expressionless but decidedly photogenic face. At sight of Laura, she stopped.

"Laura," she called, "remember me?"

"Don't be silly, Ginette. Of course I remember you," Laura answered. "How are you?"

"Dying to speak with you. Only just this very minute I heard that you were here."

She was speaking English with a strong French accent. She was the daughter of a French father and an American mother; she had been educated in France, but had paid frequent visits with her mother to their relations in California.

She had been one of the least popular members of the school. Some of the dislike she evoked might have been the result of envy, for she was extremely rich and always beautifully dressed—but there were other factors that contributed to her unpopularity. Sex was her sole interest and her sole topic of conversation—not sex in general, which might have won an attentive audience, but sex as applied to herself. She had an unsurpassed technique for entrapping any man who took her fancy. But her most irritating trait was her way of turning everyday events into melodramas in which she acted, or overacted, the chief part.

She came up to Laura and spoke in low tones.

"I've got a whole lot to tell you—but not here." She threw a cautious glance round the empty hall. "I don't want anybody listening. Let's go to the grotto. Remember how we used to, to talk secrets?"

"You did the talking," Laura corrected.

The grotto was a cave-like retreat at the end of the garden. It was built of large white pebbles and furnished with wrought-iron tables and chairs. Lining the walls were tiles depicting religious scenes. It had been used by the girls only on the hottest summer days, and by Ginette as a headquarters for her plots.

"Last time we were in here," Laura recalled, "we were fined for speaking English."

She pulled forward a chair and sat down. Ginette, after walking to the entrance and peering to right and left, joined her. "You haven't changed," she said.

"Nor have you."

"I may look the same, but I'm much older inside. You don't know what I've been through since I left this place."

Laura leaned back resignedly. "Go ahead and tell me," she invited.

"Did Mademoiselle Justine tell you I'd been married?"

"And divorced."

"She doesn't know it all. Twice."

"Twice?"

"Wait till I tell you. First, when I left here, I went home to my parents. I couldn't stand it. You know from before that all my father had when he married was this château he thinks is so historic because Madame de Sévigné put it into one of her letters. All my mother has done since she married him is to spend her money restoring it. All they ever speak about is what they have done to it, and what they will do next. And because I was so bored, bored, bored, I agreed to marry a man my father had chosen for me from many years ago. It was a terrible mistake, terrible. I don't want to tell you how I suffered. He was insatiable. After six months, I was worn out."

"You mean he was worn out."

"I mean both of us. So I said I was going to divorce him. My father was furious, of course, and he said I should go to America and see if I liked American men better than Frenchmen. So I went to California. It was terrible."

"What was wrong with it?"

"Everything. But one of my cousins was engaged. Could I help it if he liked me better? So we were married. It was—"

"—a terrible mistake?"

"Yes."

"Insatiable?"

"No, no, no. Yes, insatiable, but for tennis only. Morning, afternoon, evening—tennis. I never saw him in proper clothes, only in a short and a shirt. When he was hot, he took off one short and shirt and put on another. And at night, when it was time to go to bed, when everyone else was waking up to enjoy themselves, where was he?"

"Worn out?"

"Yes. On his bed. *His* bed, not my bed. So I divorced him and I came back to France, and I was going to stay for a little while in Paris and I remembered that this is now the Eugénie Hotel, so I came here. For three months I am here. And now I am going to tell you my secret. I am going to be married."

"Again?"

"Please, Laura, don't speak so loud."

"Well, congratulations. Why the secrecy? Don't your parents approve?"

"My parents know nothing. Nobody knows, only you. You mustn't say a word to anyone, promise?"

"I'll have to tell Jess when I get back to England. Who's the man?"

"You know him."

"I do?"

"Yes. Can't you guess?"

"No. Who?"

"Monsieur Philippe."

Astonishment kept Laura silent. "Monsieur Philippe?" she repeated at last.

"Ssh! Not so loud."

"But—"

"I was in love with him when we were here, you remember?"

"No. I only remember that you were in love with Pierre and Raoul and Henri and—"

"Oh, Laura, they were just boys! I was only really in love with Philippe."

"But isn't he—"

"I know what you are going to say. You think he is too old for me, no?"

"Yes. Let's face it, Ginette, he must be at least twice your age."

"What does this age, that age matter?"

"I suppose you're the best judge. At least he doesn't play tennis. Why have you got to keep it so secret?"

"The reason is that we have got to keep it from Mademoiselle Justine."

"Why?"

"Because if she knows he is going to be married, it might make some difference to her plan."

"Plan?"

"She has promised to make Philippe a partner in the hotel. That is why he gave up teaching, because she wrote and asked him to come here as manager, and then after a year to become her partner. He hasn't got money to give, but he has got something she needs more: a businessman, somebody with what she calls *présence*. Is that the same in English?"

"Yes. Presence. He's certainly got that."

71

"She has enough to do to manage the domestic part. Philippe is useful, and he is also what my mother would call a good shop window."

"Why would Mademoiselle Justine object to his marrying?"

"First of all, because she does not like me. She didn't like me before, and now she dislikes me more because I am divorced. She is religious; she does not recognize divorce. She will tell Philippe he cannot marry me because it will not be a true marriage."

"But she doesn't know that—"

"—it was twice? No. Certainly she doesn't know that. I didn't even tell Philippe. I will tell him afterwards, when we are married."

"He'd swallow one divorce, but not two?"

"I can't be sure. It's better to take no risks."

"But Mademoiselle Justine will have to know that—"

"I have told her that I am going away. I said to Philippe that it is best for me to go until the partnership is fixed. It is not going to be long before this is done. I had prepared to go home to my parents, but when I heard that you were here, I said to myself that I would ask you if I could come to stay with you until everything is arranged."

Laura looked at her in silence. Ginette in small doses was one thing. In a larger dose, and at close quarters . . . But if she became a nuisance, there was always the working kitchen as a retreat. Into that, visitors were forbidden to set foot.

"You'll find it very dull," she said.

"Yes, I am prepared for that. It will not be for long. Did Mademoiselle Justine tell you about an Australian woman who was here?"

"She mentioned her, yes."

"Your father painted her portrait. I think he has gone after her. When are you going back to England?"

"Probably tomorrow. You do know, don't you, that we

72

sold our house, and I'm living in a very small one?"

"But there is a bedroom for me?"

"Yes."

"And a bathroom for me, naturally?"

"Naturally."

"Then that is all right. Where is Jess?"

"She lives in London."

"I would not go to stay with her. She didn't like me."

Laura made no attempt to deny this. "Will you live in the hotel when you're married to Monsieur Philippe?" she asked.

"*Mon Dieu*, no! No, not! That I couldn't stand. I am going to buy a house in Vauzel. In that way, we shall be close to the hotel but not close to Mademoiselle Justine."

"How do you know she hasn't changed her mind about the partnership?"

"I know because it was agreed between them that if she did, she would at once tell him. The same would be for him, if he changed his mind. But he has not changed his mind, and as she has said nothing, she has not changed hers. So everything in that way is all right."

"You think that she has no idea that you and he—"

"Ssh! No, certainly she knows nothing. We have been very careful."

"Well, I hope it works out." Laura rose. "And now I've got to go."

"You'll tell me which day you are going back to England?"

"Yes."

They walked back to the hall. Ginette took the lift. Laura went to the reception desk and asked Gaston to make a provisional booking on the London flight for the following day.

It was warm, almost too warm when she left Vauzel. The suburban train was full, and even with the windows opened to their widest extent, stuffy. When she reached Paris, she found the streets stifling, and took off her light jacket, leaving her arms to cool under their short sleeves.

She had no difficulty in finding the McClure apartment. It was in a block in the Passy district, and the entrance, the hall, the luxurious lifts all indicated that these were apartments for the well-to-do. She went up to the third floor, rang the bell of number 324, and waited. There was no response. She rang again, and after a brief interval the door opened. She saw a short, middle-aged man in a purple dressing gown and, behind him, a beautifully furnished drawing room and a glimpse of a dining room beyond it. Both rooms were littered with clothes, trays on which were cups and glasses, plates of uneaten food. She knew that she could make no claim to being tidy, but she also knew that she could not have endured this degree of mess.

"Hello, there", he was greeting her. He was pear-shaped, with a flabby, good-humored face. He was unshaven and looked in need of sleep. He must, she thought, be the husband; it was no wonder his wife preferred Claud.

"Good morning," she said. "I came—"

"Come in."

She took two steps and he closed the door behind her.

"An unexpected vision," he said. "What can I do for you?"

"My name is Laura Seton", she told him. "I happened to be in Paris, and I was told you would probably be able to tell me where I could find my father. Is he by any chance here?"

He had begun to lead the way farther into the room, but he stopped and turned to stare at her. "You don't mean Claud?"

"Yes."

"You're Claud's daughter?"

"One of them, yes."

"He's got more?"

"One more."

"Well, by God," he said in wonder. "And I thought he was just another of those single guys on the loose. Come on in and sit down. There's nobody but me, but I'm more dressed than

74

I look. My wife's on her way to Australia. She took off yesterday afternoon."

"I can't stay, I'm afraid. I haven't very much time in Paris, so if my father isn't here—"

"He's been here. He dropped by this morning, to pick up his paints and whatever. My wife took the portrait with her. He hadn't been as cooperative as she'd hoped he'd be, so she said she was going to take the portrait and forget to leave the dough. Who gave you this address?"

"Mademoiselle Justine."

"Who? Oh, yes, yes. She runs that hotel my wife discovered. Well, Claud was never here, not staying. He came and went. He was invited to move in, but he didn't."

"Do you know his address?"

"I do not. And if the next question is, Did my wife know it? the answer's no; she did not. He wouldn't tell. Very cagey, was Claud. If you'd come and sit down, instead of standing on the doorstep, I think you and I could do a pretty interesting Identikit of your father. I've enjoyed every moment, and I've learned a lot, too. That man is the slipperiest customer my wife ever made the mistake of picking out, or should I say picking up? Maybe I shouldn't tell you this, but you're in a hurry and I won't get another chance to inform you that you've got a father in a million. Never lost a hair of his dignity, all the way through. We won't see him again, either Dodie or me, but we've both learned a lot, and that's why I decided that he rated a fee. So I handed over a check this morning and I said to him: 'Claud, this isn't so much for the portrait as for enlarging my experience.' So Dodie's got something to hang on the wall, and Claud's got a check to put in his pocket, and so all's well that's fair in love and war, as the saying goes. And you can't go until we've had a drink on it. Come and sit in this nice, comfortable chair."

"Thank you. I have to go."

"Why? What's ten minutes one way or the other? See that

ice bucket? I put in a bottle of champagne to cool. I was going to celebrate. I was going to celebrate all by myself, but it'll be more fun celebrating with you."

"I'm sorry. I—"

"Oh, I forgot to tell you. She isn't coming back. Dodie, I mean. She's taken off more than once, but this is the first time she's ever said she's not coming back, and that certainly calls for a celebration. What's the matter? You're not afraid I'll tear that pretty blouse, are you?"

"No."

And if you did, she thought between anger and amusement, you'd be sorry, because I'm three inches taller than you are, and probably four times as fast, and that marble paperweight on the table looks just the thing to make a nice deep dent in your skull.

"Look." He waved towards the champagne. "One drink, nice and cool and bubbling. Don't act the ice maiden, Laura; you're among friends."

She was standing beside a tall-backed chair on which, at her entrance, she had put down her coat, intending to take out of her handbag a paper on which she could write Claud's address. He advanced and took a grip on her arm, and at his touch, her amusement vanished; she saw only a seedy, far too self-confident reveller who refused to take no for an answer. She pulled her arm free.

"Good-bye," she said.

"Hey, wait!"

He lunged after her—but she had turned, opened the door and let herself out. As she slammed the door behind her, the long strap of her handbag caught; she gave it a pull and it came away from the bag. She left it hanging and walked rapidly to the lift. Behind her she heard the padding foot-steps of Mr. McClure. She went round the corner of the cor-ridor; the lift came up, the door opened and a woman stepped out. She slipped in and pressed the ground-floor button. The last she saw of Mr. McClure was his stout figure retreating to his apartment.

The lift stopped at the ground floor. She got out, and then halted with an exclamation of dismay; she had left her jacket in the apartment.

For some moments, she stood irresolute. She would have to go back. It was one thing to leave the strap of her handbag; it was quite another to sacrifice the upper half of one of her only smart suits. The thought of confronting the frustrated Mr. McClure was not attractive, but it had to be done.

"Oh, hell," she murmured—and then noticed that one of the passersby had stopped beside her.

"Trouble?" inquired Finch Falconer.

For some moments she could only stare up at him, too surprised to speak. Then she shook her head.

"No, no trouble," she said. "But what on earth are you . . . Oh, your architect. He lives here?"

"Never mind about the architect. I asked if you needed help."

"No. Yes. I just . . . I've got to go back to the third floor. I left my jacket in number three twenty-four."

He took in her slight breathlessness, her reluctance to return. Then his eyes went to her handbag. "Strap?" he inquired.

"It . . . it fell off. I know where I left it. I can get it when I get my jacket."

For answer, he took her arm and led her outside. His car was at the door.

"If you'll get in and—"

"Thank you, no. I—"

"—and wait a few minutes, I'll go up to number three twenty-four and get—"

"No. It's—"

"—your strap and your jacket."

He was holding open the car door. She got in. He turned

away and then, turning back, reached in and took her handbag.

"Your passport's in this?" he asked.

"Yes."

"And your air ticket?"

"Yes."

"Then I'll take it as insurance that you'll be here when I
come down again."

He was not away long. He returned with her jacket and
the strap of her handbag, handed them to her and took the
wheel.

"I don't know where you're going," he said "or how soon
you want to get there, but I've got to have a long, cool drink.
Nobody told me that Paris was in the tropics. Will you
please direct me to a nice, cool café?"

She told him where they could sit under trees and drink
aperitifs.

"Not aperitifs." He started the engine and followed her di-
rections. "I said a long drink, not a short drink. I didn't come
prepared for this weather. I went to a shop and bought myself
this jacket. Like it?"

"Yes."

"Summer weight. I was never charged anything like the
price of it in England. Where are we heading?"

"The Bois de Boulogne."

"That sounds cool enough."

When they were seated at a table under the great trees, he
spoke. "Could you ask them if they've got a quart or two of
a good German lager?"

"English breakfast, German beer?"

"That's right. What are you going to have?"

She ordered lager for him and a fresh lemon drink for herself.

"*Citron*," Finch repeated. "Lemon squash, right?"

78

"Yes."

She gave a quick little sigh of contentment. He had gone away, but here he was, back again. She was no longer alone in Paris. For this half-hour or so, she had his company, and only now was she beginning to understand how much she had missed it.

"You saw your architect?" she asked.

"I saw him and I spoke to him. He's coming back to the job. He made conditions, but they weren't hard to accept. So that's done."

"It was odd that he was staying in that apartment block, wasn't it? A coincidence."

"It would have been, if he'd been staying there. But he wasn't."

She waited until the drinks were placed before them. "If he wasn't there—" she began.

"I didn't go there to see him. I went there to see you."

"But—"

"Excuse me." He lifted his glass and did not put it down until it was empty. Then he wiped his lips, drew a long breath and asked her to order another lager. When she had done so, he resumed the conversation.

"As I said, I went to that apartment block to see if by any chance you were still there. I wanted to see you. I had an idea that I wanted to talk over with you. So when I'd finished my business with the architect, I drove back to the Eugénie Hotel to talk to you. But you'd gone out. Mademoiselle Justine told me where you'd gone, and supplied the address. So that's why we met in the entrance of that particular building."

"Thank you for getting my things. I hope . . . I hope there wasn't . . ."

"No bother at all. And look." He held out his knuckles for her inspection. "No blood."

His second drink was brought; he let it stand.

79

"Didn't you tell me," he asked, "that you knew Paris inside out?"

"Yes."

"Well, I kept that claim in mind. When I'd got through with the architect, I thought I'd take a chance and go back to the hotel and ask you, when you'd finished your business with your father, to stay on for a few days and show me round Paris. All I want you to do is show me places I've always wanted to see, always felt I ought to see, but never saw—or if I saw, didn't enjoy seeing because I wasn't in the mood. If you could take me to a few of the celebrated spots, I'd provide transport and meals. We could spend the days in Paris. I took my luggage to the Eugénie; they can give me a room if I don't mind a kind of attic."

"It'll probably be Jess's old room."

"So after sight-seeing, and dining, we could go back to the hotel and get ready for the next day's expedition. If you got bored, you'd only have to say so, and the tour would end. Yes or no?"

He leaned back and drank, waiting for an answer. She tried to think clearly, but she came to the conclusion that her quiet life in the country had slowed down her reactions. Things had moved too fast for her since she left home. She had become embroiled with M. Coulin and his family. She had been rescued by Finch Falconer. She had planned to rescue her father from Mrs. McClure and had ended by being, if not rescued, at least assisted by Finch. She had even let herself in for a visit from Ginette Strauss.

Her mind went to her cottage. If she stayed on for a few days, her animals would be well cared for; the orders for deep-freeze meals would be noted and kept for her. But these matters did not seem as urgent as they had done yesterday. A part of herself seemed to have become detached. To stay, or to go? She wanted very much to stay; it had been foolish to want to hurry home. She would like to see something of her father, if she could find him. And she would enjoy taking Finch Falconer round Paris.

He had finished his second drink. He signalled the waiter for a third. "Well," he asked Laura. "Will you?"

"Yes."

"Thank you."

"But I'd like to do something about finding my father. There's a small hotel not far from here where he used to stay before the Eugénie was opened. I think they might be able to help."

"You didn't get his address from that apartment?"

"No."

When his drink was brought, he raised his glass. "To the future," he said. "Yours and mine and Claud's."

She raised her *citron*.

"If we were in Germany," he told her, "you'd be drinking French wine and I'd be doing the translating. My German's good. I enjoyed learning German—a good, strong, masculine language. French pronunciation was beyond me. And now"—he signalled for the bill—"unless you have to go back to Vauzel, you could begin your duties as a guide by finding us a restaurant as cool as this place turned out to be."

"What sights do you want to see?" she asked.

"You fix the program. I just want to see enough, learn enough to be able to show off next time people start talking about Paris. What do you suggest?"

"The Louvre. That'll take two weeks and four pairs of shoes. Notre Dame. Versailles, inside, not outside like last night. Malmaison. Fontainebleau, palace and forest of. Les Invalides. Carnavalet Museum. École des Beaux-Arts. Jardin des Plantes. L'Opéra."

"That's all?"

"For a start."

"Then I'll begin by buying myself some more tropical clothes."

This was the point, she reflected, at which Jess would without any hesitation have said: "And what about your fiancée?" It needed saying. He was engaged. If his engagement was broken, he ought to say so. If it wasn't broken, he ought not to be in Paris sight-seeing with another woman. But she had never had, never would have Jess's courage, or Jess's directness. And dragging in his fiancée would break the spell—for spell it was. There had been many happy times in her life, but there had never been anything like this combination of sunshine, good companionship, freedom and fun. He was old enough and he looked sensible enough to know what he was doing. He had said that he wanted to see Paris, and he had picked himself a good guide.

They walked to the car and got into it.

"Where's this small hotel?" he inquired.

"I'll direct you. It isn't far. If my father happens to be there and if he asked us to lunch, would you accept?"

"If that's what you'd like, yes. And as we're on the subject of Claud, could I ask for a few more details? He doesn't live with you at Crossford?"

"No. He bought his studio in London before my house was built—that's to say, before it was finished."

"Does he look like you?"

"No. Except that we're both fair. He looks very English, but he's really a Frenchman. He's much happier when he's over here—partly, he says, because they know how to pronounce his name. He hates being called Clawed."

"He sounds a restless type."

"He isn't really. He moves around, but it's all in the way of work. When we lived at Seton's, we got used to seeing him coming and going. He didn't talk about his plans—not to us. Nor to my mother, because she always seemed faintly surprised when he went, and even more surprised when he came back. Only the other day, my sister and I were trying to decide what sort of marriage you could call it."

"They were happy?"

"Very. But they were both rather detached people. My mother was wonderful, everybody liked her; everybody liked my father. Both of them were good painters, both of them got completely absorbed in whatever they were working on. They met at an art school—she was studying and he gave lessons there, and they fell in love, but I can't imagine either of them planning marriage as most people plan it: a house, children, a regular job, social contacts. Neither of them seemed to need friends. The only people who visited us were people they'd known in their student days, and they couldn't stay with us, not for long anyway, because conditions in the house were pretty stark. My aunt, Mrs. Pennerley, used to—"

"Your uncle's wife."

"Widow. She used to drop in on visits of inspection. She loved my mother but she loathes my father. She thinks he married my mother for her money. She gave up her house in Bath and took to hotel life in Waterside and she still drops in on visits of inspection."

They had reached the hotel. It was quiet and looked well kept and comfortable. They had, the lady at the reception desk told them, seen M. Seton only a week ago. He had called, as he always did when he was in Paris, to see them all again. They missed him very much. But no, since that day, they had not seen him and they did not know where he was.

They drove away.

"Dead end," Finch remarked. "You might think of another lead during lunch. You were talking about Mrs. Pennerley. She wrote to me and offered to sell me a picture—but that's as far as it got. Do you know anything about it?"

"She mentioned it, yes. Have you any idea what sort of restaurant you want to go to?"

"Yes. A good one."

"I'd like a light lunch—wouldn't you?"

"If you mean because it's hot, I can eat whether it's hot or cold. Do I turn right or left?"

"Left. The restaurant is halfway down. Did I warn you that it's very expensive?"

"If I can't pay the bill, you'll have to bail me out."

They arrived and got out of the car; it was driven away by a uniformed employee. They walked up steps under a pale-green, fringed canopy. They entered a hall, at the end of which was a terrace that overlooked the river. They decided to go straight into lunch, and were led outside.

And at a table in a shady corner, deep in conversation with the wine waiter, was Claud.

Chapter 3

Claud Seton sometimes referred to himself as a hybrid. His father had been English, his mother a Frenchwoman who after sampling marriage, and life in England, found them equally disagreeable and returned to France, taking with her her infant son. As he grew older, Claud came to realize that in the subsequent contest waged by his parents, he was the trophy.

His mother won the religious fight: he had been baptized a Catholic. His father won the battle over his education: he had been sent to Eton. He had gone on to read history at Cambridge, and later studied painting in Paris. In his twenty-fifth year, he married, and adopted a way of life that, half hobby, half profession, gave him great satisfaction but small financial return.

He was in appearance English—slightly above middle height, fair, lean, with a quiet manner and a pleasant voice. But his tastes, habits and inclinations were French. He regarded the French as the most highly civilized of all races, and felt at home among them.

He had loved his wife. For his daughters, neither of whom he knew well, he felt affection and a measure of respect which might have been pride if he had not known that their development into competent and attractive young women had come about without any assistance from him. He had gone his own way. His wife had divided her time somewhat disproportionately among her home, her children and her painting.

His surprise at seeing Laura enter the restaurant was shown

by a smile and a lift of one eyebrow. Her reaction was her usual glow of pride in a father so presentable.

He stood, extending a hand across the table.

"My dear Laura! Did you by some extraordinary chance know I was here?"

"No. We just came. This is Mr. Falconer, who bought Seton's."

Claud turned to Finch, shook hands and gave a slight bow. "We should have met before," he said. "But I always missed you between the house agents and the lawyers. Are you meeting anybody here? If not, won't you join me?"

Finch glanced at Laura; she answered unhesitatingly. "We'd love to."

Claud gave an order; two extra chairs were brought, two extra places laid for the newcomers.

"What are you doing in Paris?" Claud asked Laura, as they settled themselves.

"I came to pay you a visit. Mademoiselle Justine said you weren't at the hotel but would be coming back, and she sent me to the McClures' apartment but you weren't there either, and then Finch and I drove round to the hotel you used to stay at, and they didn't know where you were."

"I was here," Claud said. "Are you staying at the Eugénie, too?" he asked Finch.

"Yes."

"He gave me a lift from the airport, and Monsieur Philippe found him a room at Madame Simon's," Laura explained. "I brought him here because—"

"Because your grandmother used to bring you here. She used to bring me, too, when I was in favour. Sometimes I wasn't. This is an extremely expensive restaurant to lead a young man to."

"I warned him."

"I am here to indulge myself. I am celebrating," Claud told Finch. "Whenever I receive what I suppose I can call a pay-

86

check, I take it straight to the bank—but I reserve, always, a percentage for pleasure. I reward myself for my industry. I am then content to let the remainder serve for humdrum living." He waited for the waiter to hand round three outsize menus, and leaned back to study his. "Laura, shall I trust you to choose?"

"No. You."

"For me, too, please," Finch requested. "I'm a learner."

"I'd like a light lunch," Laura said.

Claud glanced at her briefly over the top of his menu. "You didn't come here for a ham sandwich, I presume?"

"Not exactly." Her eyes were on the menu. "What's *mousse à la russe?*"

"You're holding your menu upside down. Why not begin at the beginning? We are going to begin with smoked fish."

"Smoked salmon?"

"No. Not smoked salmon. And after that, something they do superlatively well here: *poulet truffé.*" He gave the order and returned his menu. "Will that please you both?"

"Anything you say," Finch answered.

It was said in his usual quiet, unemphatic way. Claud's eyes rested on him speculatively for a few moments. Then he gave his attention to the wine waiter.

While they waited for the food to be brought, he addressed Finch in a reminiscent tone.

"There's another reason why I come to this restaurant," he said. "For a number of years, my mother lived not half a mile away from here. When I was an infant, this building was not a restaurant but a private residence and it had—this is hard to believe—a large garden surrounding it. The garden was open to the public, and it was a favourite meeting place for nannies and their charges. I used to be brought to it by a nurse who wore a long blue cloak and a cap with streamers; at first I came on four wheels, later on my own two legs. The perambulator was a very high one; the bodywork, the so to say chassis, was elaborate canework—very fancy. If I stroll through public gardens today, I see no uniformed nurses, but I sometimes see the same type of perambulator. Very rarely, but they do still exist. When I see one, I remember, very dimly, a clutch of nursemaids and a great noise of chattering. I think my earliest memories, apart from nursemaids, were of my father's visits. I grew to dread them."

"Why?" Finch asked.

"They were so very dreary. He never ceased to lecture. He was trying—I realized long afterwards—to counteract my mother's levity. He was trying to teach me that life was not all enjoyment, not all *mousse à la russe*. He made me think of England as a place in which nobody ever laughed. It was not until I went to an English school that I found there was, after all, another side to the nation's disposition."

"You liked it?" Finch asked.

"I was happy at school, if that is what you mean. But it was too late to make an Englishman out of me. I was French. I thought in French. I worked out English problems by turning them into French and then translating them back into English. That was why, when my mother came forward with an offer to pay for her two granddaughters at a boarding school, I said I would agree only on condition that the school was in England. I didn't want them to become split personalities, like me. The reason I sent them, in time, to the École Eugénie was to develop their French side—if they had a French side."

"She was a wonderful person. Jess and I loved her," Laura said.

"Your grandmother? Yes, she was wonderful. For some years," he told Finch, "she had to lead a fairly quiet existence. When my father died and left her his money, she revealed a hitherto unsuspected liking for luxury. She bought her clothes from the most famous couturiers. She found her way unerringly to the best tables in Europe and to the most comfortable suites in the most renowned hotels. She often took the two girls with her—not a very good preparation for travelling on a low budget, as they had to do when she died."

There was a pause as a waiter wheeled a trolley to their table. Attention became centered on the paper-thin slices of smoked fish. The wine was cool, dry, delicious. Claud tested Laura's knowledge by asking her where it had come from. She told him, correctly, and he nodded approval.

"Not a very useful accomplishment, perhaps," he told her, "but women are making their way into new spheres. You might—who knows?—become a wine steward."

When the next course was served, Laura told Finch that if he did not like it, he could order something else.

"He doesn't have to like it," Claud said. "Didn't he say he was a learner? He must learn what he doesn't like, as well as what he does like. That," he went on, allowing the waiter to serve him with tiny peas glistening with butter and resting on a bed of tender green, "that is how I came to discover, at last, what I wanted to do, what I wanted to be."

"You paint portraits," Finch stated.

"Only when I have to. Only when a long, luckless period eats up my financial reserves and forces me to replenish the store. I've just finished a portrait of an Australian woman—a rather troublesome sitter. My real work, my chief interest, what some people choose to call my hobby, is . . . or perhaps Laura has told you?"

"No. Go on," said Laura.

"I'm a kind of picture detective. I am—apart from portraits—not perhaps a very good painter, but I'm an excellent judge of painting. Not only painting, but period. I can date a picture fairly accurately. I spend long, happy hours in out-of-the-way antique shops which are full of an assortment of not very good china, silver, ornaments, oddities and—almost out of sight, almost forgotten, standing forlornly in dusty corners—pictures. I don't look for Old Masters. I look for works by long-dead minor painters. I can recognize their style, I can guess the dates. I do some research and I can sometimes find out where the picture was painted, and learn how it came through successive owners into the little junk shop. I can recognize merit. I buy what I know I shall, after some touching-up, be able to resell. One doesn't make a fortune, but no man ever enjoyed his work more than I enjoy mine. I work in London and Paris; I don't go further afield."

Laura was listening with almost as great interest as Finch. It was seldom that Claud had talked so frankly and at such great length about his life or his work. It was only when he came to a stop that she remembered, with a cold feeling of apprehension, why she had come to Paris. They were talking of painting; what more natural than that Finch should mention the Zollard that he had been offered by Magda? She felt her appetite leaving her.

"I don't know much about pictures." Finch was speaking in his deliberate, unhurried manner. "I was brought up by my grandfather, in his house near Sheffield. He didn't have much time for what he called arty-crafts."

Claud turned pale.

"The arts . . . arty-crafts?"

"He was like your pram; no, not like your pram. There was nothing fancy about him. I mean that, like the pram, he went out of date. You don't see anybody like him nowadays. He believed that work was the only worthwhile thing in life. Work kept you healthy, work earned you your bread, work kept you from getting into mischief. That was his . . . his creed, I suppose you'd call it."

"No leisure? No amusement?" Claud asked.

"Bible reading on Sundays. He wasn't a churchgoer or a chapelgoer. He didn't believe in sermons—he thought they should be preached to the people outside, not the ones inside."

"He was right. But wasn't it rather a bleak boyhood for you?"

Finch gave his slow, rare smile—the smile that Laura was learning to wait for.

"I didn't think so at the time," he answered. "It wasn't until we got to arguing about my joining the family firm that I found I had ideas of my own. Now I'm located part of the time up north, and the rest of the time in London."

"And you bought Seton's, I suppose, because it was about halfway between the two?"

"No." Finch did not pursue the topic. "We were talking about pictures. Most of the ones in my grandfather's house were the usual reproductions."

"What do you call the usual reproductions?" Claud asked.

"Well . . . there was the boy blowing soap bubbles, and there was the small dog looking at the big dog, and there was Christ with the lantern—that kind of thing."

"You liked them—at the time?"

"I don't remember looking at them much. The picture I knew best was the one that hung opposite my chair in the dining room. My grandfather didn't like it, but he kept it because my grandmother had bought it at a sale and thought it was a good picture, and had been told it was an original. It was painted by somebody called Amos Lipp."

"Eighteen eighteen to eighteen seventy. He didn't paint many pictures. He was a naval captain. Which picture was it?"

" 'The Sinking of the *George*.' There were supposed to be two—a pair—but the other one was burned when the sale rooms caught fire. I brought my grandmother's to London with me. I'll hang it at Seton's. They say it's worth a lot, but my grandfather wouldn't have paid much for it."

"Anything by Amos Lipp fetches high prices today. Are you quite certain the other one was lost?"

"Burned. It was to be put up for sale and my grandmother had made up her mind to buy it. Then the place went up in flames."

Claud was frowning. "The mate to that picture you've got was called 'High Winds,'" he said.

"That's right."

"I should be willing," Claud said slowly, "to place a very large sum, if I had it, as a bet that the picture was not in the sale room at the time of the fire, and did not get burned. I've seen it . . . somewhere. I can't recall where, but I'm certain that somewhere, recently, I've come across it. In a gallery? No. On exhibition? No." He paused, trying to remember, and then shook his head. "It's no use; it's gone out of my mind—but it'll come back. If I find it, do you want it?"

"I'd be glad to buy it, yes. That's what my grandmother would have liked."

"I'll keep an eye open. Where did you say the other was?"

"Hanging in my flat in London." He paused. "Speaking of pictures reminds me that Mrs. Pennerley offered me one."

Laura held her breath.

"Oh?" Claud finished his wine. "Which picture?"

"It was one she had in storage. A Zollard."

Claud put down his empty glass. "A Zollard?"

"Yes. I didn't see it. She sent me a cutting from an art magazine—an article about some of the pictures she owned. There was a small coloured reproduction of the Zollard."

"You agreed to buy it?"

"Well, subject to the usual—"

"There has been nothing definite as yet?"

"No. Only the—"

"You must not buy it."

Finch looked at him in silence. Then: "Why not?" he asked.

"Because it is not genuine. It is a copy."

"Mrs. Pennerley assured me that it—"

"She believes it to be genuine. But I know that it is not."

In the ensuing pause, Laura drew a deep breath and expelled it slowly. So much, she thought, for rushing over to Paris to warn Claud. So much for his daughters' first attempt to interfere in a matter that concerned him.

Claud was waiting for their wineglasses to be refilled. "You will want to know how I know," he went on to Finch.

"Please."

"The picture was to be put into storage. The firm that acts for her in these matters advised her to have the picture cleaned first. They asked me to do the cleaning—I have done work of that kind for them now and then. When I was sent the picture, I saw that it was not, as was claimed, an original. It was a copy. I would have told Mrs. Pennerley so, but we are not on good terms. I paid a visit to the firm's office in London, and told one of them—one of the sons—that I was certain the picture was a copy. He told me he thought I was mistaken, but that he would bring the matter before his father and his brother. He never got in touch with me again; shortly afterwards, I heard that he had left the firm. I returned the picture and it went into storage. I advise you to be very careful before parting with any money."

"Thanks. I will be. In cases like this, where would one be likely to come across the original?"

"Probably in private hands. Or in any one of the hundreds of small picture galleries up and down the country. Or in the States. Countless canvases are taken out of their frames and cross the ocean rolled into a small compass. There are buyers always on the watch for stolen originals that would be almost impossible to trace. They're helped, of course, by the fact that even the experts are sometimes wrong. They were certainly wrong in the case of this Zollard."

Relief flowed over Laura. She and Jess had made a great fuss over nothing. In a few sentences, Claud had cleared up the matter and had put Finch Falconer in his debt. She might just as well have stayed at home—but if she had done so, she would not now be sitting in a Paris restaurant enjoying *poulet truffé* and the company of Finch and her father. God certainly moved in mysterious ways. . . .

"What will the firm—Mellish and Son—do now?" she asked.

"If they're wise," Claud answered, "they'll accept the fact that the experts were mistaken, and they will tell your aunt so."

"She won't—"

"—believe them? I daresay not. She paid money for the picture, and we know that she doesn't spend money painlessly. But a revaluation will cost her more money, so she may well decide to cut her losses."

Laura was no longer afraid of what her aunt might do. Claud was competent to judge. Magda tore his character to shreds, but had never gone so far as to disparage his professional knowledge.

The meal ended. The bill was brought; Claud paid it.

"What," he asked them, "are your plans for the afternoon?"

Finch produced a paper from his pocket. "Louvre," he read. "Les Invalides—"

"No, no, no," Claud broke in. "On a perfect afternoon like this, there is only one place: Fontainebleau."

"Come with us," Laura suggested.

"No, my child. I have had my percentage of pleasure. Now I shall go back to work."

"Shall we do Barbizon, too?" Laura asked.

"Don't talk about 'doing,' Laura, my pet. You can drive back by way of Barbizon. This is a day for looking at nature."

They rose.

"Can I drop you anywhere?" Finch asked.

Claud shook his head. "Thank you, no."

"Thanks for the lunch."

"It was perfect; thank you," Laura said. "Incidentally, Monsieur Philippe put me into my old room, as you weren't using it. Finch was told he could have Jess's room—but if you're coming back tonight, we'd better let them know."

"I'll ring the hotel and tell them," Claud said. "I shall be going back, but only for tonight."

"And after that?"

"I've got to go to Guernsey for a few days."

"It's time you paid a visit to Crossford. You've never spent a night in my house."

"Soon, Laura, my dear, soon." He turned to Finch. "Laura will give you the address of my studio in London. It's in Deptford, where our friend Samuel Pepys spent so much of his time. I hope you'll come and look at some of the pictures I've collected. Where can I get hold of you if I ever come across that Amos Lipp? You're not at Seton's yet, are you?"

"No. You can always get me at my London address. It's easy to remember: Napoleon Mansions. Number eight."

"I'll remember."

They said good-bye and drove away. Laura's spirits were high: Paris, perfect weather, Claud at his best—a father to be proud of—a comfortable car and a companionable driver.

As they drove back to the hotel that evening, Finch broke an easy silence to tell her that it had been a day he would remember.

"We should have done the palace," she said.

" 'Don't talk about "doing," Laura, my pet,' " he said, in a surprisingly good imitation of Claud's voice and manner. "We can see the palace another day."

"You haven't learned anything. You've only looked at scenery."

"Time enough."

"Haven't you got to go back to . . ." Should she say Crossford, or his fiancée? "To Crossford?" she ended.

"No hurry. I shan't be going back there until the end of the month. I've got to be in London for a time." He paused. "I liked Claud."

95

"I'm glad. Most people do, but some regard him as a kind of dilettante."

"Nice word. But according to him, he doesn't dabble; he works."

"But not all the time, and only at the things he likes working at. I think people are puzzled because he doesn't take money very seriously. When he's got enough to tide him over for the next few months, he—"

"—knocks off. Why did he choose Deptford for his studio?"

"I don't know. I think it must be somewhere where it's difficult for people to drop in to see him. He doesn't like droppers-in. I haven't seen it yet."

"Why not? London's not so far from Crossford."

She hesitated. "It sounds silly," she said at last, "but Claud isn't like other fathers. Up to a point, there was family unity. Beyond that point, he was in a way a stranger. Jess and I don't . . ."

"Step in uninvited?"

She smiled. "I suppose that's what I mean. Jess and I arranged all my mother's pictures, and some pictures that Claud had left at Seton's, in the attic bedroom I had built for him—he said he'd come and see it, but he never came. He came to Crossford to take away the pictures, and that was all. Now he's in London part of the time, and in Paris part of the time, the way he always was, the way he's happiest. The job I do is rather like his—I work when I want to, and not when other people think I ought to."

"What exactly do you do?"

"I suppose you could call me the local deep-freezer. It wasn't my idea—it was my mother's. She didn't put it forward as a serious proposition; all she said was that someone could make a living deep-freezing ready-to-eat dishes, and selling them to people who couldn't or didn't want to cook for themselves. That stayed in my mind, but for a time it seemed

96

to me that it wouldn't work because everybody had his own freezer and all the people I knew froze their own produce. Then I discovered that most people don't freeze ready-made meals. Young people do; old people as a rule don't. Many of my regular orders now come from old people who've realized that all they have to do is pick up a phone and place an order, and I'll deliver a dish or dishes they can put straight into their ovens. The big orders come when there's an official or a festive occasion in Waterside."

"You enjoy doing it?"

"Yes. I cook in bulk—a dozen of this, two dozen of the other. Then I knock off, like Claud. At first, I didn't do many things—I didn't have a big enough freezer or a big enough stove. And I didn't know whether the idea was going to pay off."

"But it did?"

"Yes. I've got a big work kitchen with two jumbo-sized freezers. The little counter-kitchen in my living room is just for playing around in."

"You must be a good cook."

"I'm a very good cook. My mother wasn't; she could never keep her mind on it. Jess could be, but doesn't like it. She thinks I'm crazy to be doing what I'm doing, but I like it."

They had talked, earlier, of having dinner at the Eugénie. Now they changed their minds and went to St. Cloud. It was nearly midnight when they reached the hotel.

Claud had claimed his room. Finch's things had been moved to a room on a lower floor and Laura's had taken their place.

When she went upstairs, she saw under the communicating door a gleam of light. She knocked, and Claud answered.

He was in bed, reading. Pushed against the wall were his two suitcases, open, packed. He had said that he would be coming back to the Eugénie for one night and then going to Guernsey, but she knew that his habit, when he went away, was to leave some of his possessions behind, to be claimed on his return. Looking round the room now, she saw that nothing had been left out of the cases.

"You've packed all your things," she said involuntarily.

He placed his book and his reading glasses on the bedside table. "Yes. I don't think I shall be coming back here," he answered. "They've made me very comfortable, but while I was painting the portrait of that Australian woman, I discovered how difficult it is to get away from people in a place like this. I shall probably go back to the hotel I used to stay in. Or I may look for one on the other side of Paris." He paused. "And there's another factor. I mention it because it's better that you should hear it from me rather than from other sources."

She waited. He moved slightly to make room, and she sat on the edge of the bed.

"I should find it difficult to stay here in future," he went on, "because I was approached last week by Mademoiselle Justine and offered a share in this hotel. A partnership, in fact."

"A . . . a partnership?"

"Yes. She was quite frank: she needs a man to take over the business side, a man who could deal with lawyers and claims and any difficulties arising with the guests. I explained that I could not bring money into any partnership. The selling price of Seton's paid for my studio in London; most of the remainder I put into an annuity for myself, knowing that you and Jess were provided for. Mademoiselle Justine said that she was not in need of a partner with money, and asked me to think it over."

"You didn't refuse?"

"Not then. On my return today, I told her that it would not be possible to accept. I thought it tactful to make you and Jess the reasons for my not accepting the offer. So you see that it would perhaps be a little awkward for me to come here in future."

"Yes, I see."

"Well, now I've told you. How did your day go?"

"It was very nice."

"You seem to like this young man."

"He's engaged."

"Oh? Where is she?"

"She lives in or near London. There was a row because she kept giving orders to the workmen at Seton's—the architect walked out and Finch followed him to Paris, and he's agreed to go back and finish the job."

"Falconer . . . was he by any chance mixed up in some kind of publicity over an actress?"

"She was engaged to someone else."

"I don't remember any details. Did you say you like him?"

"I didn't say so, but I do."

"You don't find him a little, shall we say, heavy in hand?"

"No."

"What is Jess doing these days? She was designing jewellery."

"She still is."

"I'm surprised. I thought six months was her limit in any job. Has she made up her mind to marry Wilfred Downes?"

"No. I think that's come to an end."

"A pity. He's a man who would have suited her—or rather, settled her. His two sisters would have proved rather trying, I daresay, but his mother's harmless enough. Have you seen anything of your aunt?"

"She came to see me last Saturday. Jess was with me."

"Did she mention the Zollard?"

"Yes. She'd had a letter saying the picture was a copy, and she went up to London to see Mr. Mellish. He was in hospital, and the son didn't know much about the matter."

"She won't get far with her complaints. It's a pity she lives so close to you. I'm afraid she'll get more and more interfering as time goes on. What has been done to Seton's?"

Question and answer, Laura thought. Careless question, brief answer. Her interest in Finch skimmed over; his interest in Finch's affairs minimal. Jess disposed of, Magda mentioned. Now Seton's.

"Conrad told me they've done wonders. I didn't go and look, but Finch says he'll show me over it when he gets back."

"I suppose he'll install his wife there?"

"Yes." She stood up. "It seems so odd to have you here. Or to be here myself."

"It was nice of you to come to Paris to look me up. I wish you and Jess would do it more often."

She bent and kissed him.

"I'll be leaving fairly early tomorrow," he said. "Perhaps I won't see you."

"I'll probably be up. If I'm not, remember that your room at the cottage is ready for you, anytime you care to come."

"Thank you. But apart from seeing you, Laura, my dear, there isn't much to take me to Crossford now. Your mother was the magnet, and she's no longer there."

She was at the door. He had put out the light and was settling himself between the sheets. As she began to close the door, she remembered something that had not been mentioned: the inscription above the door of the chapel at Seton's. While she was wondering whether to bring up the subject, he spoke.

"I enjoyed our lunch together."

"So did I. I'm afraid it cost you a lot."

"Not more than my percentage of pleasure. To tell you the truth, I allowed myself an extra percentage, because after threatening to go away without paying for her portrait, my sitter relented and gave me a check before she left."

"She . . . paid you?"

"Yes. At the very last moment. A silly woman. I didn't

enjoy painting her portrait. Close the door, will you, Laura? The light's in my eyes."

She closed the door and stood in her room, one hand still on the latch, on the point of opening the door again to clear up her confusion. Mrs. McClure had paid for the portrait. But Mr. McClure had stated clearly that he had that morning written a check and given it to Claud. There could not be two payments for one portrait. But Mr. McClure had said that his reason for writing the check had been . . . had been what? She could not remember. She could recall clearly the details of the geometric design on his purple dressing gown, but his conversation had merged into an inextricable medley of Dodie, champagne, Claud and celebration.

Why, she wondered, beginning to undress, couldn't she be like Jess? Why couldn't she, like Jess, ask questions without any qualms or hesitations, without any worry about answers that might prove embarrassing? Jess would have said at once: But I spoke to Mr. McClure this morning and was sure he said he had given you a check. Then Claud would have explained and the confusion would have been cleared away.

And the inscription over the chapel door . . . had she really forgotten to mention it, or had she deliberately put it out of her mind?

She got into bed, thinking of her last talk with Jess. What, Jess had asked, did they really know about Claud?

Tonight's answer seemed to be, not very much.

Chapter 4

Claud had not, after all, left the hotel when Laura went downstairs on the following morning. Meeting her in the hall, he told her that he had had his breakfast and was waiting for a taxi to take him to the airport.

She could see, in the garden, Finch Falconer seated at the table at which they had breakfasted the day before. She saw no sign of food; perhaps he had finished.

Claud had followed her glance.

"I had a talk with Falconer this morning," he said. "He asked me about the inscription that used to hang over the chapel door at Seton's. He wanted to know what had become of it. I told him I had removed it, and I told him why. How long do you think of staying here?"

"I haven't decided. Why did you take away the plaque?"

"Because I didn't regard it as a fixture, to be sold with the house. Here's my taxi."

He kissed her on both cheeks. Mlle. Justine came out of her room and wished him a good journey. M. Philippe came from the direction of the dining room, and said good-bye. There were last words, handshakes but, to Laura's surprise, also firm assurances on Claud's part that he would soon be back.

He was driven away. Mlle. Justine paused to say a word to Laura.

"You amused yourself yesterday?"

"Yes, thank you. I'd like to stay on for a few days. Could I keep my room?"

"That is something you must arrange with M. Philippe; it is his department. You must sometimes speak English with him; he wishes to improve. When you were here before, English was forbidden, you remember? But no longer. Will you take lunch with me?"

"I'm sorry—I shall be lunching out."

"Then we shall perhaps meet this evening."

She went into her room and closed the door. M. Philippe, at the reception counter, said that Laura need not vacate her room.

"We are glad," he said, "to have you with us."

She wondered whether he knew that Ginette had spoken to her of their engagement. If he knew, he was not, she saw, going to mention it. She found herself feeling sorry for him; she realized that he was in something of a dilemma. He had given up teaching because Mlle. Justine had held out the prospect of a partnership that would give him financial security and a stable future. For all his fluttering, for all his fancy attitudes, she agreed with Jess's assessment of him as a shrewd operator. It was unlikely that he had given up his teacher's profession without testing the soundness of the partnership offer. The presence and popularity of Claud must have given him some uneasy moments, but he had doubtless noted Claud's preparations for a permanent departure and could assure himself that there was no more to be feared from that direction.

But if Claud, after all, returned, and if he accepted Mlle. Justine's offer, there would be no place in the establishment for M. Philippe; he would have to make other provision for the future. Ginette Strauss could not have been his idea of a suitable wife, but he knew, as everyone at the school had known, that she had at her disposal funds which were rumoured to be inexhaustible and which were secured from any action on the part of her mother. If the partnership went to Claud, Monsieur would still have Ginette. Ginette plus the partnership would be a double prize, but if Mlle. Justine raised objections to the marriage, he might find himself driven to choose one or the other.

It would be interesting to know the outcome. In the meantime, M. Philippe was performing a skillful balancing act.

"If you ever come to England," she said, "I hope you'll come and visit us."

"Thank you. Do you remember all the French history I taught you?"

"Most of it, I think."

"I used to enjoy the classes." He sighed. "It is a pity that such pleasant things cannot go on forever."

"I suppose it is."

He gave her a graceful bow, and left her. Whatever his future, she thought, he would never cease to maintain his theatrical poses. She went into the garden, to find herself joined by Ginette. They walked towards the table at which Finch was seated.

"I want to talk with you," she told Laura. "You had lunch with your father yesterday, didn't you?"

"Yes. We walked into a restaurant, and there he was."

They reached the table. Finch rose and said good morning.

"I waited for you," he told Laura.

"You shouldn't have done. Weren't you hungry?"

"Yes."

"Ginette, this is Mr. Falconer. Finch, Ginette Strauss, who was here when Jess and I were."

"You live in London," Ginette told him. "I saw the name you wrote in the hotel register. That address, was it a joke?"

"No. Napoleon Mansions."

"Living there, you should speak good French. Do you?"

"No."

"Can you say enough to order breakfast for yourself and for Laura? I want to talk with her for a minute. I've had my breakfast, so I won't join you."

"Coffee and croissants?" he asked Laura.

"Yes, please. I'll be back before they arrive."

After leading the way to a deserted part of the garden, and casting round it cautious glances to make certain that they could not be overheard, Ginette addressed Laura.

"I don't know whether your father has told you or not—but he is not coming back. How I know, he asked Philippe for an account of everything he owed, and he left money for the special servants, which he has never done before. So he has gone, and I am glad because Mademoiselle Justine was showing him too much attention. I don't know whether Philippe noticed this or not; in some things, he does not tell me what he is thinking. But I noticed. Coffee and music in her sitting room in the evenings, and invitations for him to take lunch or dinner. He is in his way attractive, your father; I was getting afraid that she might soon begin to think of him for a partner, instead of Philippe. He has no wife, he is free, he likes France, he likes the hotel. Even I suppose he likes Mademoiselle Justine, though she is so old. But he has gone, and when he had gone, Mademoiselle Justine telephoned to her lawyer. So everything is going to be all right for Philippe. As soon as she speaks with him about it, I will go away and stay away until all the papers have been signed. You haven't changed your mind about receiving me to stay with you?"

"No."

"Then that's all. Now you can go and have your breakfast."

Over breakfast, Finch showed Laura the guidebooks he had bought. After some discussion, they decided that their first expedition should be to the Palace of Versailles. But when they reached it, she found that what he wanted was not a guide but a companion. He was, he explained, quite capable of assimilating facts and figures; all he needed was someone who could convey atmosphere more successfully than the professional guides.

"In other words," she summed up, "I take the horse to the water and watch him drink?"

"That's about it."

The days that followed were for her not so much a new approach to familiar sights as a re-treading of paths that she had followed when she was at the École Eugénie. His knowledge of the places they visited came to him through the guidebooks; his knowledge of Laura grew as she recalled and related the small adventures, the occasional mistakes or mishaps of that Parisian past.

He asked her about Ginette. "French?"

"American mother, French father. She was brought up in France, but she spent some time with her American relations and prefers to speak English."

"Was she a special friend of yours?"

"No. Nobody liked her much, but in any case we didn't keep in groups; we were rearranged every day and put in the charge of this or that professor. Sometimes we had to go round on our own and take notes and hand them in when we got back to the school."

"All-day expeditions?"

"Yes. We had to buy our lunch—it was fun to go to cheap little restaurants in small back streets. Some of them were pretty rough, but it widened our knowledge of the language."

"How many of you altogether?"

"Fifty. About fifteen were non-French. Jess and I were the only English. The others were mostly German or Scandinavian—and there were three Spanish sisters from San Sebastián who I think were making up for a restricted upbringing. The French girls were from all parts of France—Basses-Pyrénées, Hautes-Pyrénées, Lot-et-Garonne, the Gironde. We were all free to come and go—we were an independent lot, on the whole. There was no resident teaching staff—just visiting professors. Monsieur Philippe taught history."

"The fellow who's the hotel manager?" he asked in surprise.

"Yes."

"Not the type you'd think could be let loose among a collection of girls."

"Sophisticated girls, most of them. He only bowled over the man-hungry types like Ginette, and when he did, he was very discreet. He was a good teacher."

"How much did you learn?"

"Everything, beginning with Caesar's armies. Franks, Burgundians, Visigoths and the Merovingian dynasty. Charlemagne. Norman invaders. The dukes of Blois, Champagne, Anjou, Flanders. You know all about those?"

"No."

"You ought to know about the Hundred Years War, because we came into it. What I found interesting was the entirely new presentation of Jeanne d'Arc. Everybody ought to be taught history from both sides."

"Be rather confusing for the Fourth Forms."

"They're taught too much that isn't documented. And I always hated that Bruce-and-the-spider, and King-Alfred-burning-the-cakes."

"That's just to make an impression on young minds."

"But not much use when the young minds have to take in solid facts. Were you happy at school?"

He answered in a slow, reminiscent manner, his eyes on a group of tourists clustered round a guide.

"I don't remember complaining. But I was a day boy; I went home every evening. It wasn't until I won a scholarship to Oxford that I got away from home. After that, I was in up to my neck—what they call going in at the deep end. I met our neighbours for the first time—the landed families in the historic mansions I'd seen from the outside, but whose sons didn't attend the local schools. I learned what people could do with money—my grandfather's only ideas were to save it, or put it back into the firm. I learned to drink, then I learned not to drink. I made friends with some of the men—and women—

my grandfather had put on his black list because he said they had more blue blood than brains. While I was studying them, they studied me. I had a bigger allowance than most of them, and no idea what to do with it. They showed me. I stayed on the fringe until I'd sorted them out in my own mind. I did some accepting and rejecting. I ended up with a lot of good friends—a nice, mixed bunch. I've still got them." He paused. "All except one."

He said no more, but this, from a man who had begun by speaking little or not at all, was a notable advance. His last words stayed in her mind and made her recall what she knew of the facts surrounding his engagement. The actress, Kate Lyons, had on the eve of her marriage to Lord Torringdon announced, in the newspapers and on television, that she was going to marry, instead, Lord Torringdon's closest friend, Finch Falconer, of the famous steel firm. Lord Torringdon was not available for interviews, having, it was said, taken his broken heart abroad. It seemed strange to Laura that she had been so little interested in the gossip—or perhaps it was strange that she knew as much of the affair as she did, since as a rule only international crises could draw the attention of Crossford away from its rural routine.

At intervals throughout these days, she felt herself to be in a situation that was, to say the least, ambiguous. But she was enjoying herself, enjoying Finch's company. She had an idea, faint but growing stronger, that he did not regard this companionship as a mere interlude, but she forced herself to face the fact that it could be no more than that: a brief season to be enjoyed but not analyzed. And not, she thought regretfully, prolonged.

It was she who decided when it should end. On the third evening, after an interesting but exhausting day at the Louvre, she said that she must go back to England the day after to-morrow.

They were dining at a restaurant in the Bois de Boulogne.

The weather, which had given them three sunny days, now offered a perfect evening, so mild that most of the tables had been placed outside.

He heard her decision without comment. They were sampling the wine; he sat gazing into his glass.

"Homesick?" he asked at last.

"No. But I don't want to stay away too long. I rang Sue Sheldon and told her I was probably going to get home before the weekend. It's time I went. I'd like to go on seeing Paris with you, but . . ."

He looked up and met her eyes. "I've enjoyed it," he said. "Have you?"

"Of course." She kept her tone light. "Heavenly weather, wonderful meals, car with chauffeur. I don't feel I've done much guiding. I expected to have to rattle off tables of statistics, like the real guides."

"Could we go back together?"

"On the same plane? Why not? But you're not going to Crossford."

"Not yet, no. When I get back there, will you let me show you round Seton's?"

"I'd love to see it. Are you going to rebuild the boathouse?"

He looked at her uncomprehendingly. "Boathouse?"

"Haven't you found it? There wasn't much of it left, but you can see quite clearly where it was."

"Why would I want a boathouse?"

"Then you haven't found it. Jess and I did. Not by chance. We were laying a trail for a paper chase through the grounds, and Jess remarked that it was strange that the monks had built a house near a river, but not near enough to fish. We'd always been told that monks made certain of a regular supply of fish. Then I remembered something: that the river makes a sort of loop round the hill, and . . . Have you got something I can make a sketch on?"

He took a small notebook from his pocket, tore out a page and handed it to her.

"Pen?"

He gave her his, and watched her making a rapid drawing. She pushed it across to him.

"Look—you see? That's the bend of the river. This is Sheldon property—and there's where the grounds of Seton's meet the river. There's not much river frontage, and you don't realize it's river frontage because it's pretty high above the water. And there"—she leaned across the table and marked a cross on the paper—"*that's* where there was once a primitive kind of boathouse, with steps dug out of the bank—only the steps had been washed away, and we had to make some more with stones, very slippery and very dangerous, but good enough to get us up and down to the water. The whole crowd of us used to gather there, and we had some wonderful times. We kept a dinghy there; it leaked, so we had to drag it out of the water every evening. Then Jess and I went to boarding school and the fishing ended. But it's a heavenly spot, with willows overhanging the water. —Oh, your pen."

"Thanks." He folded the paper and put it into his pocket.

"Speaking of Seton's," she said, "you asked my father about the plaque above the chapel, didn't you?"

"Yes. Just before he left the hotel. He was talking to the hall porter when I came downstairs, and I thought it a good opportunity to bring up the subject. He explained that he'd taken the plaque away because it wasn't the original one. The wording on the one that used to be there had worn away, and he'd damaged the stone when he was trying to work on it. So he made another, and he took it down because he felt it belonged to him. He said if I wanted it, he'd sell it to me. I'm thinking it over."

She gazed thoughtfully at her plate, trying to remember a time when Claud had worked on the plaque. As far as she knew, it had never been touched, far less taken down. She would ask Jess about it—and in the meantime, it was a relief to know that Claud had been able to give a good reason for taking it away.

"Does your sister often visit you?" Finch asked.

"Jess? No. She's grown away from Crossford. She was happy when we lived at Seton's. It was rough, but we didn't notice, or didn't mind. Not when we were young. It was only when we were sent to school in Sussex that she began to think about fitted kitchens and tiled bathrooms and chintzes and carpets without holes. When we went home after leaving the École Eugénie, she decided to get a job in London. She lived in rooms for a time, until my mother died and left us some money. Then she bought a flat, and I built my cottage. She wouldn't like to live in it, and I wouldn't like to live the way she does, so we're both happy."

"But she doesn't often come down to see you?"

"No. One of the reasons being that as soon as the news gets round that she's home—everybody still thinks that she thinks of Crossford as home—there's a gathering of all our old gang. She likes them, but she doesn't feel one of them anymore."

"But you do?"

"I never left, as she did. And perhaps I always liked Seton's better than Jess did. Some of the rooms were so beautiful. When we were at school in Waterside, I used to do my homework in what I think must have been the monks' dining room. It opened out of the big, south-facing room. You know the one I mean?"

"Yes."

"All its windows faced south, and it was nice and warm while the sun was shining. Then suddenly I'd feel chilly and find that there was no more sun because it had gone round to the west. I used to be furious—I felt there should have been a big window in that west wall, so that I could have gone on enjoying the sun until it began to set—and then I could have watched the sunset."

They were silent for much of the rest of the meal. At his request, their last day was spent at Malmaison.

"As I live at Napoleon Mansions," he said, "I may as well visit the house he lived in."

"That was when he was First Consul. He said he spent the happiest days of his life there. He used to go back whenever he could after he became Emperor."

"Didn't Josephine live there after her divorce?"

"Yes. But after she died, it was neglected; then the Empress Eugénie restored it. It was sold eventually, and divided into lots. The principal lot, which included the mansion, was bought by someone who presented it to the nation, and it was opened as a museum of relics that had some connection with Napoleon or Josephine."

It was a sunny day when they arrived. They visited the church in the nearby village of Rueil, to see the graves of Josephine and her daughter, Hortense. They saw the coach collection, and the summerhouse which Napoleon used as a study. But though Finch looked and questioned and commented, it did not seem to her that he was taking in very much. But it was not easy to guess his moods—and she had learned that he was not afraid of silence.

"You've had enough sight-seeing," she told him on the way back.

He glanced at her. "What makes you think so?"

"I feel as though your mind has gone home, in advance."

"It hasn't. Have I said thank you?"

"What do you have to thank me for? I haven't done the driving, or paid for the lunches and the dinners. You're the one who's been handing out benefactions. I hope that next time you're in Paris, you'll show off all your newly acquired knowledge and be a credit to me."

He did not answer this. He could not, she mused, be regarded as a man who made the most of his opportunities. He did not pick up allusions or carry a conversation across the dividing line between a casual exchange and something more intimate. Part of her felt grateful for this restraint—if restraint it was. The other part experienced acute disappointment.

They drove away from the hotel the next morning after farewells characteristic of those they were leaving behind. Mlle. Justine's manner was a mixture of warmth, dignity and regret. M. Philippe expressed flowery sentiments. Ginette leaned into the car and in a conspiratorial whisper told Laura to expect her soon.

"She's going to stay with you in England?" Finch asked, when they were on their way.

"So she says. There's a kind of plot being hatched."

"Secret?"

"Only from Mademoiselle Justine. Monsieur Philippe has been offered a partnership in the hotel, and Ginette doesn't want Mademoiselle Justine to know that she and Monsieur Philippe are going to be married."

"She thinks it would prejudice the offer of a partnership?"

"Yes."

"She's right. It would."

She looked at him curiously. "Why?" she asked.

"Because having those two married and in her establishment wouldn't seem to her a good idea. He's too old for Ginette. He's just the right age for Mademoiselle Justine. Ginette should stay there and keep her eyes open."

"She thinks Mademoiselle Justine's too old to be regarded as a rival. And she likes a melodramatic approach to life. She used to bribe Louis to carry letters to her admirers. He made a lot of money, because she was never out of love."

"Then I don't suppose Monsieur Philippe was the first," he remarked casually.

This was so unexpected that she asked him to repeat what he had said.

"You heard me. I'm surprised you didn't hear him, too.

Her room was just below yours. I used to hear him coming up the staff staircase. I didn't hear him going down again. You must be a heavy sleeper."

She did not answer. She had begun to realize that he could surprise her. It was a pity, she thought, that she was not going to have the opportunity to learn more about him. He had said nothing about any future meetings, and she felt that there was an air of finality in this drive to the airport. Her only hope of seeing him again lay in his offer to take her over Seton's.

They were sorry to give up the hired car. Watching it being driven away by the hire firm's driver, she thought that with it had gone all but the memory of those days spent in Finch's company, days full of pleasure that had sometimes seemed close to intimacy.

The journey was the usual routine of checking in and waiting for takeoff. England, when they came down on its soil, was cold and inclined to be misty.

"Is anybody meeting you?" Finch asked.

"No. I rang Jess. I'm going to her flat for lunch."

"Can I drive you there?"

His car was as large and as comfortable as the hired one they had left in Paris, but there was nothing in the atmosphere to re-create the mood of the past few sun-drenched days.

They reached Jess's apartment block to find the forecourt occupied by a vast furniture-removal van. Coming out of the building were the removal men, carrying articles of furniture which Laura, to her surprise, recognized as belonging to Jess.

"Where are they taking those things?" she asked the porter.

"Into store." He was leaning against the wall, watching operations. "Your sister's got another of her moving capers. This time, it's out. That the lot?" he asked the foreman.

"That's the lot."

"Then you can get that pantechnicon out of here. You went to Paris, didn't you?" he asked Laura.

"Yes."

"Wish I could pop over now and then. I think I'll call a porters' strike and get me some time off. Tell your gentleman he can't park his car there."

"He isn't staying."

"That's all right, then."

It was not a moment, nor was this a background, for prolonged farewells. She thanked Finch for the lift, added "and for everything," and he was gone. She was back at her starting point—without him.

She walked to the lift, depression settling like a black cloud all around her. The door of Jess's flat was closed. She rang the bell. Jess opened the door and ushered her into a living room that was almost completely empty.

"If you wait a minute," she said, "I'll get you something to sit on."

She unrolled two rush mats and laid them on the floor. From one of two red lacquer cabinets which Laura saw had taken the place of Wilfred's china cupboards, she took some cushions and threw them onto the mats.

"There you are. Make yourself at home."

"I sit on those?" Laura inquired.

"Yes. You'll get used to it. I have. Almost."

"But why—?"

"Bernard. He's gone all Japanese. I've stored my furniture. Wilfred took his things away."

"You mean you're going to live on mats?"

"The Japanese do, don't they?"

"But the beds went, too. I saw them in the van."

"Of course. Mats for sitting, mats for sleeping."

Laura, shifting from side to side in an attempt to find a comfortable position, found nothing to say. She missed the sofa, the cushioned chairs, the rugs. From a certain edginess in Jess's manner she guessed that she, too, would have liked to see the furniture back in place. But this was not the first time that the flat had undergone a change. She thought of Iain, who had shared Queen Victoria's liking for furniture covered in tartan. She thought of Ivan, who had swept out the tartan to make room for his Cossack saddles and boots, his balalaikas, his icons and his collection of Imperial china. This Japanese phase, too, would in time be superseded.

"No housework," Jess was saying defensively. "Plain, clean, austere. Are you comfortable?"

"No."

"Keep trying. And start talking. I didn't expect you so early."

"I got a lift from the airport."

"Anyone I know?"

"Finch Falconer."

"You met him on the plane?"

"We met in Paris."

"Was Claud at the Eugénie?"

"Not at first."

"But you saw him? You told him about Magda's picture?"

"There wasn't any need to tell him. He said it first. He knew it was a copy; he found out when they gave it to him to clean. He told one of the Mellish sons that it wasn't genuine, but he never heard any more about it. So I needn't have gone to Paris."

And, she added to herself as a wave of loneliness almost overwhelmed her, I'm beginning to wish I hadn't.

"What was Finch Falconer doing there?" Jess asked.

"He had a row with the architect, and went over to Paris to talk to him. He persuaded him to come back to the job."

"The job must be practically over. Tell me some more about Claud."

"There's something puzzling me. He painted a portrait of a woman who'd been staying at the Eugénie. She went back to her apartment in Paris, and Claud had to go, too, because she wanted some alteration done. So that's why he wasn't at the hotel when I arrived. Next day, Mademoiselle Justine gave me the address of the apartment and I went there. Claud wasn't there; there was only the husband. The wife had gone back to Australia, but he—the husband—said he'd given Claud a check that morning. But that night, when I was saying good night to Claud in his room, he said that the wife had paid him just before she went away. How could there be two checks for one portrait?"

"You've got it mixed up."

"No, I haven't. That's what Claud said—she paid him at the last moment. The husband said—"

"Well, what?"

"I can't remember exactly. I think it was something about giving Claud a check because he'd learned a lot from him."

"He was probably handing over his wife's check."

"That wasn't the impression I got. But Finch had asked me to take him to a good restaurant, so I did, and when we went in, Claud was there and he—"

"Which restaurant?"

Laura told her.

"Claud was there? Paying for himself?"

"Yes. He paid for us, too. Out of his paycheck, he said, which must have been the one the wife had given him before—"

"Laura, you're in one of your muddles."

"I know I am. I'm confused, that's why. The last few days have been pretty crowded."

"What with?"

"Sight-seeing."

"With Claud?"

"No. Claud went to Guernsey. Finch wanted to get to know Paris better, so he asked me to show him round."

"Was he staying at the Eugénie?"

"No. Well, yes, he was at Madame Simon's. Monsieur Philippe sent him there."

"Monsieur Philippe?"

"Yes. Then after he'd seen the architect, he came back and—"

"Had he heard about the hotel from someone?"

"Yes. Me. He didn't know about it until he took me there the evening we arrived from England. He—"

"He offered you a lift when you landed?"

"Yes. I refused, because I'd got tied up with Monsieur Coulin and—"

"Monsieur Coulin?"

"Yes. He used to supply the Eugénie with stores, and he still does, and he lives quite near, so he said he'd drop me there."

"Then why didn't he?"

"He bumped into another car, the one belonging to Jean-Paul. It was raining terribly hard, and it was misty and nobody could see anything, and we had to stop because Monsieur Coulin's old mother wanted to go to the loo, and Nicole, she's the daughter, she's married to Jean-Paul, she took her mother to a café, and while she was waiting for her, she had a drink on an empty stomach and after that she wasn't driving too well and it wasn't her father's fault that he bumped into their car, and just as it happened, who should go by but Finch Falconer in a hired car, and he stopped and he took me to dinner in Versailles, or rather, I took him, because—"

"Stop," commanded Jess.

Laura fell silent.

"I don't want to hear another word," Jess continued, "until we've had a drink. If you haven't had several already."

"I haven't drunk anything."

"Then you ought to be able to give a clearer account of yourself. I knew there was something the matter with you, the moment you walked into this room."

"There's nothing the matter with me."

"Yes, there is. Nine hundred and ninety-nine women could spend the inside of a week with a man and treat it as an episode, but you're the thousandth. You're different. Why you had to get yourself mixed up with this Falconer, I can't imagine. He filched that actress from his best friend. That ought to be enough to make you keep clear of him."

"Why make it sound as if—"

"Oh, Laura, for heaven's sake! Haven't I always been able to guess when you're keeping things back? Something's wrong. It may be Claud or it may be this Falconer; whichever, you've quite obviously tied yourself into an emotional knot."

"I've done nothing of the—"

"You went to Paris specifically to ask Claud about Magda's picture."

"I've explained all that. Claud cleared it up in the restaurant. The next day, he went away and I—"

"Where was Finch Falconer's fiancée?"

"I don't know. He didn't mention her."

"And you didn't ask?"

"No."

"Then you're crazy."

"There's nothing crazy about showing someone round Paris, is there?" Laura protested.

"There's nothing crazy about going round with a man who's engaged, either. If it was anybody but you, I wouldn't give it another thought. But you're . . . it isn't *like* you. It's not like you to spend so much time with him without so much as mentioning his engagement."

"He didn't, so I didn't."

"I see. Sit back and relax. I'll get the drinks."

"Sit back and relax on a mat?"

"Pretend you're a geisha." Jess went to the small bar, which, to Laura's relief, was a fixture and had therefore not been removed. She returned with two glasses, handed one to Laura and sank cross-legged onto the mat beside her. "Drink that," she said. "White port, very expensive, all the way from Oporto, a present from Wilfred."

"You still see Wilfred?"

"Of course. Why not?"

"I thought you said he was over."

"He moved out when asked. That didn't mean I never saw him again."

"About Bernard—"

"Well?"

"Are you serious about him?"

"I don't know. Why do I have to be serious about him? If I ever felt like getting married, he's the kind of husband I'd choose. His job takes him to Japan every two months, and he stays there for three months."

"But you don't like travelling."

"Who said I'd travel? He'd do the travelling." She got up, brought the bottle of white port from the bar and placed it on the floor between them. "I'd stay here."

"What would be the use of a husband who was in Japan more than half the time?"

"He'd come home now and then. Like Claud. You and I," she explained, "reacted in different ways to Mother and Claud's version of marriage. You decided, consciously or unconsciously, that you'd want something closer, something more continuous. I decided, consciously, that I'd settle for a Claud who came and went. I don't want to live in the mess that Mother lived in, but I want the freedom that she had. All Bernard wants is his job, which he's crazy about, and me as I am now, leading my own life. What are you fidgeting for?"

"I'm getting cramp. Isn't there a chair I could sit on?"

"No."

"You can't design jewellery sitting on the floor, can you?"

"I've given that up. I'm going back to work in that day nursery. Remember I substituted for a couple of months for a woman who went to America? They've offered me a permanent job, and I've accepted."

"Full time?"

"Yes. They won't pay me much, but the kids'll make up for that, poor little things."

"Why poor little things? You said it was a wonderful place, with—"

"—all the trimmings, yes. With everything but parents—and all those children want is their parents. I'm a poor stand-in, but I'm going back. Go on about Paris."

"I met Ginette Strauss. Remember her?"

"Unfortunately, yes. Where did you run into her?"

"At the Eugénie. She's been staying there. Two divorces since we last met her, one in France, one in California."

"What's she doing at the Eugénie?"

"Going to get married again. It's no use asking you to guess who the man is—you wouldn't get it in a thousand years. Monsieur Philippe."

"Not . . . not Monsieur History Philippe?"

"Yes. He gave up teaching because Mademoiselle Justine offered him a partnership. She made the offer to Claud, too, but he turned it down. So she sent for her lawyer, and Monsieur Philippe's ready to sign, and Ginette thinks it's wise for her to get out of the way until the negotiations are over, in case Mademoiselle Justine learns about his wedding plans, and raises objections."

"Imagine anybody wanting to marry Monsieur Philippe. Does he still trail round in a long cloak and flowing ties?"

"No. Black coat and trousers, but he still looks romantic."

"Can he really be in love with that girl? He at least has a brain. Did you point out that he's twice her age?"

"Yes. She asked if she could come and stay with me until—"

"I hope you lobbed that one right out of the court."

"Well, no. It won't be for long."

"No comment. Do you want another drink?"

"No."

"Then tell me all about your trip. I said all. Begin at the beginning and keep it in sequence. Talk."

Laura talked. She kept nothing back except her as-yet-unanalyzed feeling for Finch Falconer. Jess listened without interrupting.

"And that," Laura ended, "is all. And now you can tell me whether you remember Claud working on the chapel inscription."

"No. As far as I know, it was never touched."

"Then why—?"

"He thought he might make some money on it, so he took it away."

"But it wasn't his to take away."

"It would have been if he'd removed it just before the sale instead of just after. Don't begin building a case against Claud. I started it, I know, but there's no point in going on. We've had him for twenty-three years without worrying about what he's up to; let's keep it that way. About Finch Falconer: your business is your business, but you're not going to feel very good if he picks up his fiancée again and doesn't give you another glance. He probably treated the whole thing as a pleasant way of passing his time in Paris, and nobody could blame him; you happened to be there, you're attractive and you could show him round. I wish I could believe you'd look at it in the same light. But you won't. Why do I worry about you?"

"I didn't know you did."

"As a rule, there's nothing to worry about. It's only when you mess up these encounters with men. Look at the way you felt when you refused to marry Miles Sheldon and go to Canada with him. One would have thought you were the one who'd been turned down. Look at the way you acted when you knew Guy Transcombe had fallen for you. I've told you and told you, but you don't listen: Men can take good care of themselves. You don't have to do their worrying for them. And now you've let this Falconer take you up and, as far as I can see, drop you. And as I've just said, no blame to him."

"What do you imagine I'm going to do now that I'm back —gaze up the hill at Seton's in the hope that he'll appear?"

"I don't know. I honestly don't know. Only God knows."

Laura was struggling to her feet and stretching her cramped limbs. "The afternoon bus goes at ten to three," she said.

"Then we'd better do something about lunch. There's cheese, whole-wheat biscuits, lettuce, water cress—and wine, donated by Hollis."

"Hollis? I thought—"

"—I'd got rid of him? I thought so, too. He departed on an assignment to one of those Middle East places, but when he got there, there was an invasion or a guerrilla attack, and he had to leave."

"So he's back here?"

"He was, until I got a bright idea." She poured wine and handed it to Laura. "I told him I might run down to stay with you—which is true, especially now I've heard about this Falconer complication. He asked if there'd be room for him in your cottage and I said no, but that you wouldn't mind if he camped in one of your fields."

"In one of my—!"

"Don't panic. If he shows up in Crossford, tell him I've changed my mind and won't be down. Then he'll remove himself."

"He'd better. Jess, about those two checks that Claud—"

"Look, Laura. I was idiotic enough to believe that Claud was mixed up in that Zollard business. Now you're casting him as a crook. Can you say with absolute certainty that there were two checks?"

"No, but—"

"Then forget them. If you could offer any proof, I'd listen —but you can't. So put it out of your mind. And hurry, if you want to catch that bus."

"There's time enough."

"Not with my car running the way it is."

Laura caught the bus with three minutes to spare. It was crowded for the first part of the journey, half full as far as Waterside and empty for the bridge crossing. She disembarked to look for Conrad and claim her car.

"It looks lovely and clean," she told him gratefully.

"She couldn't have looked dirtier than when you left her with me, now could she?" he asked reasonably. "I've done some tinkering—you'll find she runs a lot better."

"Thanks, Con. Shall I pay now, or do we let it run up?"

"I'll add it to the rest. Did you have a good time?"

"Wonderful."

"See your dad?"

"Yes. Everybody all right here?"

"There's no news, if that's what you mean. Did you see Jess as you came through London?"

"Yes. And I saw Clive at The Bell and Bottle. He said to tell you he'd found a nice girl."

"That's the ninth in quick succession. If you find the brakes a bit stiff, let me know."

She drove away. Rounding the hill, she kept her eyes turned from the road that led up to Seton's. An episode. An incident. A few days that she could remember with pleasure— or forget.

There was no sign of any of the Sheldon family when she drove past the farm, but she was seen, and before she had disentangled herself from the wildly excited dogs, Sue Sheldon was at the gate.

"Welcome home," she called. "No, I won't come in, Laura. I just came over to tell you that everything's fine."

"I can't tell you how grateful I am, Sue."

"Was your father well?"

"Yes. He's in Guernsey at the moment."

Sue turned away, and then came back for a last word. "Oh, about your visitor," she said. "I didn't know which field you'd told him he could camp in, so I told him to put up his tent in the corner of the half-acre. That all right?"

Laura stared at her with growing apprehension. "Visitor?"

"He thought you were here. We all thought you were coming back a day or two earlier, until you phoned. You can't see his tent from here—you'll have to look through one of your back windows."

She came across the yard and followed Laura into the house. They stood looking out at the fields; in the corner of one was something which Laura at first took to be a house. It had a red, sloping roof that looked tiled, two windows with panes of what could have been glass, and a wide front door. Close to it was a very expensive car painted blue and white.

"What . . . what in the world . . ." Laura began breathlessly.

"That's just what I said when I saw it. It isn't till you get close that you see it's all canvas. He showed me inside it— two rooms and a kind of cubbyhole bathroom. He's got water in a fiber-glass container on a stand, and he pipes water into the bath. He had a bit of a job getting his car across the field, but he managed it in the end."

"Is he there now?"

"No. He's up at the stables. He knows a lot about horses. He seems to know a lot about a lot of things. Do you want to walk across and take a closer look at the tent?"

"No. I think I'll wait until he comes to see me."

"Then I'll be off. I put milk in your fridge, and eggs. And there's a home-baked loaf in the bread bin. If you want anything, give me a ring."

"Thank you again, Sue."

125

Left alone, Laura stood staring out of the window at the tent, but she was not thinking of Hollis. Depression, which had lifted for a while when she was with Jess, was creeping over her again. She felt that she had let herself be trapped in a situation from which the joy was rapidly departing, leaving only misery. It was all very well to tell herself that she had been happy here before she went to Paris; she could argue that Finch Falconer had been coming and going for the past few months without making the smallest difference to her life. That was before Paris. Now she was back, and she would have to get herself in hand and go on with her life.

The tent began to tremble and swim before her eyes. She made an effort to pull herself together. Brooding wasn't going to help.

She was making tea for herself when she heard the dogs barking. Glancing out into the yard, she saw that in spite of the noise, their tails were wagging furiously. Walking to the window, she saw vaulting over the enclosing wall a young man dressed in boots of soft leather, a pale-blue shirt with a scarf of darker blue, and tight blue jeans. He was red-haired, had a thick, bushy beard and was wearing glasses with very large square frames. He crossed the yard and beat a tattoo on the door.

"Laura! Are you there, Laura? It's Hollis."

She opened the door. Before she had time to speak, he was in the room, clasping her hands and shaking them warmly. His eyes were brown, his nose prominent, his manner that of someone completely certain of a welcome.

"I'm so glad we've met at last," he told her. "Jess has told me all about you, and I daresay she's given you my dossier. You saw her today?"

"Yes."

"Then she must have told you I was here. She assured me you wouldn't mind my putting up my tent in one of your fields. So that's what I did, and I hope you'll come and see it.

I had it made to my own specifications. It's lightweight, featherweight in fact, so I can take it with me when I'm on a job. Why don't we sit down and make ourselves comfortable? Do you want the dogs in or out?"

"Out."

"And the cats?"

"In."

He got the dogs out without difficulty. He let the cats in, closed the door and turned back to the room.

"Oh—tea," he said. "How nice."

There was nothing to be done but ask him to share it.

"That's nice of you. No, no, let me do the pouring. You sit over here and talk. I had a nice welcome from your farmer neighbours; splendid people. I went up and looked at the horses—Mr. Sheldon tells me you often ride them. We must fix up something; there's a beautiful mare I'd like to try out. Milk? But not sugar." He brought her cup to her. "There you are; drink that up. I suppose you're wondering how long I'll be here? It's difficult to say. I've just come back from what should have been an interesting, not to say lucrative job. I suppose Jess told you what I do?"

"She—"

"I'm a pedologist. Do you know what a pedologist is? So many people don't. I used to ask them to guess, but I stopped doing that because they came out with the most extraordinary answers—some of them thought I was something to do with measuring distances, some thought I had something to do with feet. All quite wrong. I'm a soil specialist." He sipped his tea. "What I do is—" He broke off abruptly, and put down his cup. "*Not* good tea. Laura, you mustn't drink it. It's not tea that you should use. If I didn't feel like an old friend, I couldn't say this, but I repeat: this is not worth drinking. This, Laura dear, is what they serve in canteens. You must use the rest of your supply on your plants or to clean carpets or whatever it is people do with tea leaves. I've got some excellent China tea in my tent; I'll bring you some and show you how to make it. You must take it with lime; *not* lemon, *lime*. What was I saying? Oh, you wanted to know what I did and I was telling you that I'm a soil specialist. That takes me to some very interesting places. Recently, I've been mostly to the Middle East, but the trouble is that the last three times I've got to my destination, I've run into the local wars. Everybody seemed to be fighting everybody else. One could understand it if they were holy wars, but not a bit of it; nothing holy about them. Just these bomb-happy fellows planting them and getting out of the way before they go off, which is what I call the dirtiest kind of fighting. I get there hoping to get down to soil analysis and useful matters of that kind, but they're too busy to listen. Which is a tragedy, because they don't know anything about the kind of thing I'm expert in. Here in England, every farmer knows his own soil—or should know. He knows it's sandy or clayey, whether it's fast-drying or slow-drying, whether it's acid or alkaline. But of course he doesn't often know anything about the Continental areas I have so much to do with. When you get on to tundra soils, podzols, black soils, you'll find he's a bit lost. Not surprising."

He had wandered to the refrigerator and was inspecting its contents.

"Farm butter; splendid. Yogurt. You make your own, of course?"

"No."

"You must, you really must. A Greek friend taught me, and I'll teach you. I'm rather keen on natural foods, you'll find. I've been landed in places where I've had to fall back on my own resources if I wanted to go on living. That's one of the reasons I designed my tent. In it, I'm safe from mosquitoes and sand flies and worse, safe from creepy-crawlies of every kind. That takes care of the outer man. I protect the inner man by doing my own cooking. Snacks only. You must come over and let me cook something for you. Will you be out for dinner tonight?"

"No."

"Then you won't mind if I join you? You mustn't on any account make any preparations, for me or for yourself. I'll bring cold salmon and a special cream cheese I got from an Italian friend in London. No, no, no, you must let *me* clear away the tea things. I'm a very tidy fellow, you'll find. I've had to be, living in my tent so much. I can see you haven't had time to tidy up here, but I'll help you. Now I'm afraid I shall have to go. It takes me some time to heat my bath water, but I'll be back soon. You wouldn't care to come with me now and look over the tent?"

"Not at the moment, thank you."

He opened the door. The dogs leapt at him in delight.

"Down, you lot, down. Can they go with me, Laura?"

"Of course."

"Then come along, all of you. No, no leaping. Just a nice, sober trot. Heel. *Heel*, I said. That's better."

The sounds died away. Laura leaned back, closed her eyes and let the silence enfold her. She thought that she had never before realized what real peace meant.

But he would be back. Some of her resentment against Jess abated. Jess had tried to keep him out, had tried to rid herself of him—but he vaulted gracefully over boundary walls, and charmed watchdogs into friendliness. Hints, even snubs would be lost on him; he would not even hear them. They would be drowned in the stream of monologue.

She opened her eyes and stared for a time at a picture, painted by her mother, that hung on the wall opposite. It depicted Seton's in an autumn storm, the surrounding trees bent against the wind, leaves blowing along the stony drive.

Seton's. Hollis Hinchcliffe Howard, she reflected, had done her one inestimable favour: For the entire duration of his visit, she had not once thought of Finch Falconer.

Chapter 5

It had been Friday when Laura returned. Hollis, having joined her for dinner that night, left her with the assurance that he would be with her after breakfast on the following morning. Forewarned, she shut herself into her working kitchen and began the preparation of a batch of pizzas, opening the kitchen door on his arrival, informing him that she could not be disturbed, and firmly closing it again. Left alone, he cleared away her breakfast things, dusted the living room, rearranged the furniture and then stowed away in cupboards everything that she had left lying about. After this he prepared a snack lunch and shared it with her when she stopped work. After lunch, he took her to inspect his tent. From there he drove her to the Sheldon stables and arranged a ride. At the end of it, he took her home and said he would come and fetch her later and give her a cold dinner in his tent.

He was with her throughout Sunday. Her living room was now transformed, swept bare of all the miscellaneous objects that had made it, to her mind, so homelike. Much of her time now was spent in searching for the things she needed.

On Monday morning, he helped her to choose the week's supply of vegetables, carried them to her kitchen and stacked them neatly. He arranged a ride for them both in the afternoon, and brought food over to the cottage for their dinner.

And throughout, he talked. She learned his history, from his birth in Scotland to his appearance in Crossford. Laura could escape only by shutting herself away and cooking; never had her deep freezers been so full.

On Tuesday morning, he came early and caught her before she had begun to work. He was carrying a large and bulging portfolio.

"I know you're busy," he said, "but do you think you could find time to glance at these verses I've brought over to show you?"

"Verses?"

"Well, I'm not going to call them poetry. They're just a few thoughts I've jotted down. I've always written verse, ever since I was at school. Some of it was printed in the school magazine, and the editor—he was the English master—said he thought I had something, if I stuck at it. A year or so ago, I got an introduction to a publisher in London. I phoned to tell him I was coming, but when I got there, he'd gone, slunk away with one of his authors, and I was dealt with by an aggressive woman who told me to leave my portfolio, and she'd look at it if she could find time, but that I'd be much better employed writing science fiction, that was where the money was, not in whodunits, where it used to be, and certainly not in poetry, where it never was. I waited months; no word. Then I went and demanded my portfolio back, and I'll swear it had never left the shelf she'd shoved it on when I left her office. I'm writing some articles on Middle East types, but when I decide to publish them, I'll look round for a publisher who knows his business. I'd like your opinion of these latest verses I've dashed off. You can read them while you're waiting for things to cook."

When he went back to his tent that night, she rang Jess. Jess listened to pleas and protests and finally gave a half-promise that she would come down soon and remove him.

"Though I don't see why I should," she added. "You could easily tell him to go."

"If you couldn't get rid of him, how can I?"

"But I did get rid of him. I passed him on to you. Now you've got to pass him on to someone else. Invent a friend at

Land's End or John o'Groat's who's got a soil problem and would like his help. In a case like this, you've got to use some imagination. Look, I've got to ring off. Good-bye."

And yet, Laura thought, as she got ready for bed, it was difficult to dislike Hollis. He clung, but he was no parasite. He talked without pause, but if one had time or inclination to listen, much of what he said was interesting. To his domestic skills like tidying rooms and cooking snacks could be added his energy in outdoor pursuits and his outstanding horsemanship, which had impressed even the hard-riding Sheldons. And in contrast to many young men who led camping lives, he was at all times neat, clean and well combed.

Before getting into bed, she went to the living room and fetched his portfolio. Sitting up in bed, she opened it. There was a daunting number of sheets, loose, closely written. She selected one towards the end, and began to read. It was a poem entitled "Lines Addressed to a Fly on the Wall."

> *Why can't you speak?*
> *You must have seen them come into the room*
> *You must have seen him take her in his arms*
> *You must have heard*
> *his passionate psalms*
> *in praise of her charms.*
> *Why won't you tell?*

She skipped the next four verses and came to the last:

> *There is no way*
> *to wring secrets from you.*
> *But if you will not tell them to me*
> *No others shall hear them.*

> *So I crush you. You do not fall.*
> *You are still*
> *A Fly on the Wall.*

Her eyes began to close. She settled back on the pillow. In the morning, she picked up the portfolio and the scattered pages from the floor beside her bed, put them together and wondered uneasily what she would say when Hollis asked her opinion of his work. She turned on the shower taps and found herself addressing them aloud: "Twin founts, merging into one/Nice and warm, sprinkling my form . . ." but when she found herself addressing the coffeepot—"See, from your spout/ Coffee comes out"—she decided that she must wrest her mind away from verse. It was Wednesday morning; she decided to go and have her car filled with petrol. Hollis had insisted on doing this on two previous occasions, and she felt it was her turn to pay. Before she could leave the house, however, she saw the Waterside hotel taxi draw up at the gate. Mrs. Pennerley got out, dismissed it and walked to the door.

"I would like to say at once," she began, stepping into the living room and draping her mackintosh over a chair, "that you might have let me know you were back from Paris. If I had known you were at home, I would have come round before. You didn't even tell me you were going."

"It was a sort of last-minute decision. Can I make you some coffee?"

"No, thank you. Did you see your father?"

"Yes."

"I suppose you didn't by any chance think of mentioning the confusion over the Zollard?"

Laura hesitated, wondering whether she should say that Claud had long ago pronounced the picture to be a copy, or whether it would be better to say nothing and leave the matter between Magda and the firm of Mellish and Son. She had not come to a decision when from outside came a chorus of barks, yelps and sharp commands. Then, with the most cursory of knocks, Hollis entered.

It was the first time Laura had been glad to see him. It

was a chilly morning; he had put on a dark, heavy, turtleneck sweater. He was holding a bunch of wild flowers.

Laura performed an introduction. Magda gave a brief nod, Hollis a polite bow.

"A great pleasure," he said. "Has Laura told you she's given me permission to camp in one of her fields?"

Mrs. Pennerley was eyeing him. She disliked bushy beards on young men. She also disliked the current fashion of too-tight jeans. Most of all, she resented the total absence of any touch of deference in his manner. She spoke in her most crushing tone.

"Campers leave a lot of mess. Great mistake to have them about."

"If you visit the site when I've gone," Hollis said, "you'll take back those harsh and, I must add, uninformed words. Many camping sites today are models of what one might call gracious living: rows of picturesque tents interspersed with well-equipped caravans. Some campers carry their gardens with them—in pots, naturally—and set them out before they've even topped up their supplies of camping gas. Speaking of gardens"—he held the bunch of flowers out to Laura—"here's a tribute I gathered from my own garden—which I don't have to tend, since it's flowering all round my tent. Aren't these beautiful?" He drew them out one by one. "Look: *Vinca minor.* I looked for the white variety, but didn't find it. And this one: *Anemone nemorosa.*"

"I suppose you know," Mrs. Pennerley said to him, "that nobody is allowed to uproot wild plants except under license?"

"Unauthorized persons may not," Hollis answered. "Authorized persons may. By authorized person is meant the owner or occupier of the land, so in this case, Laura and I can claim double indemnity—she being the owner and I being the occupier. Look, isn't this one lovely? *Caltha palustris*, or, if you prefer, marsh marigold. Or kingcup. And here's a rare find: *Convallaria majalis*. Lily of the valley. There's a German folk story—did you know this, Laura?—describing how it grew from the tears Mary shed at the Cross. Give me a jar or a glass—no, that's too large; this little one will do. I'll arrange them for you. I shall take you on a hunt for some more. I had no idea I'd find such a fascinating variety down here."

"You're a botanist, I presume," said Mrs. Pennerley.

"No, no, no. I used the botanical names only because they're so much more euphonious. But botanist, no. I'm a pedologist. I shouldn't be picking wild flowers in an English field; I'm a soil specialist and I should be, at this moment, in a wild region in the Middle East, discussing the podzol zone with brown, burnoused gentlemen. I was in fact there, but the gentlemen were busy machine-gunning one another, so I felt it wise to leave them. I shall go back shortly, and advise the survivors how to treat the soil of their region with a view to making it productive."

"I don't—"

"—know very much about soils? So few people do, which is a pity, since the world needs food, and the soil yields food. World problems apart, it's a fascinating subject."

"I don't want—"

"—to go too deeply into it; of course not. And I shouldn't be talking shop, like the actor who tells you all about his latest part. Speaking of actors, Laura, there's a play on now which I'd very much like to take you to see. It's on at the Prince Albert Theatre and—"

"I'm surprised," Mrs. Pennerley broke in, "that you should offer to take a young woman to a play of that kind."

"You've seen it?" Hollis asked her.

"I saw the first act. That was enough."

Hollis looked astonished. "We must be at cross-purposes," he said. "I'm talking about *Ancestors*."

"So am I. I left at the end of the first act. I would have left before if I hadn't been sitting in the middle of a row and

135

having to clamber over people's feet on my way out."

"But if you left before the second act, you missed the most brilliant part. It was even better than the first act."

"I saw nothing commendable about the first act. I expected the play to be about ancestors. I had no idea that I should find the cast completely nude."

"But that was merely symbolic. They—"

"—had no clothes on. One felt rather sorry for them, up there in those drafts."

"But the—"

"I saw no reason for dispensing with clothing."

"You were shocked?"

"Not at all. People of my generation, young man, do not shock easily. We have become accustomed to the debased standards of today."

"Debased?"

"Certainly. Music, painting, literature. Debased."

"But a play like the one we're talking about—"

"—draws a public less interested in drama than in deshabille. With so much for the voyeurs to enjoy, I daresay the poverty of the language went unnoticed."

"But you must surely have—"

"—wished I had stayed away? I did, very much."

"But the second act was so fine, so moving."

"I had already moved. My sole interest in the production is to know why, when the action took place in Kent, nobody wore any clothes. Kent is not a warm county, and this is not a climate which encourages people to go about unclothed."

"If the thing had taken place in a warm climate—"

"There are of course countries in which the inhabitants wear little or nothing. But if this play had, as you suggest, taken place there, I would have expected to see different-coloured skins. Brown, for example, or black. I do not ex-pect—"

"But if—"

"Kindly do not interrupt. I was about to say that I do not expect, did not expect to find English squires and their wives going round naked in their Kentish homes."

"But if you see nudes in, say, the National Gallery—"

"They do not come out of their frames and cavort. And their flesh tones are far more pleasing than the pallid and peeled-looking bodies of the unclothed ladies and gentlemen of Kent. That is all I have to say on the subject."

Laura, mute but fascinated, was growing uneasy at the increasingly flushed countenances of the combatants. She got up and went to the counter, returning with a tray on which was some lemon tea.

"Come and have some of this." She put the tray on the table. "Lemon tea—you like it, Aunt Magda."

Mrs. Pennerley, breathing heavily, accepted a cup. Then she rose and asked Laura to drive her back to the hotel. Hollis offered his services and received a curt negative and a cold bow as she swept by him to the door.

"Where," she demanded as she got into the car, "has that young man come from?"

"London. He's one of Jess's friends."

"That explains it. She knows far too many peculiar people. I'm not going to comment on his clothes; one has got used to carnival attire—but I see no reason for wearing windowpanes instead of normal spectacles."

The subject filled her mind until the hotel was reached. To Laura's relief, there was no mention of Claud or of pictures.

When she stopped at the garage on the way home, Conrad spoke sympathetically.

"Saw you going by with Mrs. P.," he said. "Cross, she looked. Where's your visitor?"

"At the cottage."

"Nice chap, he seems. Car going well?"

"Yes, thank you. Would you mind checking the tires?"

"Be a pleasure. That architect's back, have you heard?"

"No."

"He's been here all week. He's waiting for the boss, but there's no sign of him yet. And not a sign of the lady either. Well, what the architect said that morning was clear enough: 'me or the lady, take your choice.' So if the boss wants to see her, he's got to see her somewhere else."

He walked towards the air supply, and then paused. The bus had come and gone, leaving a solitary passenger. She stood with a large, battered-looking suitcase on the ground beside her—a girl of about twenty-four, no more than five feet in height, with a broad, muscular body that looked as strong as a wrestler's. Her hair, under a small woollen cap, was brown, and cut in pudding-basin style. Her eyes were blue, and slightly protruding; her nose was broad, her mouth large and her teeth strong and white but rather uneven. Straining the buttons of her cheap brown coat were full breasts. Her manner was calm.

After looking about her, she took from her purse a paper, unfolded it, approached Conrad and held it out.

"Know where that is?" she asked him.

Her tone was as flat as her vowels. She waited, studying him while he studied the paper.

"Yes," he said, handing it back. "It's that house up on that hill."

He waved an arm. She narrowed her eyes, measuring the distance.

"Not too far to walk," she said, "but not with my case. I'll have to send down for that. Or maybe you know somebody who'd take it up?"

"Up where?"

"Didn't you read the paper?"

"Yes, I read it. It said Seton's. I told you where it was. But you can't go there."

"Why not?"

"Because it isn't ready."

"I know it isn't ready. It's just been rebuilt, hasn't it?"

"Yes. But—"

"And Mr. Falconer's moving in, right?"

"Right. But he's not here."

"I know that, too." She sounded indulgent, like one dealing with a backward child. "I've got to come first, see?"

"No, I don't see. What's the use of going up there? There's a room kept for him, but none of the other rooms are ready, and there's nobody there except the workmen."

"The rooms won't be ready," she told him, "until I get them ready. Understand? When a house has been done up, you can't just walk in and hang your hat on the hallstand. You have to wait till it's all cleaned up."

"I know that, but—"

"My job is to do the cleaning-up. I've got to see the last of the workmen out, and then I've got to start scrubbing. There's no use Mr. Falconer being here till all that's done."

"You're going to work for him?"

"I am."

"Does he know you're here?"

"He knows I'm on my way. My mum'll have told him. She's the cook; she's coming later. If you want to know, my family's been working for Mr. Falconer's family since before your great-granddad's day. Now will you tell me how I can get my luggage up there?"

"You can't stay there with nothing in the house. There's no shops. There's no neighbours. There's nothing. Nothing to eat, no water laid on yet, I don't suppose; just builder's mess. You've come too soon."

"In that case," she said, her calm unruffled, "I'll need a room till I get sorted out." She turned to survey the peeling facade of the inn. "This is a pub, isn't it?"

"Yes. The Three Pigeons."

"There's only two on that sign. Where's the owner?"

"Talking to you."

"Do I arrange with you about getting a room, then?"

He hesitated, and then looking at one of the upper windows, raised his voice in a shout.

"Auntie Min! Here, Aunt Minnie!"

While he waited for a response, he turned with an apology to Laura. "Sorry. What was it I was going to do for you?"

"Test the tires. I'm not in a hurry."

The window opened; a woman's head appeared, the hair in rollers.

"What're you yelling for?" she asked Conrad.

"Someone here wants a room."

"Well, tell them they've come to the wrong place." She looked at the girl. "There's lots of places over the bridge," she informed her. "You go and try there."

"Too far," replied the girl calmly. "I'm going to work up at that house, Seton's they call it, but your nephew says I can't go there yet. So I'll want a room to stay in."

"Well, you can't have one here."

"Yes, I can," the girl told her. "It's a pub, and it's got rooms to let, and if they're empty, you can't turn people away. That's the law."

"Then go and fetch a policeman," advised Aunt Minnie, retreating and closing the window with a bang.

Conrad spoke. "She used to run the place when my dad was alive," he explained, "but after that, she packed it in. If you want to stick your neck out, you can have a room, but you'll have to look after yourself."

"I can do that all right. What d'you charge?"

"Same's anybody else. Will you cook your own meals?"

"There's a kitchen, isn't there?"

"Yes, but—"

"Don't tell me; I know: I'll have to give it a good clean-out first. I want a bed with clean sheets, that's all. I won't bother you, don't you worry. I can see after myself."

"Then you're booked in. What's your name?"

"Dorrit Moat."

"Dorrit? Your mum got that out of Dickens."

"My mum got that out of my great-great-grandmother. Now we've got that sorted. Where's this room?"

She picked up her suitcase and turned towards the house. Conrad, after a momentary hesitation, went forward and took it from her—and dropped it with a yelp of surprise.

"What've you got in there—tombstones?" he asked indignantly.

"What's in there is everything I've got in the world." She swung the case up easily. "You're not very strong, are you? What's your name?"

"Con Lester. Conrad."

"Are you going to show me which is my room?"

"In a minute, when I've seen to these tires. If you don't want to wait, it's the one on the left as you go in."

"Thanks."

She went into the house and closed the door, and Conrad gazed after her solemnly. "Stay here and count twenty," he said to Laura, "and you'll see her coming running out again."

But she did not reappear. Conrad checked the tire pressures, cleaned the windshield and said good-bye to Laura with an absent air. His mind, she saw, was indoors.

She drove away. As she passed the turning that led up to Seton's, she saw a car coming down the hill and had time to see that the driver was making signals—of warning or distress, she was not close enough to decide. She slowed down; the signals became more frenzied, and she stopped. Soon the other car drew up beside hers, and from it stepped a man of about fifty, short, inclined to stoutness, his hair beginning to recede. He was wearing a tweed suit. He came up and addressed Laura through the window of her car.

"You're Miss Seton and you don't know me," he stated in a loud, firm voice. "My name is Chawton, David Chawton, and I'm—"

"You're the architect who's in charge of the alterations at Seton's." She got out and stood beside him. "I've heard about you, but we've never met."

"And I thought we never, never would meet," he told her in his vigorous manner. "You are, may I say, a most elusive young lady. Are you *never* at home?"

"Yes. I—"

"Let me explain. I've been down here some days. Before I came, I promised Mr. Falconer that I would show you over the house. He said he had promised to take you over it himself, and when he comes to Crossford he will redeem his promise, but in the meantime he asked me to make a point of taking you round. I told him that it would be a pleasure, and no trouble at all. But the trouble was in finding you. Twice I telephoned. Twice I got into my car and drove down to your cottage. At last I voiced my despair to the young man at the garage: How, I asked him, did one get hold of you? And what should he tell me but that you had just been at the garage and you were on your way home. So I threw myself into my car, drove down the hill—and intercepted you."

This speech, almost as long as one of Hollis's, left him a trifle breathless.

"A few months ago," she told him, "you couldn't have driven fast down the hill. My sister and I named it Boulder Boulevard. I'm sorry you had trouble finding me. I've got a visitor who likes to be out most of the time; I've been going round with him."

"Where in Crossford," Mr. Chawton asked in surprise, "can anybody 'go round'? Inspecting all the animals on the farms? Don't tell me now—wait until we get up to Seton's. Will you follow me up?"

He led the way up the hill. The road was at first smooth and free of traffic. As they neared the house, it became wider and was lined with piles of building material. When they reached the top, he got out of his car and walked back to meet her.

"Well?" he asked. "What do you think of it?"

She could not reply. She was gazing at a frontage that she did not recognize. The old windows, the old front door had been removed; in their place was a long, glassed-in veranda. The broken stone steps which in the past had constituted a perennial hazard for visitors was now a sweep of shallow granite steps between curving balustrades.

"It's . . . it's completely different," she brought out at last.

"Not completely. Let's start in my office," Mr. Chawton suggested.

He led her past the steps to a small new wing built at right angles to the house. Opening a door, he ushered her into a small room fitted out with a large desk and stands for plans.

"This is where all the arguments have taken place," he told Laura. "He's a good client, is Finch; he made all his objections and suggestions at the very beginning—and then left me alone. Not so his bride-to-be. You know her?"

"No."

"You will. That is, if she ever lives here, which I'm beginning to doubt. He couldn't have had her in mind when he decided to buy this place. She doesn't like Crossford, and, if you'll forgive me, doesn't like the people in it. Every time she came down to see what was being done to this house, she turned the place upside down: not a word to me, but orders to the workmen and assurances to them that she had my authority for what she told them to do. Finally I gave Finch a choice: Keep her off the site, or get yourself another architect. It wasn't only this house, you see. I'd agreed to convert Finch's house near Sheffield. It was built in his grandfather's day, solid as a lighthouse, not a cheap or a bad bit of workmanship anywhere, but stark. That's the word: stark. Bleak.

A barrack of a place. If I were a poet, I'd say it was a place whose very stones breathed endurance, fortitude. And, of course, continuity. Now I must stop talking. Shall we go round? As you've seen, there are still a few workmen on the site, but they won't be here long; their job will soon be done—and so will mine."

It was, for her, a fascinating hour—and his interest in the tour was scarcely less than hers. He was not in a hurry. He was presenting the rooms as they now were, but he was seeing them through her eyes, learning what they had been in the past.

"Could it," he stopped once to ask, "could it really have been in that semi-ruined state when your parents bought it? Yes, it must have been; you were only here for—how long?—twenty-odd years. Twenty or thirty years couldn't reduce a building of this kind to the state it was in when Finch bought it. I thought at the time that he was making a mistake. I told him so. But the conversion was a challenge, and so I took it on, and I'll admit that the longer I've been on the job, the more I've come to see that he acted wisely. Crossford, as you come over the bridge, looks unpromising, but the views from here are beautiful, and nobody will ever be able to obstruct them. Come and see what I've done upstairs."

The old shaking, quaking staircase had gone. Laura saw in its place a curving one with a graceful railing. The large, high-ceilinged rooms on one side of the long corridor were now bedrooms with lowered ceilings and adjacent bathrooms. On the other side of the corridor were north-facing rooms: studio, storage, service, Mr. Chawton explained.

"And along here, in the new wing, the servants' rooms. When Finch told me the accommodation he would need for servants, I raised my eyebrows, but he explained that half the population of his native village, or his grandfather's native village, is queuing up to come down here and sign on. I didn't believe it, and said so, but Finch didn't argue the point. If you know him well, you'll know that he never troubles to argue. Unless he wants to."

"The first in the queue has already arrived," Laura told him. "Her name is Dorrit, and her mother's the cook. As the workmen were still here, Dorrit took a room at the inn."

"I'll go and have a word with her. Let's go downstairs. I want to show you the main rooms, what the house agents would call a fine set of communicating reception rooms. That glassed-in veranda is not a usual feature of English houses, but it ought to be. Uninterrupted views, and no winter blasts. It's to be furnished with comfortable chairs and sofas and will be a perfect place to use all winter. Do you recognize these rooms?"

"Yes."

"The men have just got to work on a slight alteration Finch asked for. Come and see. That was a blank wall in your day. Now it's having a large window put into it. Finch said he wanted to watch the sunsets, and he's got a point; I would have put the window in the plan if I'd realized he had a leaning towards sunsets. He told me I was to show you this particularly. Perhaps you've got a leaning towards sunsets, too?"

She made no reply. She was standing motionless, staring at the wall, unable to speak. The men working on the window had paused, and as Mr. Chawton turned away, resumed work. But Laura could not move.

A view of the sunset. Here, she had told him, was where she had done her homework. Here was where the sun had warmed her—until it began to set. She had said that there should be a window, and a window was being made, and he had told the architect to show it to her.

She felt a touch on her arm.

"Tired?" Mr. Chawton asked.

She came back from Paris. "No, not tired at all," she said.

"Then come and look at something I'm rather proud of. Did Finch tell you that I'd given him a picture gallery?"

"No."

"It was my idea. He had the space, and he was beginning to take an interest in collecting. I was sure he'd be pleased when he saw it finished—and he was." He threw open double doors. "Look."

She went in. It was not large. It had been, in the past, four unused rooms overlooking the woods at the back of the house. It was now a long, beautifully proportioned gallery.

"You like it?" Mr. Chawton asked.

"I think it's beautiful."

"It is. I'm not going to pretend, or disclaim; it's beautiful. I'm so glad you agree. Now let's end this tour by taking a look at something outside."

In the hall, Mr. Chawton paused. "Will you excuse me for a moment? We're going to have rather a muddy walk."

He returned wearing heavy boots and a workman's overall.

"My working clothes," he told her. "Now mind how you go. This is a woodland path, and it's slippery. Just follow me. Did you have picnics in these woods? I expect you did. Now, you see, it's becoming rocky. Do you know where you are?"

"Yes. Above the river."

"Quite right. I'm having the path cleared on this side, to give a view of the water. Did you often come here as children, you and your sister, or was it considered too dangerous?"

She was standing at the edge of the path, staring down at the river. Mr. Chawton was still speaking.

"You're on the site," he told her, "of something Finch discovered only a week or so ago—a kind of boathouse used by the monks. Come and look."

She looked. There were the original blocks of granite, still forming a floor. There were the stones that she and Jess and their companions had carried laboriously through the woods. There were the logs, filched from many a farmer's fireside, used to construct a series of steps down to the water. There on that tree was the remaining half of the branch that Fred

Weatherstone had clutched as he slithered suddenly into the river, taking the other half with him. There was the rope that Chrissie Transcombe had dragged up from the water and tied to the trunk of the tree, to moor the leaky dinghy.

"Finch thought you'd be interested to know that he was going to rebuild the boathouse and make a stairway down to the river. I confess that I wouldn't have thought of it myself," said Mr. Chawton, "but I only found the site after Finch talked to me in London and showed me a rough sketch of where it was."

A rough sketch . . .

Was it, she wondered, the sketch that she had made, the few lines passed across the table as they sat at dinner? Were the boathouse and the west window merely additions that he had considered worthwhile adopting, or could they be read as a message from a man who had left her without saying anything of future communications?

She found herself walking back to the house with Mr. Chawton. She heard her thanks, her invitation to him to come and see her at the cottage whenever he wanted to; she heard his warm and seemingly sincere intention to take her at her word. Then she was driving down the hill and struggling to bring her mind into some kind of order.

He had directed the architect to draw her attention to those two additions. She did not understand why he had done so, but the nearer she drew to the cottage, the more convinced she became that he had sent her some kind of message. Whether he meant to or not, he had repaired a link that had been broken on their return from Paris. He was no longer absent from her, living his own life in London, close to the woman he was to marry. He was here in Crossford, asking her to interpret a message sent in a private code.

Before she reached home, she realized that never, since he and she had met, never, since he removed her from M. Coulin and his family and drove her to Vauzel, never had she believed that their association was to be a fleeting one. She had feared, she had sometimes doubted, but the doubts and the fears had never reached down to the depths of her mind, to her strange, strong confidence in the future. She had never been good at concealing her feelings; she had let him see that she liked him. She knew that he liked her, and she was certain that he was not a man who would let her risk her happiness by prolonging an association that would end in a parting.

Now she was completely certain that her confidence was justified. She would see him again. Everything would be all right. Jess would call her crazy. Jess would ask what this confidence was based on; her only reply would be that it was rooted in the trust she felt in a man she had known for barely a week.

Everything would be all right. How, she could not guess. But she was content to wait.

She entered the cottage to a scene that had become familiar: Hollis making preparations for lunch.

"Come in, come in, Laura. Stuffed eggs, and a cheese-and-onion concoction of my own invention."

"It looks good," she said absently.

"I'm afraid I didn't make much of a hit with your aunt." He laid plates and knives and forks on the counter. "I don't understand how people holding those views can be walking about among the living. One of my aunts is rather the same. Mention any musical work later than 'The Blue Danube,' and she goes quite peculiar, like your aunt. By the way, did you by any chance find time to glance at those verses of mine?"

"Yes. I was reading them last night."

"Did any one of them stay, so to speak, in your mind?"

"I think the one about the fly on the wall—"

"Ah, that. Purely experimental. That came towards the end, so you must have got through quite a lot of them; good. Did you get any kind of picture of what I was trying to convey?"

"Well, I . . ."

To her infinite relief, the telephone rang. Answering it, she heard Conrad's voice. There were also some confused noises in the background.

"Laura? Can you hear me?"

"Yes. There's a sort of buzzing—"

"That's not buzzing, that's screeching. She's locked my aunt Minnie out."

"She's . . . ?"

"Dorrit. Aunt Minnie got a bit insulting, and she just picked her up and dumped her outside and locked the door. I'm shut in my office outside. Can you hear me?"

"Yes."

"Well, there's someone here wanting to know where you live."

"That's all right, Con. I met him."

"Speak up, love; there's a lot of thumping and shouting going on here."

"I said I met him."

"Met who?"

"The architect. He came down the hill and I stopped and—"

"I'm not talking about the architect. This is a girl. She's in a state."

"Who is?"

"I've just told you. This girl who's here."

"Dorrit?"

"No, no, *no*. Not Dorrit. Dorrit's inside. This girl just arrived, and she was in a state when she arrived, and what with Aunt Minnie and all raising Cain, she—"

"Can you speak louder, Con?"

"She had your address, but she lost it, and she's been wandering round London all alone, and then someone took her to the Crossford bus and put her on it, but she got off at Waterside by mistake, and then she took a taxi, but the taxi wouldn't wait because my aunt Minnie was throwing things, and so this

149

girl's going to stay here with me until you come and fetch her, and you'd better come soon."

"What's her name, Con?"

An unnecessary question, she thought. This had all the Ginette hallmarks: lost in London, picked up, sent on, rescued, in a state.

"She'll talk to you herself," Con said. Then Ginette was on the line.

"Laura? I'm here, in this terrible village. There is a mad-woman screaming and kicking the door to get into the house, but I am outside, shut in a little glass office. I can't tell you what I've been through, what even now I'm going through. I was—"

"Stay where you are," Laura directed. "I'll be right there."

"Visitor?" Hollis asked, when she put down the receiver.

"Yes. A girl I used to know in Paris." She had a sudden inspiration. "She's at Conrad's garage. Would you go and fetch her?"

"From the garage?"

"Yes. You'd better hurry; there's a row going on there. Conrad's aunt has been locked out of the inn. This girl's called Ginette. Ginette Strauss."

"Does she speak English?"

"Yes."

"Good. I can only speak a couple of Balkan languages and a snatch or two of Arabic. Shan't be long."

Ginette, stepping into the house, threw her handbag onto the sofa, gave a loud exclamation of relief and kissed Laura on both cheeks.

"*Ô mon Dieu, enfin!* I am exhausted. Never, never have I had such a journey, never. But at last I am here. Please give me a drink. Do you have whisky? I need something like that, to recover myself."

"Hollis brought his own; he'll give you some of it," Laura answered.

He poured out a measure and added a dash of soda. Ginette disposed of it in record time. While Laura completed the preparations for lunch, he brought in the luggage: a large suitcase, a smaller suitcase, a large Mexican basket, a Basque canvas bag and a Portuguese linen bag embroidered with a large, colourful cockerel. He took it up in stages to the attic bedroom, and then filled the order for a second drink. Sipping it, Ginette told them that there had been no question of her coming by air; she would have had to pay too much in excess luggage.

"I tried to call you last night, Laura. You didn't answer. I decided to come because everything was being settled with Philippe and Mademoiselle Justine and the lawyers. I said good-bye to Mademoiselle Justine and I stayed up half of the night, packing everything. Philippe was going to drive me to Paris and put me on the train, but at the last minute she said it wasn't necessary, so I had to call a cab. And the sea crossing! Please believe what I say, that ship did everything but only didn't turn over. I was too ill to go down to a cabin. I stayed up on top, and a man brought me a drink and then he got me a rug for my deck chair, and when we were going to land, he took me to have some food. Then there was this terrible confusion to go onto the shore, and I was struggling with my luggage and a man took me to the train and got me a seat and then he took me to the dining car to eat something. And then the most terrible part of all: When I got to London, I didn't have your address and I couldn't remember what place you lived in, and I didn't know where Jess lived, to ask her. And then suddenly I remembered that man, Mr. Falconer, who was with you in Paris, how he said he lived in Napoleon Mansions. The cabdriver took me there, and I didn't know the number but we went up in the lift and rang the bell the porter

told us to ring, and there was this servant who knew everything—Crossford, and how to get to the bus to take me there.
The bus journey was terrible, but a man sitting next to me
gave me a drink when we got to that place called Waterside,
only he didn't know that I had to get onto the bus again to
come here, so I got another cab and I got to a garage where
there was this old woman who was shouting and banging on
a door with her fists. Can I have another drink?"

"Not until you've eaten something," Hollis told her in
brotherly fashion.

"I'm not hungry. I'm only thirsty."

"No food, no drink. Laura, who is this girl who locked
Conrad's aunt outside?"

"Her name's Dorrit. She's going to work at Seton's. Did
you see her?"

"She opened the door—nice clean white apron, great surprise against that dirty background. She said: 'Come and get
it,' and the aunt tried to push past, but the girl put out an
iron bar, I mean her arm, which had the same effect, and said
that if she had any more trouble, she'd lock her out again.
So the aunt went in quietly, and Conrad went in after her.
Solid muscle, that girl."

"Are you staying with Laura, too?" Ginette asked Hollis.

"I'm camping in one of her fields. I'll take you to see my
tent."

"I don't like tents."

"You'll like this one."

"Laura, can I go up and see my room?"

"Of course."

Ginette went up to inspect it. Hollis watched her as she
went up the stairs, and something in his expression told Laura
that salvation was at hand. It was not Ginette's way to waste
time on a woman when there was a man in the vicinity. If
she could get Hollis to stop talking and listen to her instead,
she would tell him, with the utmost secrecy, about M. Philippe

and the partnership. And while she was telling him, she, Laura, could resume her normal life.

Ginette went up to unpack after lunch. Hollis went away, but returned for dinner. Ginette, coming downstairs in a robe of almost total transparency, lay on the sofa and listened to some of the trials undergone by soil specialists in remote and dangerous places. Then she told him what misery it had been to have been brought up in a château miles from civilization. Laura went contentedly about the task of serving dinner.

Hollis had gone when the telephone rang. Ginette came out of her room and hovered at the top of the stairs.

"I hope that is not Philippe," she said, frowning. "I said to him that he wasn't to call me."

"No. Not Monsieur Philippe," Laura answered.

Ginette went back to her room and closed the door. Laura stood staring at the wall in front of her and trying to control her breathing. Not Monsieur Philippe.

"Are you still there, Laura?"

"Yes, Finch."

"Have you got a visitor?"

"I've got two. Which one are you interested in?"

"When I came home this evening, I was told that a young French lady had been here. Ginette?"

"Yes. She lost my address but remembered yours."

"She got to you safely?"

"Yes."

"Everything all right?"

"Yes, thank you."

"Did Chawton show you round the house?"

"Yes."

"I'll take you round myself when I get down to Crossford."

She did not want to ask the question, but heard herself asking it. "You're coming down?"

"Yes. Earlier than I expected. Who's your other guest?"

"His name is Hollis Hinchcliffe Howard and he's a friend

of Jess's and he's camping in one of my fields. Thank you for ringing about Ginette."

"She gave me an excuse to ring. I told you I wouldn't be down until the end of the month—remember?"

"Yes."

"I'm coming down at the end of next week. For two days. I wondered if you'd drive back to London with me. I've heard from your father—twice. Once to tell me he thought he'd found that picture he said he'd look for—the mate to the one my grandmother bought. The next time, he rang to say he'd got it in his studio but would like me to look at it before we make a deal. Would you come, too?"

She hesitated. Her doubts were not concerned with him, but with her father, and they were too complicated to unravel in the course of a telephone conversation.

"I'll be able to give you a definite answer when you get here," she said.

"I hope you'll come. Are you well?"

"Yes, thank you. Good-bye."

"Not good-bye. Au revoir. French. It means that I'll be seeing you again soon."

She put down the receiver.

Chapter 6

Ginette's presence freed Laura from Hollis, but not completely, for he was too well-mannered to treat Laura—as Ginette clearly did—as a mere provider of bed and board. By the end of the week, he had made his own assessment of the situation.

"I don't know how much Ginette has told you," he said to Laura. "I've had some long talks with her, and she asked me not to repeat what she said, but she won't mind my telling you. My opinion, if anybody wants it, is that she's got herself into a kind of trap."

"Trap?"

"Well, for a start, take the age of that fellow. Old enough to be her grandfather. If he's as smooth as he looks in that photograph she showed me, it's no wonder she thinks she's in love. She says she's been in love with him since he taught history in that school."

"It was a long time ago. She managed to forget him once or twice in the interval."

"You mean those two marriages? Mistakes, both of them. It's a pity there wasn't someone around who could have stopped her from getting involved again."

"I don't see any trap."

"She's going to marry him, isn't she? And live to regret it."

"Why? She likes Paris. She says they're going to buy a house near the hotel. At any time she—"

"He'll be working long hours. She'll have to put in a good deal of time on her own."

"But not surrounded by armed bandits. You mustn't worry about her too much."

"Oh, she's been around; I know that. But I don't like the way this fellow's let her go away just as things were coming to a head."

"It was her idea, not his."

"He shouldn't have agreed. And he shouldn't have agreed not to ring her. Now she's stuck here without news."

"Why don't you take her out and try to get her mind off Paris?"

"I didn't want to leave you alone. And she's not easy to amuse. She hates walking, she's frightened of horses and she isn't interested in wild flowers. All she really wants is to get up to London and take a look at the shops."

"Then why don't you drive her up?"

"You think I should?"

"Yes."

"Then I'll fix it. We'll go up on Monday and she can do a bit of shopping, and then we'll have lunch, and after that I'll take her to a museum or an exhibition, and then we could fit in dinner and a show."

Ginette changed the program by substituting some more shopping for the museum or exhibition. She and Hollis drove away early on Monday morning—but before leaving, he drew Laura aside and addressed her in the conspiratorial manner he appeared to have caught from Ginette.

"Did that chap ring last night?"

"No. She doesn't expect him to. She told him not to."

"Would you keep away from a phone, in these circumstances? No, you wouldn't. You'd—"

"Hush, she'll hear you."

"You'd call every night to find out how she was getting on. Anyone with any feeling would—"

"Hush!"

"You're right; it's better to say nothing. But see if I'm not right—there's something wrong somewhere."

He drove away with Ginette, and Laura breathed a sigh of relief. She got into her car and drove to the garage to ask Conrad for the latest news of his aunt and Dorrit. Nothing there seemed changed. Conrad was changing the tire of a car. The windows of the inn were open, but no sound issued from the building. Only Conrad's face, as he raised it to look across the yard, seemed to have lost its cherubic look. He straightened and came across to speak to her.

"I don't want anything," she said. "I just came to ask how things were."

"Terrible. Have you ever, as long as you've known me, heard me say a kind word about Auntie Min?"

"No."

"Well, I'm feeling sorry for her. She's had it coming to her for years. My dad let her have things too much her own way, and she's always walked right over Clive and me. It was time someone paid her out—but I didn't think it would be a girl who just walked in from nowhere, like this Dorrit."

"Any more lockings-out?"

"Two. She'll take so much of Auntie Min's insults, and then she'll pick her up, the way you'd pick up a shopping bag, and dump her out here. Auntie Min took the bus into Waterside and tried to get a policeman, but they all know her; nobody'd come. She tried to climb in a window—at her age!—but Dorrit locked them all. She could get in through the pub entrance, but not through to the inside rooms—Dorrit locked all the doors. And I don't blame her. Soon's she got a room to rights, Auntie Min would start messing it up. And what that girl's got through! She started on the kitchen. She just looks at things, and they get up and clean themselves. Floor, stove, walls—why don't you go in and take a look? It all looks like new. No, don't go in. Auntie Min's in there. She stays in her room now, but it's no use risking running into her."

The door of the inn opened. Dorrit, her head tied in a duster, a large apron enveloping her small, stout frame, came out and joined them.

"'Morning, Miss Seton."

"Good morning, Dorrit. Conrad's just been telling me that you've taken charge."

"I had to eat," Dorrit explained. "How Con could ever swallow anything that was cooked in that kitchen, I'll never understand. I feel sorry for his dad, whoever he was."

"Things were all right when my dad was alive," Conrad told her. "The trouble was that dough he left Auntie Min. It went straight to her head. She said she was going to start living, and . . . well, you've seen."

"I'll do what I can while I'm here," Dorrit promised, "but I've got to find out when I'll be wanted up the hill. How does anyone find out when Mr. Falconer's going to come?"

"I think he'll be down next weekend," Laura said.

"Good. Then I can talk to him," Dorrit said. "Con, I need some groceries."

"Gimme the list, and I'll see you get everything."

She went into the house and he looked after her with regret in his eyes.

"I suppose it was too much to hope she'd be permanent," he said philosophically. "All the same, it doesn't seem right, does it, me all alone down here, and Mr. Falconer setting himself up at Seton's with a string of Dorrits? Someone ought to tell him he's behind the times; gentlemen do their own chores now. By the way, Laura, Wilfred's in town—did you know?"

"No."

"Visiting his mum. It ought to be a happy visit—I think one of his sisters has got herself a husband. I don't know whether it's bass or treble."

This last remark, which might have puzzled a stranger, would have been clear to anybody living ·in Waterside or

Crossford. The two Downes sisters were professional pianists who appeared on concert platforms to perform duets. There was little difference in their ages and even less in their appearance: each was large, fair, loud-voiced and hearty; both had smooth hair done in a bun, snub noses and determined chins. To all but their intimates, they were indistinguishable, identifiable only by their position at the piano.

"I think it must be Audrey," Laura guessed. "She's been going round with the new doctor for a long time."

"I asked Wilf about Jess, but he changed the subject. Is it on or off?"

"Off, I think. I'm sorry. I like him."

"Me, too. This is the second time she's given him the push. If you run into him, tell him to drop by and tell me all about it."

She met Wilfred on the following morning. Neither Ginette nor Hollis had appeared for breakfast; she had been delivering orders in various parts of Waterside. She was crossing the bridge on her way home when Wilfred brought his car alongside and signalled her to stop. Then he got out and walked over to speak to her. He looked depressed.

"I was on my way to pay you a visit," he said. "But as you're here, why don't we go into The Bell and Bottle and talk over a drink?"

They sat in a corner of the lounge. Wilfred ordered beer for himself; Laura asked for coffee.

"Is one of your sisters engaged?" she asked.

"Yes. Audrey. How did you hear?"

"Conrad told me. He'd like to see you."

"I'll go along. How are things with you?"

"Fine, thanks."

"Seen Jess's Japanese decor?"

"Yes."

"Did you enjoy sitting on the floor?"

"No."

"I don't understand it," he said bitterly. "I don't. I can't follow her reasoning anymore. I don't know what she's after, or if she's after anything. When she bought that flat in London, she seemed all in one piece: She was going to fix it up the way she wanted it, and she was going to come down here to breathe nice fresh air whenever she needed it. She was even going to marry me—I thought. I haven't much to offer in the way of manly attractions, but you know I can claim to have been in love with her and ready to marry her long before she set eyes on that bunch of performers she picked out in London. You saw them. Remember them? There was that chap Iain, spelled the hard way, who claimed to be descended from Robert the Bruce—did you ever meet a Scotsman who wasn't? Remember that fake-Russian fellow who filled the flat, *her* flat, with all his paraphernalia? And now she's tied up with this fellow who thinks he's Jimmu and—"

"Who's Jimmu?"

"Not is; was. The direct descendant in the fourth generation of the grandson of the Sun Goddess. First Emperor of Japan. What was I saying before I got on to emperors?"

"You were talking about Bernard Shotton."

"That's right. Well, she can have him. I'm sick of it, Laura. I'm through. I'm going to get Jess out of my system and I'm going to look for a girl who wants to settle down, like me, and raise a family. It's been too long, this hanging round her and watching her experimenting. I've had enough. You can tell her so, if she ever notices I'm not there, and asks where I went."

He paused, looked absently at his glass, then lifted it and drank deep. Laura watched him with compassion. His was not a face that lent itself to an expression of misery, being rugged and somewhat pugnacious, but there was dejection in the droop of his shoulders and in his eyes.

"I think," she hazarded, "Jess won't enjoy sitting on the floor for long."

"So the Japanese craze will end, and she'll pick up a pig-tailed Chinaman."

"Chinamen don't have—"

"—pigtails anymore. I know. If I hadn't known, my grand-mother would have told me. She's here on a visit, like me, and we're having it all again—her young days in Shanghai and Rangoon and Kuala Lumpur, falling in love with my grand-father when they were riding in a howdah on some rajah's elephant, honeymoon in Kashmir, trotting along the Mall in Simla escorted by ADC's straight out of Kipling, ayahs and bearers and khidmutgars, snakes and scorpions, Burra Mem-sahibs and dinner with the Viceroy. It never stops. It goes on and on, and my mother joins in because she came in for the tail end of it. To look at them both, you'd think they'd never travelled farther than Folkestone or Dover, but just come and listen. My mother was once carried about by a hill woman who wore nose rings."

"My father had a French nurse in a blue uniform. And my aunt was once, if you can believe it, the pet of I forget which Indian regiment."

"The picturesque past. Pity there's not more written about the domestic aspects of it. Did I say I was going to get Jess out of my system?"

"Yes, you did."

"Fat hope. You'd better have another coffee. I'm going to reminisce."

The coffee was brought by Conrad's brother, Clive. He lingered, leaning on their table, relaxed, carefree, with some of Conrad's overgrown-schoolboy look.

"Don't often see you two together these days," he remarked. "What's he after, Laura? Is he trying to switch from Jess to you?"

"I was just about to recall," Wilfred said, "that the first time I ever saw the Seton girls was when they staged that fire on the clearing behind Seton's."

"They didn't stage it. Con and I did." Clive, ignoring the customers to be seen through an archway, waiting to order drinks at the bar, drew up a chair and sat down. "Con's idea, it was. We weren't going to tell any of the girls, but we couldn't have the fire unless Jess and Laura agreed—it was on Seton's property. It was me who built the fire and—"

"Let me tell it," Wilfred broke in.

"Then speed it up. Look at that queue at the bar."

"I'd heard a lot about the goings-on of the Crossford teen-agers," Wilfred went on, "but I'd never been invited to join any of the parties. But that night, I was asked to be the chief of the fire brigade."

"Only because you were the only guy we knew who could lay his hands on a lorry. Remember the fireman's hat Jess made you?"

"It was when I saw myself in that hat that I signed on. How old were we?"

"Jess and Laura were around thirteen. You were about seventeen. More. Old enough to know better. That fire was one of the best-organized things we ever put on. The only hitch was when the borrowed garden hoses leaked."

"After that night," Wilfred said, "I came over to your side, and didn't listen to any more complaints about wild goings-on."

"There was nothing wild about anything we did," Laura objected. "We liked outdoor games, that's all. And we liked moonlight bathes in the river, and picnics at midnight in the Weatherstone barn."

"And I liked Jess," Wilfred said. "And she liked me."

"And you thought it was forever, and you're sitting here moaning because you can't tie her down. Be thankful, boy, be thankful." Clive rose reluctantly in response to angry shouts from the bar. "Be thankful you didn't pick a girl who clings. Well, so long."

"Wait a minute. Have you seen Dorrit?" Laura asked him.

He threw back his head and gave a shout of laughter.

"Once. She said I shouldn't have got out and left Con alone. I reminded her that he hadn't been left alone—he had Aunt Minnie. What's the betting Aunt Minnie won't give in and get out?"

"Who's Dorrit?" Wilfred asked.

Laura told him. "If their aunt does go, do you think Clive will go back to The Three Pigeons?" she asked.

"No. Crossford's too quiet for Clive. Even if he went back, he wouldn't stick it for long."

"Speaking of sticking, do you know that Hollis is here?"

He stared at her.

"Hollis? H. H. Howard?"

"Yes."

"Here in Waterside?"

"No. In his tent, in one of my fields. Jess sent him. He was encamped when I got back from Paris."

"So she finally thought of a way of getting rid of him. Why do you let her pass her problems on to you? He'll drive you crazy."

"No, he won't. He's busy looking after a French girl who came to stay with me. When's Audrey going to be married?"

"Soon. My mother doesn't like long engagements. She's happier than I've seen her for a long time, making plans."

His mother had more than one reason to be happy, Laura reflected; she was marrying off a daughter, and her son was showing signs of extricating himself from his long attachment to Jessica Seton. Not many mothers liked Jess, but Lady Downes had more cause than most mothers for complaint. She was a gentle, ineffectual woman who, like many of her contemporaries, was engaged in a struggle to reconcile what she had been taught by her parents with what she was now learning from her children.

Laura rose. "I've got to go, Wilfred. Drop in and see me while you're here."

He walked over to pay the bill, and then saw her to her

car. She reached the cottage to find a note from Hollis propped against the coffepot: he and Ginette had decided to go up to London again. They had taken overnight bags and would ring to let her know when they were returning.

She dropped the note into the wastepaper basket, and thought that things were beginning to look bad for M. Philippe. If Ginette gave him up, there was no guarantee that Hollis would offer to take his place. He was friendly, he was interested, he had shown concern—but Laura did not think he had any plans for settling down with a woman. But that was his problem; in the meantime, the cottage was once more peaceful and private.

She looked forward to a quiet, solitary lunch, but she was not destined to have it. The telephone rang, and she heard Mr. Chawton's voice.

"Miss Seton?"

"No, Mr. Chawton. My sister's Miss Seton. I'm Laura."

"You recognized my voice?"

"Yes."

"Will you come and have lunch with me? No notice, I'm afraid, but I was too busy to get to a phone. Are you by any chance free?"

"Free, and making a lovely light cheese soufflé, if you'd care to come and share it. Avocado to begin with, and a fresh green salad to fill the corners. Does that tempt you?"

"Did anyone ever ask you to marry them and share the cooking?"

"Yes. One o'clock?"

He arrived with a bottle of white wine, and she chilled it while they drank sherry. She learned that he had been married twice, second time lucky, had children too late in life, and was one day going to retire and live in Switzerland. He ended by praising the layout of the cottage.

"Who was your architect?" he asked.

"I didn't have one," she confessed.

"Why not? You don't trust the breed?"

"If I'd thought about it, I would have decided that this was too small a project to interest an architect."

"So you told the builder what you wanted, and believed you'd get it? That's how I met my second wife. She told a builder what she wanted, and I was called in to take over the job when he'd made a mess of it. But you appear to have been lucky. Do you think Finch is going to be happy living in Crossford?"

She hesitated. Then: "I don't think I know him well enough to answer that," she said. "The house is lovely; he ought to be happy living in it. If he finds Crossford dull, he's got a nice fast car to take him out of it now and then. And in any case, he's got to spend a lot of time in London, hasn't he?"

"As much or as little time as he wants to. He's his own boss. Isn't Mrs. Pennerley your aunt?"

"Yes."

"She drove up to Seton's in a taxi and asked me to submit plans for the new school they're putting up in Waterside. She said she had come on behalf of the education sub-committee, but she seemed to have the biggest say in the project. Would I find her easy to get on with?"

"Most people don't, but—"

"But what?"

"I imagine you'd find it stimulating."

"May I take that as meaning that I have a way of managing difficult people?"

"You dealt with Mr. Falconer's fiancée, didn't you?"

"Oh, you remember that?" He laughed. "Yes, I got rid of her. But I think your aunt would be a tougher proposition. All the signs go to show that she's a seasoned warrior."

Laura filed this for use next time Jess referred to Magda as an old battleax. She looked at her watch and decided that she could serve lunch. They spoke of many things during the meal, but Finch's name did not come up again, and she concluded that he had said nothing to Mr. Chawton about coming down at the end of the week.

As he was leaving, he mentioned Magda once more.

"I forgot, when I was speaking of your aunt, to tell you that I first heard of her through a young nephew of mine who's just gone to work for a firm called Mellish and Son. Do you know who they are?"

"Yes. They've acted for my aunt for some years."

"So my nephew told me. He's getting promotion earlier than he expected. Old Mr. Mellish has just died, and his son has taken his place. That means there's to be a reshuffle, and my nephew will take a step or two up the ladder."

And it also means, Laura told herself, that Magda will get less assistance in her inquiries about the Zollard.

She saw Mr. Chawton off, cleared away the lunch things and then drove to the Sheldon stables to see if she could find a horse that needed exercise. She was out for more than two hours, and returned to the cottage by way of the farmhouse, where Sue Sheldon gave her tea and freshly baked scones.

She was drinking her after-dinner coffee that evening when Jess telephoned.

"Laura? How are you?"

"I'm fine. So is Hollis. So is Ginette."

"My God. I rang to say I was coming down at the end of the week, but I don't think I could stand it. How are you keeping sane?"

"He's going round with Ginette, so I don't see much of either of them."

"Isn't it time she went back to Paris?"

"There's been no summons. She told Monsieur Philippe that he wasn't to ring until everything had been fixed up."

"She ought to go back and see what he's up to. Or is she thinking of letting Mademoiselle Justine have him, and helping herself to Hollis?"

"I've no idea. Are you coming down or not?"

"I'm thinking. Can't you get rid of your incubuses?"

"Incubi. I doubt it. But you won't see much of them—if anything. Ginette's one idea is to get out of Crossford."

"Then I'll risk it."

Laura had been trying to decide whether she should mention the fact that Finch Falconer would also be coming down at the end of the week. The call ended, and she had said nothing. He would be up at Seton's; Jess would be at the cottage. They would have to meet, but she did not look forward to seeing them together. Jess had formed her opinion of him, and it was not a favourable one—and what Jess thought, Jess usually said, or if she didn't say it, it was plain in her attitude and manner. There would, she knew, be no verbal duel. Finch's weapons, so far as she had seen, were his calm front, his frown and his monosyllabic replies. These did not sound an effective armoury, but she thought they might be enough to subdue Jess.

Ginette and Hollis came back the following day—to unpack, repack and go away again. They were not specific as to where they had been or how they had amused themselves, but it was clear that they were on a more than friendly footing. Ginette asked whether there had been any word from M. Philippe, and did not seem interested in the answer; she was busy trying to decide between the attractions of a trip to Jersey or a visit to the Isle of Man.

Laura did not miss them. Her mind remained fixed on the coming visits of Finch and Jess.

She had decided to keep them apart if possible. They were to arrive on the same day, but it was not likely that they would arrive at the same time.

However, they did. She thought it a mean trick on the part of Fate. Jess drove up, left the gate open and parked her car at the door. Through the open gate drove Finch.

Laura made the introduction as brief as possible. "Hello,

Jess. Hello, Finch. You two haven't met. Come in."

The two stood where they were, each at the door of a car, each subjecting the other to a frank survey. Jess spoke first.

"Now that we've met," she said, "I can tell you how much I want to see what you've done to Seton's. I'm not here for long—could you take me to see it?"

"Yes," said Finch.

That was all. Why, Laura wondered irritably, couldn't he do what everybody else did, what the commonest forms of courtesy demanded: look pleasant? Why stand there, grave, unmoving, expectant, as though waiting to deal with the next question? Polite exchanges—hadn't he ever heard of them?

"Look, do come in," she urged.

Jess took a small case out of her car; he held out a hand to take it from her. She relinquished it and preceded him into the living room.

"You drove down from London?" she asked him.

"Yes."

"I wish they'd widen that last bit of road leading into Waterside. You get a nice, fast stretch and then you find your-self crawling along behind buses and lorries. Couldn't you get hold of someone at the top, and get them to do something about it?"

"Perhaps."

"You've already done a lot to boost local firms. Conrad, at the garage, dealt with all the vans going up and down to Seton's—and your carpenters and plumbers and electricians filled his pub. Are you going to deal with the Waterside firms when you're living here?"

"Yes."

Jess, seated on the sofa, looked up at him. "I talk too much. Have you noticed?" she asked.

For the first time since their meeting, he smiled—his slow, transfiguring smile. "Keep on," he said.

She shook her head. "I'm no good at monologues. Laura,

do we get tea, coffee or something to drink?"

"Whichever you ask for."

"I'll have a pre-dinner sherry."

"How about you?" Laura asked Finch.

"I'm sorry. I can't stay. I came," he explained, "to ask when I could take you over the house. As your sister's here, I could—"

"—take us both. Good idea," Jess said. "What's the matter with tomorrow?"

"Are you free?" he asked Laura.

"Yes."

"What have you done with Ginette and Hollis?" Jess asked.

"They've gone to the Isle of Man. They didn't say when they'd be back."

"Draw a line through Monsieur Philippe's name," Jess advised. "Is tomorrow on?"

"If you cared to," Finch said, "we could look over the house before lunch, and then perhaps you would both go somewhere to lunch with me."

"Take Laura. I hate threesomes, thanks all the same. Unless"—suddenly, Laura knew what was coming—"unless your fiancée would make a fourth?"

"No."

"What a pity. Didn't she come down with you?"

"No. Midday?" he asked Laura.

"Thank you."

"I'll call for you."

The door closed behind him. They heard him drive away.

"Why did you have to drag in his fiancée?" Laura demanded.

"Curiosity. You don't appear to have any on that subject, but surely you'd like to know what he's after? You won't learn anything by looking at him, and he won't give anything away unless it's prized out of him."

"I knew you wouldn't like him."

"Did I say I didn't like him? You wouldn't call him exactly sparkling, would you?"

"Does everybody have to sparkle? Does everybody have to have a supply of smart sayings, or small talk? He gives a perfectly polite yes or no to questions; does he have to spin out his answers if it's not necessary?"

"Magda called him a rough diamond, didn't she?"

"Yes, she did, and he isn't rough and as you've just said, he doesn't sparkle. But I like him."

"You more than like him. And if I'm any judge, he more than likes you. That's what's worrying me. If he didn't have this elusive fiancée, I'd try to like him, for your sake. I'll admit he's got looks—face and figure. There's a lot of him, and most of it seems to be muscle. Where's that drink?"

Laura brought it to her, with one for herself. She switched on a table lamp and sat down.

"Wilfred's here," she said.

"If you'd said that earlier, he could have made a fourth at lunch tomorrow. Does he know I'm here?"

"I don't think so. When I saw him, I didn't know. He went back to London, but came back to help his mother with wedding preparations—so Conrad told me. I forgot to tell you that Audrey's engaged."

"To that doctor, I suppose?"

"Yes."

She paused, wondering whether she should relay some of the sentiments Wilfred had expressed over his beer at The Bell and Bottle. She thought not. Jess would phone, he would arrange to meet her—or not. It was between the two of them.

But Jess, instead of ringing, decided to drive round and congratulate Audrey. While she was out, the telephone rang. Laura answered it, to hear Finch's voice.

"I'm at Seton's. I've only just come in. I passed your sister on the way. I didn't make a very good impression, did I?"

"Did you want to?"

"Yes. Did you think I wasn't trying? Don't you know me yet?"

"I'm beginning to."

"Are you like your mother—in character, I mean?"

"People used to say so. I was never as vague as she was."

"Your sister's like your father."

"Jess—like Claud? I don't see the slightest—"

"—resemblance? It's there. Listen. When I left your house, I drove out to see that new restaurant about four miles beyond Waterside. It's good. It's being run by a friend of mine. We'll go there, and he's promised to give us what we had when your father gave us lunch. He wants to know whether he can compete."

"Why are you so much more talkative on the phone than you are—"

"—face to face? I don't know. Do you?"

"No. I've got to serve dinner. Till tomorrow."

When Jess returned, they had a light dinner and then settled down to look at television. After ten minutes, Jess got up and walked over to the set.

"Want any more?" she asked Laura.

"Not unless Miles Shotton is coming on."

"Very funny." She switched off and returned to her chair. "Why haven't you asked me about Bernard?"

"What's there to ask? I know it all. He's gone Japanese and you sit on the floor and he goes to Japan and comes back and—"

"Not anymore."

"He's given up Japan?"

"He's going to live there."

"For good?"

"Forever. I hope. Go on—say it."

"Say what?"

"Tell me it didn't last long. Tell me I'm a fool for going into something without knowing what I was getting into."

"Look, Jess." Laura spoke reasonably. "It's your life. You don't have to account to anybody for what you do. If you want to change your life-style every now and then, why not? If you tried to live as I live, you'd die of boredom. The only thing I don't understand, in this case, is how you could get tired of Bernard if he was never there."

"He was there too often. And as to life-styles . . . do you know anything about Japanese cooking?"

"No. I read something about it—it sounded rather complicated."

"Complicated? Every time I wanted a cup of tea, I had to go through what Bernard called the time-honoured ceremony. He produced sixteen—*sixteen*—utensils and spread them out and sat down to tell me what I was to do with them. A family in Osaka had taught him the ritual. I said all I wanted was some boiling water and a tea bag, but he sat there with his eyes half-closed, sniffing the—I'm quoting—the subtle fragrance and arranging the things in—quoting again—a harmonious pattern. Special bamboo teaspoon, two silk napkins, a fan, a bamboo whisk, you name it, we were using it. So I told him if he felt so strongly about it, he ought to go and make his home there, so that's what he decided to do. He thought I'd go, too, but I decided I couldn't take all that politeness and ceremony and floating round in kimonos. Speaking of kimonos, I've brought you one. Wait till you see."

She got up and took from her case a rolled-up garment. Shaking it out, she revealed a kimono of purest silk, embroidered with dragons. The material, the work, the colours were so beautiful that Laura, with an exclamation of delight, gathered it to her and hugged it.

"Jess, you can't give this away!"

"Can't I? I never want to see another one as long as I live. Put it away and let's make some coffee and lace it with cognac. I think Wilfred might drop in. I didn't see him when I went to the house, but he knows I'm here, so he'll be over."

But Wilfred didn't come. They were settling down to sleep when Jess mentioned him again.

"I suppose he had to go out to dinner," she said "But it's odd he didn't ring, or come on here afterwards. It's the sort of night he likes for those brisk walks he's so keen on."

"I'm sorry you quarrelled with him. I always thought he was the nicest of all the men you knew."

"That's not saying much. I'm beginning to think that all the men I know are freaks. Weirdies. And I didn't quarrel with him. I just told him to get out, that's all. Good night."

Chapter 7

Jess was restless and irritable at breakfast the next morning. Ten o'clock came, then eleven, and there was no sign of Wilfred. The omission was so strange that Laura's heart sank. He had been devoted to Jess from his boyhood. They had quarrelled frequently; Jess had more than once announced that everything between them was over forever—but on every previous occasion the sequel had invariably been the appearance of Wilfred to plead or argue. For him to be in Waterside now, for him to know that Jess was at the cottage, and to make no move to see her, was something Laura had never known before.

At half past eleven, Jess walked to the telephone and for the third time that morning, picked up the receiver and put it down again without dialling.

"I'm going out," she said. "I'll wait for you and Finch at the bottom of the hill at midday."

Laura did not ask where she was going. Half an hour later, she saw Finch's car and opened the door to let him in.

"I'm a bit early," he said. "Your sister's car isn't outside. Has she changed her mind about coming to see the house?"

"No. She's meeting us at the bottom of the hill. Coffee?"

"I'd rather have some beer."

She found, after some searching, glass, bottle and opener.

"Usually I know where to find things," she explained, "because I leave them where I can see them. But Hollis has a mania for tidying. He even finished the bookshelves I was putting up, so that he could get all the books out of the way. Is that beer cold enough?"

He nodded. "Cold enough, but not large enough. If there's another—"

He got it for himself and settled down to enjoy it.

"Do you know a girl called Dorrit Moat?" she asked him.

He looked at her in surprise. "Yes. She and her mother are coming to work for me. How did you hear of her?"

"She's here."

"In Crossford?"

"Yes. She got off the bus at the garage and said she'd come to get Seton's ready for you to move into."

"My fault. I didn't anticipate any holdup in the building program, and forgot to let her know that she wasn't to come until I could give her a definite date. Where's she now?"

"She's got a room at The Three Pigeons."

"From what I've seen of it, it's not in a state to cater for customers—except the pub part. Who's looking after Dorrit?"

"She's looking after herself. Conrad's aunt used to be in charge, but she decided to retire, and that's why the place got so neglected. She didn't want to let Dorrit have a room, but Conrad gave her one. There's been a clash or two, but Dorrit dealt with the situation by locking the aunt outside. Don't move Dorrit too soon; she's cooking Conrad's meals as well as her own. I don't suppose he's had anything done for him since his father died. If the aunt got out, he might find a wife, but nobody's prepared to move in while the aunt's there."

She paused; a car had stopped at the door. She glanced out of the window.

"Ginette and Hollis," she reported. "Back from the Isle of Man."

She opened the door and they entered, brisk and alert and not at all travel-worn. Ginette gave Finch a smile, but Hollis advanced on him with outstretched hand.

"I know you; you're Falconer," he told him. "I recognized your car. I was talking to the chap at the garage, and he told me there was only one of them round here, and it belonged to you. Tell me, do you find it as—"

"Oh, Hollis," broke in Ginette impatiently, "please stop this talking about cars. I'm going to faint from hunger. Look at the time we had to get up, before six o'clock, and no fresh bread and no good coffee. Now I want to eat. Laura, did Philippe ring?"

"No. Could you two look after yourselves? I have to go out."

"Leave it all to me," Hollis said. "But before you go, Laura, I've got to tell you something. It's been wonderful being here. I'm sorry Jess didn't manage to get down, but as things turned out—"

"Oh, hush!" shouted Ginette. "We said that I would tell it, and now look, you're—"

"All right. Go ahead and tell it," he invited.

Ginette leaned in a graceful pose against the counter. "What it is, Laura, is this: You know how I have always loved Philippe? Well, I still do in one way. But from the beginning, Hollis said I shouldn't marry a man who's so old, and when I thought about it, I knew he was right. Hollis said—"

"I told her she'd been too impulsive. She let him talk her into it, and—"

"Why do you interrupt me all the time?"

"Because you're rather given to circumlocution. The point, Laura, is that I'm going to Turkey on a job."

"I was going to say that, if you had waited," Ginette said angrily. "I was going to tell them. Yes, Laura, he has to go to Turkey. A telegram came before we left this house to go to that island. It said—"

"Marching orders," said Hollis. "There'll be a confirmation in the post, but the telegram set it all out. I've got to leave straightaway. I'm sorry to go, but—"

"What is the use of telling anything," Ginette demanded, "if you tell it all wrong? The telegram came, but before that, we talked together, and that is what you should have told first. You see, Laura, Hollis and I have not known each other for a long time, but we were very quick to like each other. From the first, I found him agreeable. And it was a change to make love with someone not so much older than me, someone not old like poor Philippe. You understand this?"

Finch spoke. "If you'd rather discuss this without me—" he began.

"No, no, no," Hollis assured him. "There aren't any secrets."

"Yes, there are," Ginette said, "but he can know about them. I don't mind. He will know soon, when I go away with Hollis."

"You're going to Turkey?" Laura asked in astonishment.

"Turkey? No, not to Turkey. Hollis wanted me to go, but I said that I didn't want to go there. Instead, I am—"

"She's going to Greece," Hollis said. "She's been to a lot of places, but she missed out on Greece. She's going to wait for me in Athens. I'll join her as soon as I'm free, and we'll sail round the islands. Nice time of year to do it."

"Don't you think that's a good idea, Laura?" Ginette asked.

"There's just one little thing you seem to have forgotten," Laura said. "Weren't you—"

"I know what you are going to say. You are going to say about Philippe. I was just going to tell you about that."

"Is he going to wait until you get back?" Laura asked.

"There's nothing to wait for," Hollis explained. "As far as he's concerned, Ginette isn't coming back. If a man talks a girl young enough to be his granddaughter into marrying him, he ought to have more sense than to let her out of his sight. He oughtn't to be too surprised when he learns that it's all off. All the same, the chap's got some feelings, I expect, and we don't want to hurt them."

"So I wrote a letter," Ginette said. "Only Hollis said it wouldn't do."

"Too terse," Hollis said. "Not enough padding to act as a shock absorber. And after all, this kind of thing is better said than written, so Ginette and I thought that as he's bound to get on the phone soon, you could tell him, as kindly as you can, that it's all off."

There was a pause. Laura was waiting to get her breath back.

"Did you say—" she began slowly at last.

"Laura, he *knows* you. He *likes* you," Ginette said. "You were his favourite pupil. You must tell him—and you will be able to tell him in French, so that he will understand without any mistake. It is very sweet of you to do this for us."

"We'll be everlastingly grateful," Hollis confirmed. "And now I'll do something about something to eat. Too late for breakfast, too early for lunch; I'll make it brunch. You wouldn't want to stay and sample some of my special coffee, Falconer?"

"Thanks, no. I've just finished two beers."

"Then this is where we part. Laura"—he kissed her cheek—"bless you for your kindness. Good-bye, Falconer."

Ginette's farewells were even briefer. She kissed Laura on both cheeks, gave Finch a limp hand and went upstairs.

Finch and Laura drove almost to the hill before making any comment.

"Well," he asked at last, "how do you feel about that?"

"Furious. What has it got to do with me? How could they stand there and tell me quite calmly to—"

"Why didn't you refuse?"

"Because there was a feeling at the back of my mind that if I didn't agree to do it, they'd do it themselves—more crudely and much less kindly. I don't like, I never did much like Monsieur Philippe, but I think he's entitled to—"

"He's well out of it."

"That doesn't alter the fact that—"

"You shouldn't have let her in. You should have put up the shutters."

She found nothing to say to this. She knew it would also be Jess's opinion.

Jess was waiting at the foot of the hill. She walked up to Finch's car.

"You're late," she told them.

"Hollis's fault," Laura answered.

"They came back?"

"To say good-bye and pack. He's going to a job in Turkey. She's going to wait for him in Athens."

"And what became of the poor professor?"

"Ditched."

"Lucky for him. How did they break the news?"

"To him? They didn't. They asked me to. They—"

It was no use going on. Jess and Finch had both become helpless with laughter.

"I'm glad you find it funny," Laura told them.

They regained their self-control, and Jess spoke.

"Let it be a lesson to you," she said. "It might end by being a lesson to Hollis, too. By the time his job's over, he'll find Ginette has attached herself to a handsome Greek. Then he'll come back and put up his tent all over again."

"Not on my land," Laura vowed. "Will you lead the way up the hill?"

Jess went back to her car. When they reached the house, she got out and stood looking round in amazement.

"Why the surprise?" Laura asked. "You knew it had been more or less rebuilt."

"I thought it would be as it was before, only propped up. But that wing's new."

"It was copied from an old print I found in the Waterside museum," Finch told them. "Before the trees grew up, the house could be seen from across the river; when the print was made, there was a wing, but the architect thinks it was taken down and the stone used to build the chapel."

Only a few workmen were to be seen, and they were at work clearing away debris. The house seemed to Laura to have already assumed a welcoming look.

It was Jess who led the way inside, who led the way from room to room, recognizing or not recognizing, reconstructing, exclaiming, lost in recalling the past. This, Laura thought, watching her, was the real Jess, the old Jess who had grown up here and who had been content with things as they were. This was the Jess who had led the teen-age gangs, who had cared little for criticism and less for the conventions. This was the Jess that Wilfred had loved.

She stopped at the sight of some workmen putting the finishing touches to a window.

"That wasn't there before," she said.

"No. It should have been," Finch answered. "It gives a view of the sunsets."

"And look, Laura—isn't this the room Claud was working in when the plaster fell off the ceiling and showered him? But it looks bigger."

"Dividing wall knocked down," explained Finch.

"What happened to the old kitchen?"

"Pulled down. It was built over an old well."

"You mean there was another well, not only the one in the garden?"

"There were three. They kept looking for water, but took some time to find it. Two of the wells have been filled in; the third will be used for watering the gardens."

"Gardens . . . We never had a garden. Unless you count my mother's herb garden," Jess said.

"And Claud's pots of begonias," Laura added.

"Heating everywhere," Jess commented. "We had the kitchen range, and a log fire in the so-called drawing room. One awful January . . . did you tell him, Laura?"

"About the icicles? No."

"Icicles," Jess told Finch. "Hanging from the leaks in the roof of one of the attics. Laura and I put candles all round the floor and made it look like an underground cave—it was beautiful. We invited a whole crowd in for a midnight feast, and they all brought food, and someone—Ted Transcombe, I think—brought a copper cauldron that belonged to his grandmother, and we made hot cocoa and the steam rose and that was the end of the icicles."

"Could we show Jess the boathouse?" Laura asked Finch.

They walked through the wet wood and stood at the edge of the property, looking down at the river. The boathouse was almost finished; the men who had been working on it were seated inside, eating their midday meal. Jess leaned against the door and addressed one of them.

"Hello, Ted. We've just been talking about you and the icicles. Did you ever imagine there'd be a real boathouse here?"

Ted, leaning comfortably against the carpenter's bench, finished a mouthful of sandwich and spoke. "I've got a boat for sale if anybody wants it," he said.

"Specifications?" Finch asked.

"I'll sail her down and you can take a look."

"If it's as hard to manage as that pony you sold us for our cart," Jess said, "you can keep it."

Ted gave Finch a conspiratorial wink. "Let me know when you're ready to look at her," he said.

"I will," Finch promised.

They walked slowly back to the cars.

"Can't you change your mind and come to lunch?" Laura asked Jess.

"No. I saw Audrey Downes last night, and sent a message to Wilfred saying I'd be at The Bell and Bottle at lunchtime today, hoping to pick up a meal ticket. I can't let two of my squires slip away in one week, can I? I suppose you didn't notice that he didn't rush round to see me yesterday. Or perhaps, being you, you noticed and didn't like to comment? Or had he already told you he was going to slice me off his life?"

"All he said—"

"Never mind. If he doesn't come to The Bell and Bottle, I'll send out troops to find him. Thanks for showing me round the house, Finch. I think it's lovely. Good-bye."

They watched her drive away.

"Wilfred?" Finch inquired, as they drove down the hill.

"Wilfred Downes, son of Lady Downes, who lives in Waterside. Her husband was a surgeon, and got knighted for something or other. One of her daughters—she's got two—has just got engaged to a doctor who's just come here."

"Jess said something about slipping away."

"She got the tense wrong. I think Wilfred has slipped away. He's been in love with her for years and years, hoping she'd marry him."

"Patience exhausted?"

"Yes." She found it extraordinary to be discussing Jess's affairs with him, but it was no more extraordinary than this unlooked-for continuation of something that had begun in Paris. "Patience, or hope," she went on. "I don't know which, but I'm sorry. He's the only one of Jess's men friends I've ever liked. Wilfred wasn't a stranger; all the others were."

"All?"

"Well, let's just say the others. Is this the place you told me about?"

"Yes."

He had stopped the car at the end of a narrow lane that led off the main road. Before them was a simple, whitewashed building set in a field, with only a narrow flagged path leading to a wide front door. Painted in bright blue letters above one of the windows were the words COME IN.

They went in. Laura saw a room that ran the length of the building, with windows along the front and the sides. Tables were set in a semicircle, facing a large counter behind which a man and a woman were working at a line of stoves. The dishes and plates warming above the heat, the ingredients, the utensils were all in plain view. Here there could be no secret recipes; the customers could follow every move in the preparation of their meal.

Only one table was vacant. The man turned, saw them and waved them towards it. The woman raised a friendly, floury hand and went on working.

"They're called Joe and Jenny," Finch told Laura. "They've been here two months; I've got shares. They had a restaurant up in Edinburgh and then decided to come south. I heard this bit of land was for sale, and bought it. The open kitchen was Jenny's idea. Running it this way, there's no ceremony—and no need for waiters. Customers fetch their own food when it's ready."

Laura got up and walked to the counter to watch the owners at work.

"Finch gave your order," Joe told her. "I'm not afraid; I was trained in Paris."

Laura looked at the two boards hanging from the counter. One was marked ENGLISH FARE, the other CONTINENTAL FARE.

"Saves menus," Joe told her. "Nice roast beef, today, with Yorkshire pudding and veg. For the travelled, *tripes catalanes* with black bread and black olives. For fish lovers, sole à la Normande. For weight-watchers, salads on the counter, help yourselves. For cheese connoisseurs, Gorgonzola, Bel Paese, Roquefort or Stilton."

When the meal was over, he came over to their table to ask her opinion of the food.

"Blue ribbon," she said. "Thank you very much."

"Thanks for your custom. Want your bill now, Finch, or shall I chalk it up?"

"Don't start that chalking-up," Finch warned. "It's—"

"I know. It's called a running account, and some customers

run and don't come back. Right, then. Gimme a couple of fivers and I'll see if there's any small change in the cashbox. Come again, Laura; with Finch or without him."

In the car, Finch switched on the engine and put a question. "Where to?"

"Home."

"No. There's only today. Tomorrow I have to go back to London. Are you coming with me?"

"Yes."

"Good. But that's only a drive and a visit to your father's studio. Today we could drive round and you could show me Waterside and we could go somewhere for dinner."

"I said home because I thought you might like to eat something that I'd cooked, for a change."

"I thought it was all in the deep freezer."

"Not my private supply. I can give you some nice steak."

"What else?"

"You could make a salad while I put potatoes into the oven."

"In their jackets?"

"Naturally."

They stopped for tea at a roadhouse, and then went back to the cottage. She left him free to roam round it while she telephoned to learn what orders had come in during the day.

"Upstairs," she told Finch, rejoining him, "is the attic bedroom-studio I had built for my father. But he never stayed in it. I'm looking forward to seeing his studio in London."

When she began the preparations for dinner, he followed her to the counter. On the way, he paused at the letter box fixed to the front door.

"You haven't taken out your mail," he said. "Not interested?"

"I forgot it. Take it out, will you?"

"Two for H. H. Howard," he said. "No, three. One very official-looking. Two for you which look like bills, and one with a French stamp."

"For Ginette?"

"No. It's addressed to you."

She held out a hand; he walked over and gave her the letter.

"Monsieur Philippe," she said at once. "I know that writing. Do you mind if I read it?"

"Go ahead."

She opened the letter. It was two pages long, but she had only to skim through the contents to get the message. Coming to the end, she folded it and put it back into the envelope.

"Want to guess?" she asked Finch.

"Easy. He's accepted two partnerships. Wise man."

"I could think of some other adjectives."

"Yes, those. But teaming him up with Ginette . . ."

"Do you know why he's written to me?"

"To break the news to her—right?"

"Quite right. He hadn't the courage, the guts to tell her himself, so—"

"He's going to marry Mademoiselle Justine?"

"No, he isn't. He's already married to her."

"I know the French for that: *fait accompli.*"

"Do you realize that he expects me to tell her that he's married? What's the matter with me?" she asked in bewilderment. "Am I some kind of messenger boy, or—"

"You just happen to be someone they know they can depend on to do what they asked. It wouldn't happen to your sister."

"You mean she's a hard type and I'm a soft touch, is that it?"

"I mean that she's a match for the cadgers and the Ginettes and the Hollises. She'd probably respond to an appeal from the deserving, but she wouldn't accept—because she wouldn't be offered—the kind of commissions you've been given today."

"That's what I said: soft touch. How does one tell a girl that the man she was expecting to marry has married someone else? I don't like her, and I wish I'd never met her and I wish she hadn't been in Paris when we were there, and I think the marriage would have been a disaster, but couldn't he have done his jilting some other way?"

"Which way?"

"Any way. Any other way. How do I know? It's one thing for her to decide she won't marry him. It's quite another for her to be informed that he's married someone else."

"You mean she gives him up, all right. He gives her up, all wrong?"

"Yes. That's exactly what I mean. So how do I tell her?"

"She's not here. She's gone. So how can you tell her anything?"

She stared at him uncomprehendingly.

"You mean . . ."

"You're not thinking straight. You've nothing to worry about. She's not here, so you can't tell her anything. He won't ring, so you won't have to tell him anything."

"I just do nothing?"

"When there's nothing to be done, that's what you do. All you have to do at this moment is feed a hungry man."

"Sorry."

When the meal was over, she put the coffeepot and cups and saucers on the tray and pushed it across the counter, and he carried it to the table. When they were seated, she handed him Monsieur Philippe's letter.

"Read it," she invited.

In leisurely fashion, in between sips of coffee, he read it. Then he handed it back to her.

"Nice, flowery style," he commented. "Mademoiselle Justine, I think, made him write to you and not to Ginette. Very clever."

There was the sound of a car which Laura recognized as Jess's. Jess came in, threw her handbag on the sofa and spoke without preamble.

"I could do with a cup of that coffee, Laura, if there's any left. Hello, Finch. I'm in a hurry; I want to get back to London tonight. You're going up together tomorrow, aren't you?"

"Yes. First to Claud's studio to see the picture," Laura answered. "Then I'm going to have a sandwich lunch in Finch's flat, and then he has to go up to Sheffield. Can you give me tea?"

"Of course."

"Then I'll catch the later bus home."

Jess drank her coffee hastily. She looked tense. Laura, watching her, felt apprehensive. Something had happened—exactly what, she could not guess.

Her uneasiness seemed to communicate itself to Finch. He rose, thanked her for the dinner and said that it was time he left.

"Wait a minute," Jess said to him. "I forgot something—a message I was asked to give you. From Conrad. He doesn't want you to be in too great a hurry to claim this girl called Dorrit. I don't know Dorrit, but I presume you do. She's got rid of Conrad's aunt."

"Aunt Minnie—gone?" Laura asked in amazement.

"Bag and baggage. To Whitby. Conrad spent most of today repainting the inn sign. It's now got three pigeons."

"Conrad tried to get rid of her. And couldn't," Laura said. "Clive tried, and couldn't. If they'd only known, all they had to do was send for Dorrit Moat."

"So the message was to leave her with Conrad as long as possible," Jess said.

When Finch went away, she spoke moodily.

"Sorry I broke up your party."

"You didn't. How did your lunch go?"

"The way lunches usually go. We ate and talked."

"Was Wilfred there?"

"No." Jess put the last things into her case and closed the zip. "No, he wasn't. We asked him to meet us for dinner, but he didn't. I left a message with Audrey, asking him to come to the flat tomorrow. If he doesn't come, that's that. If you're interested, there's news about your friend's fiancée. She's in a new play. Not film, play. Tryout in Brighton. The show comes to London next week. She's been busy, so that's why he's been free to take you round. Have you mentioned her yet?"

"No."

"Who am I to call you crazy? I don't understand you, but more important, I don't understand him. All I know is that I've caught your confidence in him. He's not playing; he's serious. And if one can judge from the way he looks at you, he's in love. I don't know where that leaves you. Now I'm going."

"Don't go for a minute. There are two things . . ."

"Well?"

"Do you think it's all right if I go to Claud's studio without telling him I'm going?"

"That would sound a pretty silly question to anyone who didn't know Claud. Yes, it'll be all right. Until he has a phone installed, you can't ring and give him notice, can you? So you've a good excuse for appearing without telling him in advance. It's an absurd way for him to act, anyway, so it's time we stopped it. I could have dropped in more than once after I knew his studio was ready, but I didn't, knowing he liked to have notice of our descents. But we're not children anymore. In future, I'll look him up whenever I feel like it. What's your other problem?"

"This letter from Monsieur Philippe." She picked it up from the table and held it out. "Want to read it?"

"No. He wrote to you, and not to Ginette?"

"Yes."

"That means he's crawled out of it, and he's afraid to tell her. That makes two of them. My God, what a pair. Perhaps it's a pity they didn't marry one another, after all. Do you want to bet that he'll marry Mademoiselle Justine?"

"No. He's already married her."

This time, Jess did not laugh.

"You're expected to break the news to Ginette?" she asked.

"Yes. But I can't. She's gone."

"You could send his letter on to her. But you won't. Anybody but you would throw it at her and let her see that for once someone played a mean trick before she had time to think one up. Why let her go round telling the world she gave him up? But you're going to tear up the letter, aren't you?"

"Yes. You told me I shouldn't have got involved. This way, I can at least get out without any more trouble."

She walked with Jess to the car. Jess got in and put a question.

"About Finch. Remember that game we used to play, trying to sum up people in one word?"

"Yes."

"How would you label him?"

"Inarticulate? Impassive?"

"How about dependable?"

She did not wait for a reply. When she had driven away, Laura went into the cottage with a heavy heart. Dependable was the label they had given Wilfred Downes.

Chapter 8

Jess had pointed out that Claud's lack of a telephone furnished Laura with a reasonable excuse for not telling him that she was going with Finch to the studio. But when he opened the door to admit them, she realized at once that she had made a mistake in coming. She could not have put into words the reason for this conviction—but it grew stronger as she stepped inside.

Claud had at first seen only Finch. Then his eyes moved to Laura, and there was a scarcely perceptible pause before he greeted her. When he did, his tone was welcoming, but he had succeeded in communicating his displeasure to her.

"Come in, both of you. You'll have to be careful how you move—there's very little fairway."

They reached a clearing and stood looking round them.

"Well? What do you think of it?" he asked.

They could only congratulate him. The studio was high, spacious, with a large skylight. At one end were small but well-planned living quarters with narrow windows that gave light but were placed above the level of prying eyes. It was difficult to believe that outside, both back and front, were noisy streets and constant passersby.

"How did you find it?" Finch asked.

"By patience. And by going for long walks round the district. There were vast warehouses; there were garages, but everything I saw was too large or too small—until I happened on this. It was part of a disused, very old shed—I think Charles the Second might have seen it when he came down to Deptford to look at his ships. It was up for sale. I put in a bid, and was turned down. I raised my price, and they asked me to go and see them, and we came to terms. After that, I had to wait for permission to convert it. Then I had to wait for workmen. But it was done at last, and I'm pleased with it. The kitchen looks too small, but there's everything I need. Oh, by the way, I made coffee. You'll have some? I made it for two, as I didn't know we'd be three. I'll show you where the coffee is, Laura, and you can make some more. And while you're making it"—he turned to Finch—"I'll show you what your grandmother would have liked to buy."

Finch followed him, Claud lifting or moving canvases to clear the way. Laura could hear them when they reached the picture, but she could not see them.

She was glad to be alone. Chagrin and resentment had begun to build up inside her. If it had been possible, she would have gone to the door, opened it and let herself out. But she was here and she would have to stay.

Perhaps, she thought miserably, she was letting her imagination run away with her. There was nothing in Claud's manner to give her the feeling of having trespassed. But in those few seconds on her entrance, she had known that the brief, pleasant association that had existed between them in Paris had ended. She was back where she had always been, where she and Jess had always been—outside Claud's life.

"I'm not," she heard him saying, "absolutely certain. That is, I'm not certain on the professional level. On the personal level, I've no doubts whatsoever. Do you want to know how I found it?"

"Yes."

"I wasn't—when I came across it—actually looking for it. I had other commitments, other commissions, other things on my mind. I hadn't made any inquiries; if you ask, the word gets round and prices go up. I knew you weren't in a hurry. Then I had—or you had—a streak of luck. I was looking at some seascapes in a little shop behind Earl's Court, and heard a chance remark made by the proprietor to a departing customer: If he liked those pictures, he told him, he might find one or two at Purdy's place.

"It didn't sound promising. I knew Purdy's place. It's a hovel of a shop off the Old Kent Road. He sells hamsters, skate boards, budgerigars, mackintoshes, his wife's homemade gingerbread—and now and then, pictures. They're holy pictures, as a rule; Madonnas in the foreground, cherubim and seraphim in the background. I'd never seen anything worth looking at there, but I've learned over the years not to neglect even the Purdys. So I strolled in one afternoon and looked at the hamsters and gradually made my way along between the junk until I came to two pictures. They were seascapes. One was worthless. This was the other.

"And then luck turned her back. When I expressed mild interest, he said the picture was sold—and sold to a West End dealer. Name? He gave it to me. The dealer, when approached, had sold the picture in his turn. To whom? He wouldn't tell me. All he would say was that he would make inquiries and find out whether there was any chance of my buying it. You'll guess that by this time somebody had made a rough, or perhaps not so rough, guess at its value. But we won't discuss price until you've seen it. Will you step back a few paces? That's right." He turned a canvas and stepped aside. "There you are."

Finch, without moving, gazed at the picture. After a time, Claud spoke.

"Well?"

"I'm no judge. But I like it, and I'll take your word that it's the mate to the one I've got."

"Thank you. But before we come to terms, I want to show it to one or two friends of mine, to see what they think."

"Did you buy it?"

"Yes. I knew that if you decided you didn't want it, I could sell it without difficulty to half a dozen other clients. So you can be quite frank if you've changed your mind about wanting it. Have you?"

"No."

"Good. The price will be stiff. Before it left Purdy's, it was known to be an Amos Lipp. And now . . . Laura," he called, "how is the coffee?"

"It's all ready," she told him.

She had set cups and the coffeepot on the small folding table Claud used for his meals. The men sat on a bench, Laura on the only chair. Claud brought a tin of biscuits from a cupboard.

"How long will it be before your phone is put in?" Laura asked him.

He raised his eyebrows. "But Laura, my dear, who said I was having a telephone put in? The last thing I want, the very last thing I need is a telephone."

"If you'd had one, I could have told you I was coming with Finch."

"My dear child, there's no need to tell me; you can always come. If I need to telephone, I walk to the warehouse next door, go into the office and use their phone. To be at the end of a line, always available, always being interrupted in the middle of my work . . . No."

"Have you ever painted your daughters?" Finch asked.

"Not since they were children. I gave the portraits to my mother. What became of them, we shall never know. They weren't among her things when she died. One of these days, when I'm in Paris, I might embark on a search."

"She always took them with her, wherever she went," Laura said.

"Except at the last," Claud pointed out.

It was said with a smile, but there was an edge to the words; he had not forgiven her for coming. She began to clear away the coffee cups, and he raised a hand to stop her.

"Leave them, my dear. This district abounds in women only too happy to act as cleaners. Must you go?"

"I'm afraid so. Finch has to go up to Sheffield after lunch."

Claud walked with them to the door.

"You're quite sure you've made up your mind about the picture?" he asked Finch.

"Quite sure. But I forgot—Laura hasn't seen it."

Before Claud could prevent him, he had taken Laura's hand and, holding it loosely in his, led her across the studio, through the stacked pictures, to the one Claud had shown him. Halting before it, he put a casual question.

"Like it?"

She looked at it—and froze. She tried to nod, she tried to speak; all she could do was stand and gaze. She knew that the colour had left her cheeks; she wondered whether Finch could feel the chill of the hand that lay in his. With an effort, she turned and led him back to where Claud waited.

"Give my love to Jess, if you're seeing her—are you?" Claud asked.

"Yes."

They were outside. They left Claud and walked to Finch's car, parked some way down the street. When they drove away, Claud was still at the door. He raised a hand in farewell.

They drove in silence. She was used to Finch's talent for saying nothing when there was nothing particular to be said, but she had never felt more grateful for silence, for the opportunity of mastering her feelings. She longed for Jess. Nobody but Jess would understand.

She had looked forward to seeing Finch's flat, but she was no longer in the mood to enjoy their proposed sandwich lunch. But by the time she had come to a decision and was about to ask if the plan could be changed, she found that they were driving into the forecourt of the apartment block. Finch was going on to the area reserved for residents' cars, when he found the way blocked by a brightly coloured Mini. Walking toward it were two women. Laura recognized them—they were Lady Downes and her daughter Margaret.

They stopped beside Finch's car, and Margaret addressed Laura.

"Well, this is a surprise!" she said.

Her voice, like her appearance, was hearty. Beside her, her mother looked like a very pretty, very well-dressed doll. She gave Laura her usual vague greeting.

"Laura dear. So nice."

Laura and Finch got out of the car. Margaret addressed him in forthright fashion.

"I know you," she told him. "Not to speak to. I've seen you round Waterside. Mr. Falconer, right?"

"Yes," Finch said.

"I recognized you, too," Lady Downes said. "We only learned, a few minutes ago, that you're a tenant in these flats."

"The porter told us," Margaret explained. "But you're up at the top, among the swells. Poor old Wilf's down on the ground floor in one of the cheap layouts."

"*Cheap?*" Her mother spoke in astonishment. "At the price Wilfred paid—cheap?"

"Comparatively speaking, Mummy, comparatively speaking. About a fifth of what penthouses cost."

Laura found her voice. "I didn't know Wilfred was moving," she said.

"It's high time," Margaret said. "He's been in those stuffy rooms of his since he first came to London. We've been looking at places for the past month or two, but we all liked this flat the best, so Mummy and I dragged the house agent here this morning and so to speak finalized the business."

"Such a relief!" sighed Lady Downes. "Such a weight off one's mind. Meg darling, look: You've left your car in the way. We must move it. I do hope, Mr. Falconer, that you'll see something of my son while he's living here."

"He's taking possession on the first of next month, and I'm coming up to help him arrange his furniture. Not that he's got much, but Mummy's sharing out some of hers between him and Audrey."

"A nucleus, a nucleus," murmured Lady Downes. "Good-bye."

They drove away. There had been no mention of Jess. Laura turned to Finch.

"Would you mind very much if we skipped that sandwich lunch?" she asked.

"Not hungry?"

"Not very. Could you take me round to Jess's flat? Then I'll catch the afternoon bus home."

He took her to the flat. As they drove into the forecourt, a furniture van drove out.

"Your sister again," the porter told Laura. "In, out. This time it was in. If she doesn't mind keeping the movers in business, that's her lookout. You parking, sir, or going?"

"I'll see Miss Seton upstairs, and come straight down."

The door of Jess's flat was open. Small items of furniture stood on the landing, and Finch helped Jess and Laura to carry them inside. Gone was the Japanese look, gone the mats and the cabinets.

"I thought you two were going to have a sandwich lunch," Jess said.

"She changed her mind," said Finch. "Just tell me where this chair goes; the porter's timing me."

Jess closed the door behind him and turned to look at Laura. "Trouble?" she asked.

"No. Yes." Laura abandoned the books she had been arranging, and sank onto a chair. "I daresay I'm making a lot of fuss over nothing—but I wanted to get here and talk to you."

"What about?"

"That picture."

"Oh, God, Claud's not up to something, is he?"

"I don't know. I think so."

"Why have we suddenly got involved? Why couldn't things have gone on as they were, with us living our lives and Claud living his? Is it my fault for getting too excited about Magda's picture? If I hadn't pushed you over to Paris, if we'd minded our own business, would you have been worrying about this latest deal?"

"It's too late to discuss that. Could I have a drink?"

Jess gave her one.

"You're pale," she said. "Don't you want to eat something?"

"Not yet. I want to talk."

"I'm listening."

"I shouldn't have gone with Finch. Not without letting Claud know. As soon as he opened the door, I realized it was a mistake."

"Claud said something?"

"No. But I knew he wasn't pleased to see me. I think Finch felt it, too—I'm not sure. Claud had made coffee—for two only, as he pointed out. While I made more for myself, he took Finch across the studio and showed him the picture, the seascape, and told him how he'd found it."

She paused. Jess raised her eyebrows.

"So far, there's not much to worry about," she commented. "What comes next?"

"Do you remember, after Seton's was sold, you and I put all Claud's pictures and all Mother's pictures up in the attic bedroom in the cottage?"

"Of course I remember. We worked like horses, carrying them into your car, and out again, and up those stairs. . . . Well, go on."

"Some of them were pictures we'd never seen before—things that Mother had copied from originals when she was at that art school. One of them was a picture of a rough sea, with ships tossing . . . it was called 'High Winds.' When

Finch and I had lunch with Claud in Paris, and the picture was mentioned, I knew I'd heard the name before, but I didn't connect . . . I was thinking of a lot of other things. But when Finch showed it to me today, I remembered it."

"You think it's the picture that Claud offered Finch?"

"The picture he said he found. The picture that was to be the mate to the one Finch had. Claud gave details of how he had found it and—"

"The one Finch has is an original?"

"Yes. Bought by his grandmother. The mate was going to be put up for sale, but was destroyed when the sale room caught fire. In Paris, Claud said he was certain he'd seen the mate somewhere."

"How do you know he wasn't telling, isn't telling the truth? He's unearthed a number of pictures in his time. Did you recognize the frame?"

"No. It was in a different frame—but I saw the frame it had been in when we took it away from Seton's. It was empty."

"And what's worrying you is that you think Claud might be—I said *might* be—misleading Finch?"

"Misleading! He told him the picture was going to be expensive. He—"

"Look, Laura, why don't you just forget it?"

"*Forget* it!"

"Can you prove it was painted by Mother?"

"Prove? No. I'm just certain, that's all."

"Look. This is a business deal between Claud and Finch. In my opinion, Finch is a man who can look after himself. He's got a hard Yorkshire head and he knows how to use it. He's been taught the value of money, and he's got the Yorkshireman's outlook on outlay. He isn't going to let Claud get away with anything. We don't know whether Claud's trying to get away with anything. I don't suppose we ever will know. I asked you, not so long ago, what we knew about Claud. The answer is that we don't know anything and never did know anything about him. If he's offering a copy and claiming it's an original, I don't suppose it's the first time he's done it. It's up to Finch to decide whether he buys the picture or not. He may decide to take Claud's word for its genuineness because Claud's your father. If he buys it, I don't suppose anybody's going to peer at it and try to prove it's a copy, and go to the trouble of collecting evidence about Finch's grandmother and the fire at a Sheffield sale room. Put it out of your mind. If you're beginning to wonder, as I'm beginning to wonder, if we've got a father whose ethics are a bit dusty, just remember that we've had him for twenty-two or -three years without losing any sleep. Now will you help me to get the rest of these things out of the way, and then we'll have lunch and . . . You're not *crying*, are you?"

"No," sobbed Laura. "How would you like it if you loved somebody and your father told him a string of lies and—"

"I'd mind my own business. And if I loved someone as down-to-earth as Finch, I'd give him credit for knowing how to recognize the Clauds of this world, and how to deal with them."

"I don't want Claud dealt with."

"I do. But that's not what you're crying about. You've been bottling up a lot of steam since you got back from Paris; it'll do you good to get rid of some of it. When did you decide you were in love?"

"I don't know. Ever since we met in Paris."

"Are you at last beginning to give some thought to the fact that he's engaged?"

"No. I can't explain, Jess, it's no use. All I feel, all I *know* is that everything is going to be all right."

"I see. Wasn't it Christ who pronounced a blessing on those who closed their eyes tight, and went on believing? Do you want another drink?"

"No."

"Then we'll eat. There's not much. I went to the super-

199

market and snatched a few things, but I had to head back in a hurry, to get here before the furniture van arrived."

Laura, now dry-eyed and on her feet, looked round the room with her first sign of interest. "I'm glad you're going to be comfortable again," she said.

"After sleeping on a mat with my neck on a wooden bolster, I'd opt for anything with springs. Why don't you stay and have tea and catch a later bus? You could move furniture with me and get your mind off Claud. I can't offer you a sofa; Wilfred took his. He's given up his rooms and he's bought a flat."

"I know. We met his mother and Margaret outside Finch's apartment block. How long have you known?"

"Audrey told me when we had lunch together. They'll be delighted to get him to themselves again. The hard part is going to be when they try to find him another girl, this time one with matrimonial leanings."

Laura looked at her, trying to read what lay behind the casual manner. But Jess was continuing.

"If he lets himself get bossed around by his family again, after having got clear of them, he'll be a fool."

"What's foolish about wanting to marry and settle down?"

"Nothing—only he doesn't want to. Not at once. He's been told he ought to. He's got a soft center, like you. They won't let him think for himself, because when he thinks for himself, he doesn't think what they want him to think. Left to himself, he'd come back here and we'd be happy, for as long as it lasted. Doing what they tell him to do, he'll end up with a muscular female who'll jog beside him while he does his measured mile. He'll get serious and stuffy, like his father— remember his father? Or fussy, like his mother."

"Will you miss him?"

"I'll miss that sofa."

"I wish I could understand what you've got against marriage."

"If I began to tell you, you'd lose your bus."

"When are you coming down again?"

"I won't leave it too long. Something tells me your affair is working itself up to a crisis. Got everything? Hand me the car keys, will you?"

They went down to the car. Immediately opposite the entrance, in the space expressly prohibited to waiting vehicles, was Finch Falconer's. At the wheel, reading a newspaper, sat Finch.

For some moments, Jess and Laura halted, too surprised to move. Then they walked across the intervening space. Lowering his newspaper, Finch saw them and got out.

"What are you doing here?" Jess asked him.

"Waiting."

"For Laura?"

"Yes. Afternoon bus, she said."

"If she'd changed her mind and decided to stay the night, would you have sat out here waiting? Freezing?"

"Animals to feed," he reminded her. "And"—he waved a hand towards his car—"adequate heating."

"You're very kind," Laura said, "but you ought to be half-way to Sheffield by now. Jess will take me to the bus."

"No," he said. "I will."

The tone was quiet, calm and inflexible. Jess turned to Laura.

"You heard what the gentleman said? Get in. All she ate," she went on to Finch, as he switched on the engine, "was a dry biscuit and an apple. You'll have to take her to a filling station. Have you seen your fiancée lately?"

"An hour ago," he said.

He waited for Jess to speak, saw that she was having difficulty, and bore Laura away.

Chapter 9

"Your original intention," Finch said, as they reached the outskirts of London, "was to catch the evening bus. That would have got you home just before ten. So we have time for tea and dinner. I suggest tea at Oxford."

"It's miles out of our way."

"So it is. Where would you like to go for dinner?"

"Joe and Jenny's?"

"No. I want to talk. You haven't asked why I didn't go up to Sheffield."

"Why didn't you?"

"Something important came up. Why did you change your mind about that sandwich lunch? I suppose the answer's the same: Something important came up. You wanted to talk to your sister."

"She knew that Wilfred was going to move."

"That wasn't the only thing on your mind. Why does your father have such a curious effect on you?"

"I didn't know he had."

"I noticed it in Paris. Does he have that effect on Jess?"

"Neither of us knows him very well. In fact, neither of us knows him at all. But Jess doesn't have any hesitation about asking him frankly about anything she wants to know. If we'd been younger when my mother died, we might have got closer to him—but I doubt it."

"So do I. From what I've seen of him, I wouldn't put him down as a family man. And Jess doesn't seem to be a family woman. Does she have a rooted objection to marrying?"

"No. She says she'll marry one day. Not yet. But Wilfred got tired of waiting, and I don't blame him."

"They were engaged?"

"For a time. I never understood why she always got engaged to the men who fell in love with her."

Later, she broke a long, comfortable silence to ask him if he remembered his parents.

"No. And I never missed them. I had, as your father suggested, rather a bleak upbringing, but it didn't seem so at the time. There was no small talk in my grandfather's house; no chat, no gossip. You said what was necessary and then you saved your breath. My grandfather believed that every time a man opened his mouth, he gave himself away. Myself, I think that eyes are more of a giveaway. Your eyes. My eyes, if you'd looked. Perhaps you did look. Why else have we been so much at ease together, so happy, so free of all worry about the future?"

She made no reply. He drew the car to the side of the road, and stopped.

"Look at me," he said.

She raised her eyes to his.

"Is this like reading palms?" she asked lightly.

"No. Palm reading's mostly for the future. This is for here and now. Do you know what I can read in your eyes?"

"Do I have to know? Can't we let it go on as it was going?"

"Is that what you really want?"

She made no answer. She had told Jess that she had no fears for the future. She had been content to trust to this strange conviction that all was going to be well, in spite of the obstacle that loomed between herself and Finch. But to drift was one thing. To stop drifting, to challenge that unknown future, to face up to the consequences of learning, perhaps, more than she wanted to know . . . was that, in fact, what she really wanted?

He did not press for an answer. He drove on, and they

stopped for tea and then drove slowly in the direction of home. It was an afternoon of sunshine—not as warm as Paris, the air not so clear. When they were a few miles from Waterside, he turned down a wooded lane, drew into a clearing and stopped.

"I've got something to tell you," he said. "It'll take rather a long time, and I won't be able to tell it very well—but I'll try."

His hands were motionless on the wheel. He was looking almost absently through the windshield to the undergrowth, wet after the morning rain.

"I've got to tell you," he went on, "about my fiancée. My ex-fiancée." He turned to her. "You see? I said I couldn't tell it well. I wanted to tell you from the beginning to the end, and I've ruined it."

"Perhaps," she said, "only the end matters."

"No. You've got to hear it all. I won't come well out of it, but that's something I'll have to face later. How much do you know of the . . . what the papers called the Torringdon affair?"

"What I heard in Crossford. What Jess told me."

"I was the villain of the piece, wasn't I? I stole my friend's fiancée. On the eve of their marriage, I broke up their engagement and sent him to nurse his broken heart on a distant island. That was how it went, wasn't it?"

"More or less."

"The truth isn't much prettier. But here it is."

He paused, possessed himself of one of her hands and held it loosely.

"Torringdon's family and mine are neighbours," he began. "But I didn't meet him until I was up at Oxford. We became friends, and stayed friends. We spent most of the vacations together. We differed in temperament, in upbringing, in aims and ideas, but none of that made much difference to our liking for one another. He used to guide me through the intricacies of the social scene, and I used to get him out of the trouble he used to get into over women. He wasn't what you'd call a womanizer, but he liked the society of women, and as he was rich, good-looking and titled, some of them ran after him and one or two almost caught him.

"Then he disappeared. We were going to Kashmir together. It had been one of his dreams; he'd had the money but never the time. Now we were to go together. I was to make all the travel arrangements, and he was to join me at my grandfather's and we were to set off. It was just after the beginning of October.

"He didn't come. He didn't phone. He didn't get in touch. I knew he'd been in Norway; I knew the people he'd been staying with. I rang them and learned that he'd left four days earlier, and gone to London.

"That was how matters stayed for the following week. His family were away; none of the staff knew where he was. I could have been uneasy, but it wasn't the first time he'd gone underground. So I waited.

"Then he rang. He was at home, and wanted to see me. I got into my car and drove over and found him . . . I can't think of a word. I think distraught would describe him. He was nearly out of his mind. Over a woman. That wasn't new—but this time, it was different. This, he told me, had been going on for over a year. And he'd come back from Norway, met her in London, and learned that it was over. She wouldn't marry him. She loved him, she wanted to marry him, but circumstances were too strong for her. She had fought it out—with herself, and then with him. It was no use, she said; it was finished. She was going home.

"Her home was in the West Indies. She was black. Black, beautiful, the daughter of a Government minister who was the leader of the anti-British bloc on the island, the head of the group which claimed to have been responsible for the island's independence. His loathing of the British had stopped short only of allowing his daughter, his only child, to complete her studies at Oxford.

"There are two evenings in my life that I won't forget. That evening with Torringdon was the first of them. I won't say that this was the only time in his life that he'd asked for something he couldn't have; I only know that it was the first time anything had gone root-deep. He was in a state that was all the worse because there was nothing he could do. She'd gone. To follow her would have meant giving everything away—giving her away. There couldn't have been any way, on the island, of hiding their association. And if it became known, her father would be finished, a traitor who'd betrayed his party—or a laughingstock who'd been deceived by his daughter. That wouldn't have worried Torringdon, but it would have killed the girl.

"There was no Kashmir. There was a sort of breakdown, and I stayed with him. And then for a time, it looked as if he was going to be all right. He didn't talk about her anymore. He picked up some of his old friends. He started going round.

"About the middle of November, I introduced him to Kate Lyons. I didn't know her well, but I knew that she'd just broken off her engagement to the film director Heybrouk. She was actress enough to carry it off, but she wasn't happy. She was in the same state as Torringdon. So it wasn't surprising that the meeting between the two of them was like some kind of coalescence.

"They got engaged a week later. They planned to marry on his birthday in February. They went everywhere, and then the publicity for her film got going and the media came into it. I would have kept away from them if both of them—he and she—hadn't made it plain that they wanted me around. It wasn't a twosome, ever; it was the two of them—and myself. And what worried me more than the fact that they needed a third was the fact that he had never told her about the other girl.

"And then one evening, on my way to his flat to meet her and Torringdon, I bought a paper and learned that the girl's father was dead. I stood in the rain and wondered whether Torringdon knew. Then I got to the flat and found that yes, he knew. He'd known since that morning. He said so in the note he left for me in the hall of the flat. He'd gone. The secret would be kept until it was safe to tell it; in the meantime, he'd gone to join her. I was to tell Kate and explain everything, and Kate—the note said—wouldn't mind because they'd never been in love with one another."

He paused. His eyes were on the hand he was holding. He was counting the fingers. He turned it palm uppermost and absently traced the lines crossing and recrossing it. Then he went on speaking quietly.

"That last bit was right. They'd never loved one another. She hadn't been able to get Heybrouk out of her mind, and had said so. Torringdon had gone on thinking about the girl on the island, but hadn't said so.

"When Kate let herself into the flat that evening, I had to tell her where he'd gone—and why. That was the other evening I'll remember. I'll skip the details. I stayed with her, as I'd stayed with him. She wasn't in a state to be left—but it wasn't because he'd walked out. What she was crazed about was her image. I'd never known what the word meant, in that sense, but I heard it enough that evening to learn. I saw that he couldn't have chosen a worse moment to walk out—or the black minister to die. The film premiere, the Fanny Burney film, was to take place in three days. Triple crown: actress, bride, future countess. Was she, she screamed, to appear as a girl who'd been walked out on?

"I had no solution. When she'd tired herself out, I went into the kitchen and heated some milk and dropped in a couple of aspirins and took it to her. She was asleep. I told myself I could leave. I put the furniture back in place and sat on the sofa, feeling washed out. I remembered the milk, and drank it. I didn't remember about the two aspirins.

"I woke at about nine. She wasn't in the flat. I went home. Four hours later, I was rung up by a reporter and asked for details of my life history. Then the evening papers came out and I read that I had stepped in at the last moment and stolen my best friend's bride-to-be. I was famous, infamous.

"I couldn't get in touch with her until late that night. She was calm and clear and quite factual. If I tried to tell the truth, she'd deny it. There was no danger of anything leaking from Torringdon's end; that, she knew, was going to be kept quiet. All she needed was a face-saver—and I was it. She told me I wouldn't be on the hook for too long; in the meantime, there it was in all the newspapers.

"She came down to Crossford now and then, to make the thing look real. A big row blew up over her interference in the architect's sphere, and she told me then that she had plans to get rid of me. Today, between my going to your father's studio and waiting outside your sister's flat for you to come out, I got what I think the French call my *congé*."

Once more, he paused. She waited.

"She telephoned to my flat. I wasn't there, so she left a message—I would have been given it if you and I had stuck to our plan of having a sandwich lunch. When I left you at Jess's, I went back—and learned that she wanted to see me. She said she would be at the restaurant next door to the theatre until three o'clock. Alone.

"I drove there, fast and full of hope. When she said alone, she meant with her usual entourage but with the general public kept away. She, or someone, offered me a drink, and when it came, I found we were drinking a toast. She married Heybrouk yesterday, in Brighton. There'll be an announcement in all the papers tomorrow, but they're both so famous that nobody, thank God, will give a thought to the fellow she threw over. I drank the toast and came away—and went to Jess's flat to wait for you, all night if necessary."

That seemed to be all. They sat in silence. After a time, he lifted the hand he had been holding, dropped a kiss on the palm and looked at her.

"Comments?" he asked.

She shook her head. There was nothing she needed to say.

"What I shall never understand," he said musingly, "is why or how you and I knew that there was no need to say anything about the future. I knew I was going to be free before long—but you didn't know. How did I know that you would know that things were going to work out? How did you know?"

"I didn't know."

"You couldn't, shouldn't have taken me on trust. But I didn't worry, and you didn't appear to be worrying."

"The only one who worried," she told him, "was Jess."

He looked at her frowningly. "I've done this the wrong way round," he said. "I should have begun by . . . Do you understand that I'm a free man? Do you?"

"Yes."

"Do you understand that we . . . that you and . . ."

"Yes."

"But there's more to be said, isn't there?"

"Yes."

"Do I begin by saying that I've loved you ever since you came across to my car on that wet Paris road, sheltered under that Frenchman's umbrella? Would that make sense?"

"I think so."

"Rain, and mist, and you very quiet, composed while the others shouted. And then we were in the car together, and I lied; dinner was an excuse. I lied again when I said that I had no hotel reservation. And the next few days . . . I hope we'll be together for the next sixty years at least, but I hope we never forget those days. What are you smiling at?"

"Your flow of speech. Did you say you loved me?"

"Yes. And I should have asked if you loved me, but you

wouldn't be here if you didn't. Just the same, it would be nice to hear it. Say it."

"This is a rather public place to make a declaration."

She was in his arms. Two youths on bicycles came down the lane, stopped to study them and went on their way. A tractor coughed and shuddered past them. They saw and heard nothing.

She roused herself after a time to ask a question.

"The only person I need tell is Jess. Magda'll have to be told, too, I suppose. Who've you got to give the news to?"

She had to shift her position slightly in order to let him count on his fingers.

"There's old Aunt Trixie. We'd better tell her first—she's ninety-six and hasn't been well, and she'd hate to miss the excitement. Then there are the three sisters: Aunt Lily, Aunt Amy and Aunt Em. They're only in their eighties. Em was the lady chess champion of Sheffield once. She can still play a good game, but you have to watch her—you think she's plotting a cunning move, but you find she's fallen asleep."

"Do they all live together?"

"Aunt Trixie's in the house my grandfather built for her. She's looked after by the village—they take it in turns, day and night. They all lived on her bounty for so long that they got together on her eighty-fifth birthday and drew up a duty chart, and they've stuck to it. If someone drops out, someone takes over; two-hour shifts. It goes so smoothly that when I'm there, I hardly notice when there's a change of duty officer. The three sisters, Lily and Amy and Em, look after themselves, with a bit of outside help. Then there's Uncle Ed. Not my real uncle; my aunt Enid's widower. He's going on for eighty, but he—"

"Why are they all so old?"

He looked down at the top of her head in surprise at the question.

"Because they're all my grandfather's generation, that's why."

"Then all these aunts—"

"Great-aunts. My grandfather's sisters. He had six: Trixie, Lily, Amy, Em, Enid."

"You missed out one."

"I'm coming to her. She's called Rosalind. My grandfather thought it was because she'd been given such a fancy name that she went astray."

She raised her head to look at him. "Went astray?"

"Keep still. She left home when she was sixteen, and stayed away for two years and then came back, but never told anyone where she'd been."

"Or what she'd been doing?"

"Or what she'd been doing. My great-grandfather thought of throwing her out into the snow, but she was good at figures and he needed an assistant. She worked for him until he died. Now she's eighty—she was the youngest—and she's invested her money in a little wool shop and still serves the customers."

"What does Uncle Ed do?"

"Cadges. He spent all his own money, but couldn't get hold of Aunt Enid's. She didn't leave him any, so the family keep him in funds. When you meet them all, don't look for any sentimental streak. Old as they are, they'll look you over and size you up. You must never, never attempt to argue or contradict when they're talking to you. They formed their opinions on every matter, social, moral and political, at the beginning of the century, and they've seen no reason to change them."

"When can we go up and see them?"

"As soon as you like."

"What happens when they're so old that they have to be taken care of?"

"All arranged. They're realists. They raised the money for

a home for the aged, staffed it, supported it and endowed it—with the condition that there's a room for them when they need it. When and where do you want dinner, if you ever decide you're hungry?"

"I can give you a nice cheese omelette."

"I know a place where they'll give me lobster, steak and salad. What's amusing you now?"

"This isn't how I thought I'd be made love to. I imagined someone telling me he loved me, and giving me time to think it over, and then the usual things: flowers, presents, plans, house-hunting."

"You're feeling cheated?"

"No. I wish—"

"Wish what?"

"I wish I had some nice relatives to present to you. There's only Jess."

"And Claud. And your uncle's wife."

"Magda doesn't count. Claud . . . for a little while, in Paris, I thought we'd made some kind of bridge. For a day or two, I felt almost like a daughter."

"No more?"

She hesitated. She thought of the studio, and her reception, and the picture out of its frame. No proof. The chapel inscription, the Zollard. The McClure checks.

"No," she said. "No more."

Chapter 10

The morning papers printed a brief notice of the Lyons-Heybrouk wedding. The evening papers had pictures of the Brighton ceremony, and television watchers were given a view of the couple taking possession of their Chelsea house.

Laura had telephoned the news to Jess the night before. Jess said she would withhold comment and deliver it in person; she would drive down early the following day. A call in the morning, however, changed this plan. Her car would not start; she would come by bus and would like to be met at the garage.

Finch elected to go there alone. Conrad, on seeing his car, went into the inn and returned a moment later with Dorrit and the morning paper. They walked up to the car, and Dorrit addressed Finch.

"Good morning, Mr. Falconer. Conrad's got all worked up about this notice in the paper."

"Conrad's not worked up; Conrad's puzzled," said Conrad. "Not a word to a soul down here, to warn them what was coming."

"I told Laura," Finch said.

"You told Laura? That it was all off with that actress?"

"Yes. That's why I'm here."

"I don't get it. Why are you here?"

"To meet Jess."

"You told Laura, and you're meeting Jess. Where's the linkup?"

"You're thick, that's your trouble," Dorrit told him. "Why

would Mr. Falconer come and meet Miss Seton if there wasn't something in it?"

"Something in what?" demanded Conrad. "That actress goes and marries another chap, Mr. Falconer tells Laura and then he comes to meet Jess. I missed something?"

"Yes, silly. He's come to meet his future sister-in-law. That's right, isn't it, Mr. Falconer?"

"Quite right, Dorrit."

They waited patiently for Conrad to rearrange his ideas. He spoke at last. "You . . . and Laura?"

"Yes," said Finch.

"Since when?"

"Since Paris."

"Paris? You mean that . . . that time she went, you went?"

"On the very same plane."

"Well, I still don't get it, but if it was Paris, that accounts for it. Congratulations."

"Thank you."

"And now," Dorrit said, "you can tell him about your aunt Minnie."

"My aunt. . . ." Conrad pulled himself back to the present. "Ah, yes. Aunt Minnie. She's pushed off," he told Finch.

"And it was me that pushed her," Dorrit added. "She ought to of gone a long time ago. She had no call to hang on here if she didn't want to work. But she's gone, and good riddance."

"So what I wanted to ask you, Mr. Falconer—" Conrad began.

"Oh, no, you don't," Dorrit interrupted. "You're going to ask Mr. Falconer to leave me here just for your convenience. You can save your breath." She turned to Finch. "As soon as you want me to go up to the house, I'm ready."

"And what about me?" Conrad demanded. "With Aunt Minnie gone, the house'll be empty. Who's going to—"

"You can find yourself a wife. The trouble was your aunt, and she's gone, and I've made the place clean and tidy, so any girl'll be glad to run it for you. But not me. I came here to work for Mr. Falconer, and that's what I'm going to do. Now if you'll stop talking, I'll go and attend to my work and you can get on with yours."

She went unhurriedly indoors, and Conrad spoke gloomily.

"She means that, every word. Oh, well, that's life. Did she leave any sisters where she came from?"

"No. They're all married."

"Just what I thought." He gave a resigned sigh. "About Jess coming. Did she know anything about this carry-on with Laura?"

"She had a pretty good idea."

"Then she should have told an old friend like me. When the news gets round, you'll get a vote of thanks."

"What for?"

"For giving a big lift to Crossford and Waterside. My dad always said that if ever Seton's got to be the leading house of the district, we'd see a big change all round. And we will, too. Living up there, maybe you won't know you're bringing a lot of new business to the place, but you'll see: There'll be more shops doing more business, more coming and going over that bridge—and me in the middle, bang between Crossford and Waterside. So it's a pity those three pigeons can't stretch their wings."

Finch made no reply. He had got out of the car. He leaned against it, giving the inn a slow, appraising survey.

"How do you manage to fill up the cars, and fill up the customers in the bar at the same time?" he inquired.

"Not many customers these days," Conrad replied. "In my dad's time, his chums used to turn up of an evening—they'd fill the place, a couple of dozen of them, or more. Cheerful, it was. They fell away when he died. My aunt served in there for a time, but she was too sour to make a go of it. Now there's only about half a dozen drop in. Pity, because it's not a bad little place."

"It needs a coat of paint."

"Can't I see? I never got round to doing the outside—there were jobs inside to see to. I do 'em at off times. But painting, that's different. You can't leave a house-painting job every ten minutes to see to a chap's tires. Dorrit and I were going to do it together, if she'd stayed. She said the inn could be made to pay, and she was right; it could. But not without anyone to run it."

"It's a pity you and your brother couldn't have stayed in partnership."

"There was never a chance of it, right from the start. We get on, Clive and me, but he never liked this place, the way I did. It was too quiet for him. He was always set on getting over that bridge, over to the bright lights. He made my aunt Minnie the excuse to get out, but if it hadn't been her, he'd have thought of something else."

Finch's eyes were still on the inn. He spoke thoughtfully. "A good businessman," he said, "might think it a good proposition. It's in a neglected state, but it's got possibilities. If someone with a little money to spare—myself, for example—knew that there was likely to be an increase in business in the near future, he might think of it as a good investment."

There was a long silence. Then Conrad swallowed, cleared the huskiness from his throat and spoke. "You were saying . . . ?"

"Not the whole place. House and pub separated. You could make this a self-service station; that would free you to run the pub. That would leave your partner to run the inn. He couldn't do it himself, having other business interests, but if he knew some reliable young woman he could put in charge, he might find himself getting a good return for his outlay."

He stopped, and directed his gaze to Conrad. The bus came

into view, but neither of them saw it. Conrad spoke in a tone of wonder. "Only the other day," he said slowly, "I was saying you were a chap that didn't talk much. But when you do talk . . . Do you know what you've just said?"

"Yes."

"Look, Mr. Falconer—"

"Laura would like you to call me Finch."

"Then look, Mr. Falconer, Finch, what you've been saying . . ."

"I made you an offer. Didn't you hear?"

"I heard. You wouldn't go as far as to put it down on paper?"

"No. Why do I employ lawyers? Now you'll have to excuse me; here's my future sister-in-law."

For once on her arrival, Conrad's comments were not heard. He greeted her, but that was all. Only when she was in Finch's car and about to leave did he find his voice.

"Years ago," he reminded her, "when you and me and Clive were talking, you two said Laura was the quiet sort who didn't go for men and who liked life on her own. I said no, she was the marrying kind. See how right I was? If you're thinking of throwing a celebration party, Mr. Falconer, Finch, I'm free all this week."

"Why didn't Laura come to meet me?" Jess asked as they drove away.

"She wants us to get to know each other."

"Then let's begin by being frank. I think you should have told her what the position was as soon as you knew you were both falling in love."

"I would have done—if I'd been quite sure what her feelings were. I knew what mine were. I knew she liked me. I didn't know how much."

"If she'd taken my advice and stopped seeing you—"

"I would have told her. But I wanted to tell her that I was free."

"Have you made any plans for the future?"

"Yes. Early wedding. All my great-aunts are old; if we want them to attend the ceremony, we can't put it off for too long."

"I suppose you realize it won't be a quiet wedding?"

"We wanted one, but Laura pointed out that if we left out anybody from Crossford, there'd be some hurt feelings."

"All Crossford and half Waterside. Wait till you see the guests. She'll ask every butcher, baker and candlestick maker. Has Magda been told the news?"

"Laura was going to ring her while I came to meet you. I don't think she'll be pleased; I didn't make a very good impression. She probably agrees with Arnold Bennett, who said the men of the North were outwardly brusque, stoical, undemonstrative and scornful of the impulsive."

"And inwardly full of sentiment. Want to make a bet?"

"Yes."

"Remember the Zollard she was going to sell?"

"The one your father said was a copy?"

"That one. She'll give it to you and Laura as a wedding present. She'll decide she can't risk selling to anybody else, so you'll get it, and that'll save her the expense of buying you something else. She's not a spender, as you'll live to learn."

"How much is the bet?"

"You mean it's a real bet?"

"A bet is a bet. If she doesn't give it to us, you pay me ten pounds."

"And if she does, you pay me. I'll make it twenty, if you like."

"Done."

"That matter settled, you can ask my blessing on your union."

"Not yet. I don't want to know how you feel about it now. I'll ask for your opinion in a few years, when I've been a model husband."

"Have you ever been in love before, or is that a silly question?"

"It's a reasonable question. No, I haven't. Women don't like me much; I'm too slow. I don't respond."

"If Paris hadn't been there, would you and she ever have got together?"

"Of course. Our first meeting—in the car park—wasn't auspicious, but she stayed in my mind. Seeing her round here, when I came to live at Seton's, I would have—"

"—set the affair in motion. Who was it who said: 'She should flee as a bird unto the hill'?"

"It's a line from a psalm."

They were at the cottage, and Laura was at the door. She led them inside, to a tray of steaming coffee. Jess dropped her bag on the floor and kissed her on both cheeks.

"Happy days," she said. "It was a good idea to send him to meet me. We discussed it all on the way here, and decided that it's going to work out. Did you ring Magda?"

"Yes."

"I suppose you got a spate about not trusting Finch because he stole his best friend's fiancée?"

"Something like that."

"She's furious because she didn't see it coming. Have you fixed a wedding date?"

"We'll fix one today," said Finch. "I'm going to start moving into Seton's in about ten days. I'm bringing some furniture up from the London flat, but I'm leaving most of the things in the Sheffield house until the last of my aunts is dead. They were all born in the house and grew up in it, and they look on it as the family home."

The telephone rang, and Jess laughed.

"That's the first," she said. "The news is getting round."

It was Lady Downes, who told Laura in her tepid way that nothing except Audrey's engagement had ever made her feel happier. Such a lovely house, such a splendid-looking man, so near all her old friends, could anything be nicer?

"No, nothing," Laura agreed, and thanked her for calling. She put the receiver down and tried to think of a way of bringing up the subject of Wilfred. Finch did it for her.

"Seen anything of her son?" he inquired.

"Wilfred? Yes," Jess answered. "He's been round to my flat twice, pretending he left something there."

Finch took her empty cup to Laura, waited for a refill, and carried it back.

"What," he asked, "is your objection to marrying him?"

"None. Now that you've asked," Jess said, "I'll give you my views. Marriage is a great institution. Marriage is the only background for a happy, united home, and happy children. It's probably because I've got such a healthy respect for marriage that I kept getting engaged—testing the water. But what I wanted, what I want before I marry, is some freedom. That's why I'm hanging back. Why does marriage have to come so soon? A few years ago, Laura and I were at school. Even the École Eugénie, free as it was in many ways, wasn't total freedom. Women go out in the big world and start learning about themselves, learning what life's all about—and then what? A man persuades them to get married, and they're back in harness. What they do in future is done in conjunction with, or with the consent of, a husband. I'm not like Laura; I couldn't give up what she's given up—a cottage of her own, a job of her own, her independence. I'm not ready yet. I can have perfectly healthy babies when I'm thirty or more. Before marrying, I want to feel that I've made it on my own. Laura's going to marry you and move back to Seton's and settle down and be contented and happy, without ever feeling that she missed a phase. If you're still listening, I like Wilfred more than any man I've ever known. He wanted to give me a shock by walking out; all right, he succeeded to the extent of making me realize that he was at the top of the list and that I love him.

But I don't want to start what they call a new life with him. Not yet."

"And if he doesn't want to play the role of gentleman-in-waiting?" Finch asked.

Jess stared at him in surprise.

"Laura, did he say that?"

"Yes, he did," Laura said proudly. "He keeps saying things."

"All I'm trying to do," Finch said, "is put in a word for Wilfred. We're going to be neighbours when he moves into his new flat. I just want you to know I'm on his side."

"I'll keep it in mind," Jess promised.

The following week was a busy one for the furniture removers. Some of Finch's possessions were brought from London to Seton's. Wilfred's furniture was transferred from his rooms to his new apartment. As his sisters were away on a concert tour—their last before Audrey's marriage—and as Lady Downes did not feel up to the exertion of going to London to help him to move in, the task fell to Jess.

The removal of Laura's furniture from the cottage up to Seton's was undertaken by volunteers until it was found that their cars were too small to fit any but minor items. Friends also came to assist with the arrangement of the furniture in its new setting, their ideas on its disposal proving as varied as their backgrounds. When they had departed each evening, Finch and Laura made the adjustments they felt to be necessary. The cottage, when empty, would be sold to Mr. Sheldon. During the sale of the land to Laura, it had been agreed that if she ever gave it up, it would revert to the Sheldons. Sue Sheldon planned to live in it and continue Laura's deep-freeze business.

For Finch and Laura, their chief pleasure, and one which they did not allow anyone to share, was the hanging of their pictures in the miniature gallery. They owned between them thirty-nine pictures; a London delivery firm brought one with goodwill messages from Ginette and Hollis, making the total forty. Eleven of the collection were pictures that had been painted by Laura's father or mother; the rest were Finch's. The present from Ginette and Hollis bore the name of a painter neither of them had ever heard of.

There was only one space left in the gallery when they had finished. Claud had not yet delivered "High Winds." Finch had offered to fetch it, but Claud said that he would bring it when he came to the wedding. He had, he explained, decided that it was time he had some means of carrying his pictures around, and had bought himself a small van.

The wedding reception, held at Mrs. Pennerley's insistence at the Waterside hotel, was an example of her talent for organizing. How much she contributed towards the cost, and how much Finch privately provided, Laura did not inquire. She had accepted her aunt's offer to send out the wedding invitations, but after catching her surreptitiously crossing several names off the list, had taken over the task. Finch found that Jess's forecast had been correct: the tradesmen of Waterside filled more than half the places in the church.

Mr. Chawton acted as best man. Claud, who was to have given away the bride, sent a message two days before the ceremony to say that he was in bed with influenza. In his absence, Laura was given away by Wilfred.

The highlight of the wedding was the arrival of three hearselike cars with Sheffield number-plates, bringing gaunt Aunt Em, plump Aunt Lily, elegant Aunt Amy and still-lovely Aunt Rosalind. But the one who stole the scene was Aunt Trixie, placed in a wheelchair decorated with orange blossoms and propelled by Uncle Ed.

Conrad reported a great feeling of flatness when the bride and groom had driven away. Not until the departure of the three cars did the local excitement die down.

The honeymoon was brief. After two weeks in Italy, Finch

and Laura were back in Crossford, to begin life in the house in which Laura's had begun. Jess came down for a weekend. Walking through the picture gallery with Laura, she stopped to look at the empty space.

" 'High Winds'?"

"Yes. Claud said he'd bring it."

"Remember how you worried about it after you'd been to his studio?"

"I still worry. Finch never told me what he paid for it."

"He wanted a pair. He got a pair."

"Yes, but—"

"But nothing. The money probably bought Claud his van, and left enough to buy several more. That's better than having a father you had to support."

"Is it?"

"Yes. Have you seen Magda since you got back?"

"No."

"I thought not. If you had, she'd have given you some news."

"About you?"

"About Wilfred and me. I've given up my flat."

Laura turned slowly to face her. "You've *what*?"

"Given up my flat. I've moved into Wilfred's. It was too big for one; it's perfect for two."

"I don't understand why you—"

"Protective measure. His sister Margaret was going to move in. Can you imagine? He was dreading it, but he didn't see any way of getting out of it. Now he needn't worry; no more room."

"But—"

"And I can keep my eye on him. I can put him on a leash next time he looks like walking out."

"Is he—are you both—happy?"

"Blissfully. How about you? Is marriage turning out all you expected?"

"Yes."

"I'm glad. Don't forget to tell me what Claud says when he sees the Zollard hanging here."

But Claud gave no sign for the next three weeks. When at last he came, he was in his new van—at the wheel of a car, he told Finch and Laura, for the first time since his undergraduate days.

They took him over most of the house. He expressed his admiration for the way in which the conversion had been done, and congratulated them on the arrangement of the furniture in the rooms.

"That's Laura's department," Finch said.

He was coming up the stairs with the picture Claud had brought.

"Come and see it hung," he said. "You haven't seen our picture gallery."

He led the way. Claud, following Laura, stopped abruptly at the entrance. Glancing round at him, Laura saw that he was too surprised to speak. Then he advanced into the room.

"I didn't expect anything of this kind," he said.

Finch was on a stepladder, hanging the picture in the place that had been reserved for it opposite its fellow. He came down, pulled the ladder aside and stood gazing.

"What d'you think?" he asked Claud. "They make a good pair, don't they?"

Claud stood looking from one picture to the other; whether he was judging the best position for them, or congratulating himself on what she thought must have been a highly profitable sale, Laura could not decide. She looked at Finch; he was walking slowly down the room, examining the pictures as he went. Claud followed him, giving each picture a brief scrutiny until he reached the one that had been sent by Ginette and Hollis. At this he stopped short.

"When did you buy that?" he asked in surprise.

"I didn't. Wedding present," Finch answered.

He had spoken carelessly. Claud stared at him.

"Have you any idea what it's worth?" he asked.

"We don't even know who painted it," Laura replied.

"You should know. How can you hope to build up a good collection if you don't know anything about painters? This is a Craymer. Perhaps I shouldn't blame you for not knowing his work; it's only just coming onto the market. He held an exhibition last month in Paris; it caused a sensation. If you ever want to sell this, for heaven's sake ask me about it first. Have you any idea where it was bought?"

"No," said Laura.

"Have you got all these pictures well insured?"

"Yes. Do you think we've hung them properly?" Finch asked.

Claud smiled. "If I say that I couldn't have done it better myself, you mustn't misunderstand me. I congratulate you—especially on the Craymer. I had no idea you had so good a collection."

Finch was walking slowly back. He reached Laura's side and took one of her hands in his.

"Small, but interesting, I think," he said. "And varied. And not many reproductions. I've only one regret: that I didn't have the gallery made a bit larger. I would have liked to fit in half a dozen more pictures. But as you see, there's no room for even one more, unless I get rid of one of these, which I don't intend to do. I think"—he turned to Laura—"I think we've got enough pictures, here and distributed through the rest of the house, to satisfy us."

Claud nodded. "You'd be silly to overdo it," he agreed. "But remember that you're talking to a man who likes to make an occasional profit by selling pictures. What am I to do the next time I pick up a neglected masterpiece—sell it to someone else?"

"Yes," said Finch.

Nothing could have been spoken more quietly, more calmly

than the monosyllable—but it had an undertone that could only be called finality. In the brief silence that followed, Laura felt Finch's hand tightening round her own.

She would have liked to look at him. He had said once that she would be able to learn the truth by looking into his eyes. What truth would she read in them now, if she had courage enough to look? He had in one word informed her father that there would be no further dealings between them. He had stated that he had bought all the pictures he wanted. Perhaps he had bought one that he had not wanted. . . .

Claud had reached the Zollard. He halted.

"Magda's wedding present," Laura told him.

He turned.

"She gave it to you?"

"Yes," Finch answered, and did not add that it had cost him twenty pounds in a lost bet. "She admitted that there was a doubt about its genuineness, but said that she herself refused to believe it was a copy."

"I assure you that it is." Claud glanced at his watch. "I'm afraid it's time I went."

"No coffee? No lunch?" Laura asked.

"Thank you, my dear; no. No time. I wanted to come and see you both, and see the picture hung. Now I must get back to London."

They watched him drive away; then they went slowly up the steps into the house. Finch stopped to study Laura.

"He always has this effect on you," he said.

She went close to him and put her head on his shoulder. "I think I've discovered why," she said.

"Could I know why, too?"

"I think I'm sorry for him."

"Why?"

"I don't know why. He must be lonely."

"He's alone from choice."

"Yes, but—"

226

"If he ever gets into trouble, we'll be here to help him."

She raised her head and looked at him. "Trouble?"

He smiled. "Something that most people run into at some time or another. I had to rescue you twice—in Paris. Remember?"

"Yes. But trouble, real trouble—Claud?"

"Nobody's immune. Though"—he took her arm and turned her in the direction of a table on which a tray of coffee had been placed—"some are more immune than others. Among those, I think we can count Claud. Come and pour out my coffee."

She hesitated, but only for a moment. She had questions, but she knew that it would be wiser not to ask them. He knew or he guessed what Claud had done. His words had been a plain statement. But she had his assurance that there would be no future dealings.

Trouble? Perhaps, one day, if Claud got careless. But with Finch as the new head of the family, she decided that she had nothing to fear.